PRAISE FOR BRANDILYN COLLINS' KANNER LAKE SERIES

CRIMSON EVE

"Collins tops herself by creating a suspenseful, nonstop thrill ride.... Truly the best CF suspense title so far this year; this book deserves a place in all collections."

—*Library Journal*, starred review

"...teeth-chattering, mind-freezing prose. *Crimson Eve* is Collins at her very best.... The pacing is so intense there was little opportunity to rest. Collins crafts an unparalleled cat-and-mouse game wrought with mystery and surprise."

—*TitleTrakk.com*

"The excitement starts on page one and doesn't stop until the shocking end ... [Crimson Eve] is fast-paced and thrilling."

Romantic Times

"The action starts with a bang, with an attempt on Carla's life, and the pace doesn't let up until this fabulous racehorse of a story crosses the finish line ... Collins's fast-paced and intriguing plot line is sensitively combined with diary entries of Carla's past heartaches. Crimson Eve will be a welcome addition to the libraries of Christian suspense fans."

Christian Retailing

VIOLET DAWN

"What a ride! Collins is a high-caliber writer. [She] spices her seatbelt suspense with a dash of humor and heart-wrenching predicaments. Don't forget to breathe."

Novel Reviews

"... features a sympathetic heroine and uses flashbacks effectively to set up this tale about child abuse and its long-term impact. With several suspense titles under her belt (*Brink of Death, Stain of Guilt, Web of Lies*), Collins knows how to weave faith into a rich tale. Possible crossover appeal for fans of Mary Higgins Clark."

—Library Journal

"Skillfully written ... Imaginative style and exquisite suspense."

1340mag.com

"... a roller-coaster ride with incredible heights and violent spiral twists that leave you quaking as it slows to a stop."

—North Idaho Lifestyle

"Collins expertly melds flashbacks with present-day events to provide a smooth yet deliciously intense flow."

—RT BookClub

"Collins's skill in handling multiple points of view and time shifts, which flow easily together and advance the plot ... interesting details of police procedure and crime scene investigation ... a promising and entertaining beginning to the Kanner Lake Series."

Publisher's Weekly

CORAL MOON

"Thrilling.... Leave the light on when you read this one.... Readers will enjoy spending time with the well-rounded characters in Kanner Lake. This is a fun read with almost no down time, one of those rare books you hurry through, almost breathlessly, to find out what happens."

—Spokane Living

"A chilling mystery. Not one to be read alone at night."

—RT BookClub, four stars

AMBER MORN

Brandilyn Collins
Seatbelt Suspense™

Other Books by Brandilyn Collins

Kanner Lake Series

1 | Violet Dawn

2 | Coral Moon

3 | Crimson Eve

4 | Amber Morn

Hidden Faces Series

1 | Brink of Death

2 | Stain of Guilt

3 | Dead of Night

4 | Web of Lies

Chelsea Adams Series

1 | Eyes of Elisha

2 | Dread Champion

Bradleyville Series

1 | Cast a Road before Me

2 | Color the Sidewalk for Me

3 | Capture the Wind for Me

BRANDILYN COLLINS

Kanner Lake Series

AMBER MORN

BOOK 4

ZONDERVAN®

ZONDERVAN.com/
AUTHORTRACKER
follow your favorite authors

Amber Morn
Copyright © 2008 by Brandilyn Collins

This title is also available as a Zondervan ebook product.
Visit www.zondervan.com/ebooks for more information.

This title is also available as a Zondervan audio product.
Visit www.zondervan.com/audiopages for more information.

Requests for information should be addressed to:
Zondervan, *Grand Rapids, Michigan 49530*

Library of Congress Cataloging-in-Publication Data

Collins, Brandilyn.
    Amber morn / Brandilyn Collins.
       p. cm. — (Kanner Lake series ; bk. 4)
    ISBN-13: 978-0-310-27641-8 (pbk.)
    ISBN-10: 0-310-27641-1 (pbk.)
      11. Hostages—Fiction. 2. Idaho—Fiction. 3. Resorts—Fiction. I. Title.
  PS3553.O4747815A84 2008
  813'.54—dc22

                                     2007042521

Published in association with the literary agency of Alive Communications, Inc., 7680 Goddard Street, Suite 200, Colorado Springs, CO 80920.

Interior design by Beth Shagene

Printed in the United States of America

---

08 09 10 11 12 13 • 23 22 21 20 19 18 17 16 15 14 13 12 11 10 9 8 7 6 5 4 3 2 1

SCENES AND BEANS™
The Kanner Lake Blog

Life in Kanner Lake, Idaho—brought to you by Java Joint coffee shop on Main

Visit Scenes and Beans at *www.kannerlake.blogspot.com.*

Want to Discuss Amber Morn *with Your Book Club?*

Insightful questions about the story and
how it applies to your life can be found at
www.kannerlake.com/discussions

*Gratefully dedicated to
the original Scenes and Beans blog writers,
who helped shape the characters
in Java Joint.*

Sabrina Butcher

Bonnie Calhoun

Rebecca Carter

Laura Domino

Bob Edwards

Stephanie Fowler

Tracy Fowler

Beth Goddard

Gina Holmes

Bev Huston

Pamela James

Jason Joyner

David Meigs

Chris Mikesell

Dineen Miller

Sandra Moore

Vennessa Ng

Kjersten Nickleby

Michelle Pendergrass

Cara Putman

Sherry Ramsey

Janet Rubin

Chawna Schroeder

Wayne Scott

Lynetta Smith

Michael Snyder

Lynette Sowell

Stuart Stockton

Kim Thomas

Jennifer Tiszai

Marjorie Vawter

Karen Wevick

When calamity comes, the wicked are brought down,
but even in death the righteous have a refuge.

Proverbs 14:32

INTRODUCTION

Dear Reader:

Here we are at the fourth and final book in the Kanner Lake Series. It doesn't seem long ago at all that I started writing the first one, *Violet Dawn*. If you haven't read the other books in this series, don't worry. You can still read this one and not feel lost.

Like the other Kanner Lake books, *Amber Morn* features the gang at Java Joint, who post on the Scenes and Beans blog. In the previous books, many of them were supporting characters. This story places them front and center as an ensemble cast.

As *Amber Morn* begins, it has been eight months since the events in *Crimson Eve* that changed Carla Radling's life—and the face of the nation. And over a year since the confounding murders that occurred in *Coral Moon*. Kanner Lake has let out its breath, settled back into peaceful existence.

That's about to be shattered.

Today the town will face the most fearful day it has ever known. Every citizen—whether as friend or family member—is close to someone caught in the trauma.

And now, dear reader, once again the ride begins. This one is a roller coaster in the dark, for its operators are volatile and unpredictable. And they do not care if you reach the end safely. So keep your hands inside the car, strap yourself in tight, and don't forget to *b r e a t h e* ...®

AMBER MORN

PART ONE

Attack

ONE

Any man going on this mission wasn't coming back.

Cluttered kitchen, cluttered head. Kent Wicksell could hardly think straight. It wasn't supposed to start like this. Dread anticipation pumped through his veins as he faced off with his second son. Vigilante Brad, gunning to take on the world. At twenty-nine, he thought he knew more than anybody.

Kent's voice seethed. "For the *fifteenth* time—this job's for me and Mitch. *You* are staying home. We ain't leaving your mom alone."

They'd been arguing for the past ten minutes. Too long. They needed to get *out* of there.

Brad stood his ground, face like granite. His cool blue eyes stabbed Kent. "I *ain't* staying here." His voice pulsed low. "I watched over T.J. since he was born, just as much as Mitch has. And I ain't stopping now."

Kent surged forward two steps, finger punching the air. "I'm telling you no! I *won't* let you—"

Lenora caught his arm. "Stop, Kent! Let him go."

He turned to her, jaw loosening. She stared back, a terrible, grim determination pressing her lips. Kent's knees went weak.

No, no, no.

Where had that look on her face come from? Just this morning she'd clutched at the knowledge she wouldn't be left by herself.

"You'd let him *go?*" Accusation heated Kent's cheeks. "You'd trade *two* of your sons for another?"

She held his gaze until her chin trembled. "It's for T.J.," she whispered. And she started to cry.

Kent's heart cracked. T.J.—their youngest son. Once their greatest hope. Smart. Well liked. Going somewhere in life. Never did drugs.

"I got four fractured ribs," he'd told them in his weekly phone call from prison two nights ago. Eyes swollen almost shut. A broken arm. His words were racked with pain. An innocent eighteen-year-old in prison, beaten—just for *being* there.

Of all three sons, this never should have happened to T.J.

At thirty-three, Mitch still lived at home, bouncing from job to job, in and out of jail on various drug and burglary charges. Meth was his latest drug of choice. Just last night he'd shot up for this special event. To Mitch, the greatest day of his purposeless life had dawned this morning. Rescue his littlest brother, betrayed by injustice. Show the world he was worth something.

As for Brad, he was unpredictable. Angry. In jail twice for beating on girlfriends. A high school dropout, like his dad.

Brad flicked his eyes from his mother back to Kent, his mouth drawn in a victorious line. "Don't forget who went with you yesterday on your scouting mission. Don't forget who took you to a computer in the library and *showed* you the blog."

On Main Street in Kanner Lake they'd watched traffic, people. Noted the police station two blocks up from Java Joint coffee shop. They went into the café and ordered coffee and pastries. Sat at a table, nerves taut, eyes roaming over the big front windows, the layout and size of the place. Kent and Mitch took turns walking down the back hall in search of the bathroom. They'd noticed the other rooms off the hall—a small office, a storage area. The rear door with no glass, a lock and deadbolt ...

Kent fixed his gaze on Lenora, watched her tears fall. *It's for T.J.*

No way. She'd lost enough. Brad was *not* walking out of here and leaving her alone. Kent and Mitch would take Java Joint, just like they'd planned. Kill every person in the place if they had to. Brad would stay with his mother.

Mitch stormed into the kitchen, a Rambo expression on his gaunt face. Wired for action. His pupils were huge. He swiveled from Brad to Kent. "What're you doing standing here? We're *late.*"

Kent planted his legs apart, hands on his hips. He wasn't about to lose this battle. Bad way to start the day, and his hostages would soon feel it. His anger was pumping all the harder—and he'd have to let it out on somebody. "Your brother thinks he's going." He aimed a burning stare at Brad. "I say he's not."

Brad's eyes narrowed. Without a word, without a backward glance at his mother, he snatched up the lightweight jacket he'd brought into the kitchen—a jacket with a bulging, heavy pocket—and stalked out the front door toward the weapon-loaded truck.

TWO

"Hey, you, ready to go?" Paige called through her roommate's bedroom door.

"Two minutes!"

Uh-huh. Two minutes meant five, more like ten. Leslie Brymes could primp with the best of them. "Better hurry! You're the last person who should miss the signing."

"Like he's going to do it without me."

Paige flicked a look at the ceiling and turned away. Anticipation hummed through her veins, thrusting her into action. She trotted outside and plucked the *Spokane Review* newspaper—Leslie's current competition, therefore carefully read every day—from the sidewalk. In the nearby field, birds chirped and a prairie dog stuck an inquisitive nose up from the ground. Paige tipped her head back and closed her eyes.

Hey, God. What a perfect day to become engaged.

So she hoped.

Back inside, she made for the kitchen and plopped the newspaper on the table, then stood staring out at the backyard, Frank West's face filling her mind. The strong jawline she loved to trace, his wide-set, large dark eyes. The thick brown hair he kept short for his work on the Kanner Lake police force. She pictured his nervous smile as he presented her a ring tonight. Why else would he book such an expensive restaurant? Besides, he'd been dropping hints . . .

When she'd stumbled into Kanner Lake two years ago—scared, running for her life, trusting no one—never would she have dreamed of a day like this.

The telephone rang. Paige reached for the receiver and read the caller ID. *Frank West.* She smiled. "Hey there."

"Hi." His voice flushed her with warmth. "You about to leave for Java Joint?"

"Yeah, if Leslie ever gets ready."

"You riding together?"

"Uh-huh, in my car. She's leaving with Ted after the party. It's about the last day off they'll have together before she moves to Seattle. She has to start packing her stuff."

Frank sighed. "I feel so sorry for him."

Not the first time Paige had heard this. "Me too." How she and Leslie had discussed the choice. Leslie had cried and worried and cried some more. "But this is her dream job, Frank, just like publishing *Starfire* is Ted's dream. Their relationship will work out somehow—if it's meant to be."

Ironic, how this happiest time in Ted's and Leslie's lives was also the most heartbreaking.

Frank cleared his throat. "Anyway, thought I'd stop by Java Joint and see you for a minute before I go on duty. Maybe catch S-Man signing the contract."

S-Man—Ted Dawson's nickname, based on Sauria, the science fiction world he'd created. After over two years of work, he'd landed an incredible two-book deal with HarperCollins.

"Oh, that's great!"

Footsteps sounded. Paige turned to see Leslie, sporting a puffy-sleeved bright pink top and rhinestone-studded jeans. She shook back her blonde hair and struck a *ta-da* pose in the doorway, then lowered her chin and pursed her mouth in a look that read—*Whatever are we waiting for?*

Paige shook her head and smiled. "Okay, Frank, Miss Seattle TV Reporter just appeared in all her glory. She needs to stop by her office for something; then we'll be at Java Joint."

He'd be there in about twenty minutes, Frank replied. Paige hung up, her anticipation fueled. She loved seeing her man in uniform.

THREE

Through a dirty living room window, Kent watched Brad stride to the pickup and climb inside. He swiped the two jackets on the seat—along with his own—onto the floor. Lenora stayed in the kitchen. Kent could hear her crying as Mitch told her good-bye.

Brad slid over to the middle of the truck's seat. Staring straight ahead, arms crossed. Immovable.

"Dad, we got to *go*." Mitch emerged from the kitchen in his jerky drugged walk. Lenora trailed him, her face splotchy and eyes red.

Kent gestured with his chin. "Go on out. I'm coming."

"What're you gonna do about Brad?"

"I'll handle it."

Mitch hitched a shoulder, then clomped out the door and down the porch steps. Kent turned back to hold Lenora.

They hugged in silence, hearts beating against each other's chest. He pulled back, looked into her worn face. Lenora used to look young for her fifty-one years. Not anymore. She'd aged in the last seven months, her wrinkles deepened, crow's-feet at her dulled eyes.

She raised her gaze to his. "Go, Kent. Do what you have to do."

He flexed his jaw. "It'll work, Lenora, I promise. And it won't take long—a few hours. It'll work."

She managed a weak smile.

Kent broke away and walked out the front door. He resisted the urge to look back.

Mitch was pacing by the open passenger door of the truck, cussing at his brother to get out. Brad ignored him. He drew up when Kent approached and cocked his head to one side. Waved his skinny arms. "He ain't listening."

Kent got behind the wheel and started arguing all over again. Brad wouldn't budge.

"Come *on*, Dad." Mitch shifted from one foot to the other. "We're behind schedule."

Kent kept talking. Brad ignored him.

"*Forget* this." Mitch clambered into the seat and slammed the door, sealing his brother's place in the middle. "Easier with three anyway." He kicked the jackets over toward Brad's feet.

Kent spat a curse and glared at his oldest son. Mitch never had the sense to come in out of the rain. This was his worst choice yet.

Brad kept a stubborn focus through the windshield. "I told you I'm going, Dad. You *need* me."

Kent pressed back in his seat. Wild thoughts flew around in his head. Like maybe they should call the whole thing off. Go back and try talking to the lawyers again.

Yeah, right. The talking hadn't worked. And it never would. And now look at T.J. — in the prison hospital. That was Kent's fault for waiting so long. *His* fault.

Rage and self-loathing twisted through Kent's spine. He'd vowed to fix this situation today. And he would.

They needed to leave. *Now.*

Kent Wicksell took a long breath — and started the engine.

FOUR

At 7:25 a.m. Bailey Truitt's spirits sang. What a beautiful morning! Dawn had blossomed over Kanner Lake in stunning shades of scarlet and peach, turning to a soothing amber glow as the sun rose. The temperature would be in the mid-eighties — unseasonably warm for Memorial Day weekend. And most of her fellow Scenes and Beans bloggers would soon gather at Java Joint for their celebration. Bailey's husband, John, who suffered from epilepsy, felt good enough to come too. That was a blessing in itself, given the side effects he'd experienced with the new medication.

Bailey smiled as she foamed a biggie nonfat latte for Bev Trexel, the first to arrive. Ah, the familiar scent of coffee and milk and sweet pastries, the sizzle-and-gurgle of the espresso machine. They tickled Bailey's senses as she pulled the drink away and set it down. "There you go, Miss Bev." She pressed a plastic top over the cup and handed it across the counter to the retired English teacher. "No waiting in line — that's what you get for being first."

"Thank you." Bev took a drink, satisfaction spreading across her powdered face. She looked mighty festive in a bright blue top and gold slacks. Quite the bold colors for Bev. Her white hair was perfectly coiffed as always. A standing weekly appointment at the beauty parlor kept it that way. "Where *is* everyone? It's almost seven thirty."

"Oh, they're coming." Bailey waved a hand. "You know this bunch. Like herding cats."

Bev's eyes glinted. "I think the saying should be 'like herding Wilburs.' Now *that* would be a trial."

"True." Bailey glanced out the window. "Speaking of ..."

Bev's expression flickered with sudden mischief. All innocence, she sidled toward the fourth counter stool and sat down. Uh-oh.

Outside, Wilbur Hucks shuffled toward the door, wearing his yellow T-shirt with the cartoon face of a stupid-looking redneck. The typical shirt that tourists loved to buy read "I-duh-ho." Wilbur hated that. He'd had his own custom version made: "You wear I-duh-ho, I tell ya where to go."

Wilbur caught sight of Bev through the window—and a glower spread across his face. He pulled open the door.

"That's my stool, woman!" He clomped across the floor, aiming for Bev's back. She sat primly, one elbow on the counter, and sipped her drink.

Wilbur threw Bailey an exasperated look. "See what she's doin' to get my goat? Three other stools at the counter, and she takes mine."

Bev raised an eyebrow. "I don't see your name on it."

Wilbur's wizened face flushed to the roots of his white hair. "We're supposed to be celebratin' today, Bailey. Why you let her start settin' me off?"

"Oh, Wilbur, you know you love it," Bailey teased him with a smile. "What would you do if you couldn't complain?"

"I ain't here to complain. I'm here for the free coffee and pastries you promised."

Bev lifted her chin, disapproval deepening her frown lines. "Sounds like good enough reason to take another stool for the day. Imagine that, Bailey, guzzling your coffee for *free*—and complaining about a little thing like where I choose to sit."

"You know it ain't no little thing." Wilbur huffed. "Either I get my stool back, or I'm goin' home to Trudy, where it's nice and *peaceful*."

In a silent dare, Bev stayed put.

Wilbur waited five seconds, muttering under his breath. Then turned himself around and stomped toward the door.

FIVE

Silence hung thick in the truck cab. Kent drove west toward Highway 41, fingers tight on the wheel. Kanner Lake was over twenty minutes from their house, which sat off Highway 95 just north of Hayden. He pressed the accelerator, on the watch for cops. They had to make up for lost time.

His mind whirled. Now that Brad was here, what should he do? Kent and Mitch had planned every move of the attack. Each second counted. Now tasks had to be refigured.

Kent mulled it over. Much as he hated to agree with Mitch, three men would make it easier. Now they could hold the hostages in the first few minutes while Brad did the busywork. Safer that way. Brad just might be a little too trigger-happy, and Kent didn't want to lose any more hostages than was necessary up front. Hostages were bargaining chips.

When everything gelled in his mind, Kent announced the revised plans. His sons agreed without argument. That was something for Brad.

They drove in simmering revenge and determination. Every mile turned up the heat.

Mitch's right leg jiggled. Harder and harder it went until the floor shook under Kent's feet. He wanted to slap the stupid thing still. Adrenaline and fear slammed around in his veins too, but he'd just as soon deny it. Seeing that nervous leg broke him out in a sweat.

The city limits sign reared its head. "There ya *go*." Mitch pounded a fist against his window. "Yeehaw, if they only *knew* what's coming!"

SIX

Welcome to your own party, S-Man.

Ted Dawson reached for the Java Joint door, memories from the past two years flashing through his head. Lying in agony in the forest during a workday of logging, his leg crushed ... The small cartoon dragon drawn on his cast in the hospital that led to the creation of his main character in *Starfire* ... Typing away on the manuscript at his regular table in Java Joint day after day ... finally finishing ... rewriting ... pursuing an agent ... And best of all—even better than landing a contract that would make him a full-time writer—the look in Leslie Brymes's eyes when he blurted that he loved her, and she responded with the same words. Stunningly beautiful, dramatic, take-on-the-world Leslie, ten years younger, loved *him*.

Ted's thoughts clouded. He paused, hand hanging in the air. This was a day to celebrate. *Don't think about her leaving. Not today.*

He took a deep breath and pulled open the door. *"Shnakvorum, rikoyoch!"* *Greetings, friends*, in Saurian. He limped inside.

"Whoa!" Wilbur Hucks pulled up inches in front of him. Ted had nearly run the man over. "You lookin' to do me in this morning?"

"Oh. Sorry. Should have paid attention. I was just ..."

"Yeah, I know." Wilbur's face was nothing but frowns. "You were in Sauria. You can get your head outta that world of yours now, you know. You done wrote the story."

"Hey, Ted!" Bailey called from behind the counter. Her sunny smile was particularly brilliant this morning. The overhead lights shone on her auburn hair and caught the swing of her small hoop earrings.

Bev turned and shot Ted a cat-that-ate-the-canary look. She sat on the fourth stool.

"Oh." Ted closed the door and focused on Wilbur.

"Yeah, oh. She won't move, neither, so I was just leavin'."

Ted pushed the strap of his computer bag farther up his shoulder. The bag felt light today without his laptop. His eyes slid from Wilbur to Bev and back. This was a character conflict for sure. What Wilbur needed was a fresh response. Something unexpected.

Ted leaned in close to the seventy-eight-year-old, voice dropping to a whisper. "I say let her keep it. That'll take the wind out of her sails."

Wilbur gave his head a firm shake. "Nope. Can't do it. It's the principle of the thing."

With all the grace she could muster, Bev rose from the infamous stool and approached Ted. Extended her arm in invitation as if the stool were a golden throne. "Ted, there you are. I was saving this spot for the guest of honor."

Moving faster than Ted had ever seen him, Wilbur scurried back to the counter and plunked down on the stool. "There!" His fingers wrapped around the bottom of the seat as if he dared anyone to pry him loose. "Ah-haaah!" He leered at Bev.

Bev huffed. "Oh, for goodness' sake, Wilbur, grow up."

"Tell you what." Ted lifted a hand. "Let's call a truce for one day. We're here to celebrate."

"Hear, hear." Bailey slapped down a palm.

Bev muttered something under her breath. Ted headed for the other end of the counter. *Conflict resolved. What'll happen next?* In a novel, that's the way it went. One conflict following another, building, building. His first science fiction novel was done, but he had a second to write, and plot ideas kept rattling around in his head.

He pulled the computer bag off his shoulder, then stood holding it, the gears in his mind starting to turn. Wilbur and Bev ... fighting over a possession ... one teasing, the other all too serious ... What if the Wilbur character lashed out, hurt the other one? What if he accidentally *killed*? He'd have to run away ... hide what he'd done—

"Where's my favorite science fiction writer?" a familiar voice called from the door. Ted snapped his head up and smiled. Leslie had arrived.

SEVEN

Kent took a quick detour off Lakeshore—up a few blocks and back down so they could pass Main. He glanced up the street as they rolled by. A bunch of cars parked around Java Joint, which was on the right side and not far from the top of the second block. Java Joint—the café known across the country, thanks to its Scenes and Beans blog. Kent's lip curled. The place would never see another day like this one.

Back at Lakeshore, Kent turned left. Almost to ground zero. Brad's folded arms tightened, and Mitch's leg bounced higher. On their right at the top of Kanner Lake rose the new hotel under construction. In three months it was supposed to be done. At the moment the site was quiet.

Good.

Two blocks up, Kent turned left again on Second Street and pulled over to the curb. Cut the engine.

The truck's digital clock read 7:55.

Tension ran like electricity through the cab. They all inhaled at the same time.

"D-day." Brad stuck his jaw out.

Kent nodded. "Let's do it."

Mitch reached into the glove box for the guns.

EIGHT

"Sheesh, what a noisy bunch." Carla Radling shook her head at her sixteen-year-old daughter, Brittany, as they approached Java Joint's door. "You can hear them out here."

"Yeah, and we'll just make it louder." Ali Frederick, Brittany's one teenage friend in Kanner Lake, shook brown bangs out of her eyes.

Carla's heart swelled as she smiled at the girls. How wonderful it was to have Brittany visit. She lived in Seattle with her adoptive parents, and Carla didn't see her nearly enough. Being around the two girls made Carla feel like a teenager again instead of her thirty-three years.

Wait, bad analogy. Not for a million bucks would she ever want to relive her teenage years.

The noise increased as they pulled open the door. Everyone was talking at once.

"Hey, Carla, finally!" Leslie broke away from S-Man and greeted them, arms out. "Ali, so glad you came."

"Me too." They hugged, Ali all grins. After being caught up in the terror of two murders in Kanner Lake last year, seventeen-year-old Ali had become like a little sister to Leslie.

"Wow, *love* your jeans." Brittany's large chocolate eyes roved over the bling.

"Thanks." Leslie caught Brittany's hands. "It's great to see you again. Carla is *so happy* every time you visit."

36

Brittany shot a look at Carla. Their eyes met in silent connection.

Amazing. A year ago Carla hadn't even known Brittany was alive. Now look at the beautiful, vibrant daughter before her.

Carla made the rounds with Brittany and Ali, reminding the girls of everyone else's name. Paige. S-Man. Hank Detcher, pastor of the New Community Church, which Carla attended. Jared Moore, owner of the *Kanner Lake Times* newspaper and Leslie's boss. Jared was sixty-seven but still worked long hours every day. Wilbur, perched on his stool as if it might run out from under him. Bailey—bustling behind the counter like a crazed chicken, making everyone's drinks. Bev and Angie, retired schoolteachers in their sixties, and best friends who met at Java Joint every morning for coffee—even though their personalities were exact opposites. Angie was as fun-loving and giggly as Bev was prim and proper. But that Bev. She could needle Wilbur almost as well as Carla.

"Ohhh, hiiii!" Angie's plump arms swallowed Brittany in a 'grandmotherly hug, her rouged cheeks flushing.

When she could extricate Brittany, Carla nudged the girls over to the counter. "Let's see." She draped an arm around each of them and looked around. "Not everybody's here."

Bailey set Carla's latte on the counter. "Jake can't come. Remember, he and Mable are on a trip this weekend. And Janet—that's Pastor Hank's wife"—she smiled at the two girls—"is also gone this weekend. One of their daughters is sick."

Paige sidled up to the counter, her striking blue-green eyes focused on Brittany. "Hi there, beautiful girl."

Carla took her arm away from Brittany so they could hug. "Hey, Paige, where's Sarah?"

Sarah Wray owned Simple Pleasures across the street, where Paige worked.

"Oh, she's coming. Sarah can't stand to miss a party."

"Hey, everybody, remember the drinks and pastries are on me!" Bailey frothed a mocha at the espresso machine.

Wilbur caught Carla's eye and pulled his mouth down at the corners. Crotchety Wilbur. Carla's favorite person to argue with. He slipped off his stool and picked up the mug at his end of the counter that held the bathroom key. Dumped out its contents. Shuffled up to Carla, turning his back on Bailey. "She and John don't have the money to pay for all this, what with his medical bills and all. Give her a donation."

A command, not a request. But Carla was happy to comply. Wilbur quietly hit up each person in turn. Brittany and Ali took the time to order their coffees.

When Bailey slid the last drink over the counter, Wilbur thrust the mug at her, overflowing with bills. "Here ya go, Miss Bailey. Best woman in the world, after my Gertrude." His lips twitched into a semblance of a smile. "We wasn't gonna let this be on your tab. Looks like you made a pretty penny."

Bailey accepted the mug, eyes gleaming. "Oh, you all, I don't know what to say."

"You deserve it!" Angie called.

"Go ahead, count them suckers." Wilbur jerked his chin toward the money.

One by one, Bailey slipped them out. Fives, tens, twenties. At the bottom was a one-hundred-dollar bill.

Wilbur. Carla would bet on it. But the old curmudgeon would deny it with his last breath.

"Thank you," Bailey whispered. "Thank you all, so much."

Carla applauded and raised her cup. "Here's to you, Bailey!" Soon everyone's cups were raised.

"Thank you again." Bailey looked almost embarrassed as she stuffed the money back into the mug and slipped it onto a shelf beneath the counter.

Pastor Hank sipped his drink, then raised it once more. "And now, S-Man, time to sign that contract!"

They all whooped and hollered. Ali and Brittany laughed.

Movement at the door caught Carla's eye. Frank West stepped inside.

"Hi!" Paige glided to him like metal to a magnet. They hugged, then pulled back to gaze into each others' eyes.

Carla leaned toward Brittany's ear. "Are they gone or what?"

She gave her head a slow shake. "Totally."

S-Man opened his computer bag and pulled out a stack of paper. Carla raised her eyebrows. "Good grief, looks like one of my real estate contracts."

"Yeah, this is three copies. Lots of pages to sign."

"Tough work there, Ted."

He smiled at her, and his serious face and dark knitted eyebrows relaxed. Carla had told Leslie all along—*S-Man's cute when he smiles.*

Ted held up the contract. "*This*"—he shook the paper—"is what I've been working so hard for during the past two years. Writing all day, learning the craft, not making a *dime*. And now …" He blinked, as if he still couldn't quite believe it.

"Now you're headed toward fame and fortune!" Leslie raised her hands in victory. "Like the publisher said, 'Stellar writing. The nation's next science fiction star.'"

No kidding, thought Carla. Seventy thousands bucks *each* for two books. That had to be a big advance for an unknown writer.

"He's already a star, thanks to our blog." Wilbur wagged his head. "Man's almost as popular as I am."

"All right, who's got a pen for this historical moment?" Pastor Hank patted his empty shirt pocket.

"Right here." S-Man already held one in his hand. "But this won't be quick. I have to sign all three copies, plus initial every page."

"That's all right, Ted. I'm clapping all the way through." Bev started to applaud.

Carla joined in along with everyone else.

Ted leaned over the counter and began the happy task they'd all come to witness.

NINE

Mitch and Kent each hid a handgun in the large right pocket of their jackets. Brad grabbed his own coat from the floorboard and patted its bulge. "Already got mine."

Kent threw him a hard look.

The three men jumped from the truck. Lifted two large duffel bags out of the back. The heavier one was filled with four MP5 submachine guns and enough thirty-round magazines to take down a small army. Kent unzipped the lighter bag and pulled out a white envelope. Brad stuck it in the waistband of his jeans. Kent closed the bag and gave it to Brad to carry. Mitch took the bag full of weapons.

They looked at each other. This was it, and God help them.

For you, T.J.

Kent checked his watch. Eight o'clock.

They cut diagonally across Second toward the corner of Main, trying to look nonchalant. The morning air felt fresh and tingling on Kent's cheeks.

Would he ever feel it again?

Sudden grief for all he would lose pierced him. Freedom, home, Lenora. He knew he'd go to prison for this. Maybe for life.

He turned his head and spat on the street.

They reached the curb of Main Street and stepped up to the wide sidewalk. Java Joint would be on their left, a few doors down.

At the bottom of the block, a man in an old Subaru pulled into a parking space. Kent kept an eye on him.

The world narrowed. The sound of their footsteps, the street, their target's front entrance. Adrenaline surged through Kent, making his fingers twitch. The *power*. Nearly beat his heart right out of his chest. Each step melted away the months of sickening helplessness.

Today Kent Wicksell would see justice for his youngest son.

He breathed in, breathed out. *Walk normal. Look normal.* He could hear Mitch sucking air, could *feel* his pent-up energy. Brad's shoulders were back, his face like stone.

Five more feet. Kent slipped a hand into his jacket pocket, squeezed the cold metal of his weapon.

Hold back. Not yet.

They reached the door. Kent threw it open and yanked out his gun.

TEN

John Truitt had just stepped onto the sidewalk, headed for Java Joint, when he saw the three men. Two carrying duffel bags. No one else on the street—typical for this early on a Saturday morning. Retail shops didn't open until ten.

Something about those men. They walked like they were in no particular hurry. But those duffel bags ... and their straight backs and roving eyes didn't—

The pen. And his cell phone. He'd left them in the car.

John sighed and turned back toward the Subaru. The new epilepsy medication really addled his brain. Made him light-headed too. He was already running late. S-Man had probably signed his contract by now—without the fancy new pen John had bought him. Should have had Bailey bring the present.

He opened the passenger door and leaned down to fetch the gift from the seat. The pen was in a nice wooden box, wrapped in green paper. John snatched it up and straightened—too fast. Dizziness hit.

He shook his head and blinked, waiting it out. With a deep breath, he closed the car door.

Back on the sidewalk, he realized he'd still left his cell phone behind.

Forget it. He wouldn't need it anyhow.

The three men had disappeared. Must have gone into Java Joint.

John smiled to himself. *Wonder if they know they're walking into a party.*

ELEVEN

Paige noticed a flicker of worry on Bailey's face and suspended her hands midclap. In front of her, Frank kept applauding. Paige leaned over the counter toward Bailey. "Something wrong?"

She tossed her head. "Oh no, it's okay. I was just wondering where John is. He's supposed to be here, but this new medication he's taking..."

Bailey's eyes focused over Paige's shoulder, toward the window. Her expression flattened. Paige turned. Spotted three men approaching the door. Two of them were carrying duffel bags.

The hard looks on their faces...

Paige reached for Frank's elbow.

The door flew open. The three men leapt inside.

Guns. They had *guns*.

"Freeze!"

"Don't move!"

"Freeze now!"

Everyone's head snapped around.

The men threw down two duffel bags, and one landed with a clatter. The last man inside banged the door shut and bolted it. Three weapons pointed.

Brittany and Ali shrieked. Frank whipped his right hand toward his gun.

The first of the three men fired.

Bam-bam-bam.

Frank jerked back, and his hands flew up.

He crumpled at Paige's feet.

No!

Paige screamed. Someone else screamed. The room shattered into chaotic wails.

Paige sank to her knees, all breath stopped in her throat. "Frank. *Frank*!"

"Get up!" The man who shot him stalked over, weapon pointed at her face. "Get up *right now* and move back to the counter."

The youngest man's face twisted. "All of you, shut up! And get your hands in the air!"

Screams choked into stunned gasps. Shaking hands raised.

The barrel jammed into Paige's cheek. "Get up. *Now.*"

She moved. Somehow. Pushed to her feet and shuffled back a step. A second. Swaying. Nausea clawing at her stomach. Her blurring gaze fixed on Frank. He wasn't moving.

Dear God, please, no, no, no ...

Her heel hit the base of a stool. Seconds ago, Frank had stood right there. Clapping.

This isn't happening. It isn't real.

Paige smacked both hands over her mouth. *Please, Frank. Move.*

The man who shot Frank backed up. His face was red, deepset eyes narrowed. "Brad, go!"

The second man stood near the first, gun pointed. He rested on one foot, the other leg bouncing. His cheeks were sunken and the pupils of his beady eyes huge. Sweat ran down his temple.

The youngest man, called Brad, slid his gun into his pocket and yanked up the bottom of his jacket. Pulled a white envelope out of his jeans waistband. He strode to Frank and bent down.

"No!" Paige lurched toward him.

The first man leapt forward and shoved her. "Sit *down*!" He pushed her onto a stool next to Jared Moore. The man's teeth gritted, cords ropelike on his thick neck. "Don't move or you're next."

The world blurred. Paige blinked hard, fighting to see Frank. Vaguely, she registered others gasping. Leslie. Angie.

Brad was stuffing the envelope halfway down the back of Frank's pants. He pushed to his feet, then grabbed Frank by the shoulders and flipped him over.

Frank's uniform shirt shrieked three crimson holes.

He was dead.

Paige's mouth opened. A primal cry rose from her soul, clattered up her throat. She slumped to her left. Jared caught her and held on.

Brad clamped his fingers around Frank's wrists and dragged him toward the door.

"No, no!" Paige struggled against Jared, fighting to get up, reach Frank. She didn't care, they could kill her. They'd *already* killed her. "Let me *go*!"

The first man turned his gun on her in cold hatred.

"Shh, Paige, stop." Jared's voice shook. His arms were like iron.

Paige went numb. Some part of her watched Brad unlock the door. The second, skinny man jerked backward, gun still pointed at the group, until he could hold the door open with one hand. Brad shoved Frank over the threshold in a sickening tumble. Closed and bolted the door.

Paige burst into sobs and collapsed against Jared's chest. The only feeble thought her mind could hold was *sixty seconds*. One minute ago, Frank had been here with her. Now he was gone.

She hung on to Jared, squeezing his arms. *Tell me, tell me this isn't happening . . .*

"All right, everybody, listen up." The shooter's voice could have cut steel. "You seen enough to know we mean business. Anybody who moves is dead."

I'm already dead.

The hitched breathing of her friends filtered into Paige's ears. Shock draped a wool blanket over the room.

Frank, Frank ...

The shooter jerked his chin toward Brad. "Get the weapons."

Brad ran over to one of the duffel bags and wrenched back the zipper.

TWELVE

As John walked up Main toward Java Joint, muffled shouts sounded. He cocked his head. What was that?

Three sharp cracks in a row.

Gunshots.

Screams followed. Yelling.

Bailey.

John's feet rooted to the pavement. Sheer, cold terror washed over him.

S-Man's present slipped from his fingers. Next thing he knew, he was running.

Java Joint's door swung open. A body clad in a policeman's uniform tumbled out.

John slid to a halt. *Frank West.*

The café door slammed shut. The deadbolt clicked.

Frank lay crumpled on his side facing the street, still as stone. Something white and flat stuck out of his pants at the back.

The screams from Java Joint stopped.

John's mind spun. What was happening? He stared at the still form. Frank had been shot. *Shot.*

Those three men. Their duffel bags. *Guns.*

Bailey. All of our friends.

Was he dreaming this?

John's stomach lurched. He had to do … something. Get Frank. Get help.

He ran toward the fallen officer.

At the edge of the café, he pulled up. Its windows were almost floor to ceiling, starting too low to crawl beneath them. Go any farther, and he'd be a sitting duck.

Frank. John had to get him out of there.

Dear Lord, give me strength.

No more time for thinking; he had to act.

John took a deep breath, stooped down, and started a crab-walk toward Frank.

THIRTEEN

Bailey clutched the counter, her knuckles white. She watched the attackers around the backs of her friends, who were all clustered on the other side. As if frozen from some other world, Ted's contract and pen lay near the other end of the counter. Had he only been signing it minutes ago?

The two older men pointed guns at them all. Shock razored through Bailey's body, shredding her thoughts. She could hardly feel, barely *think*. Couldn't hear anything over the rush of blood in her ears, the skid-pound of her heart.

Frank. Paige.

God, help us.

Brad reached into the open duffel bag on the floor.

Bailey tore her eyes away. She couldn't bear to see what was in there. Numbly she stared at the other two men with guns. *Remember their faces.* The thought pulsed like a dim light through the fog in her brain. Yes—remember. Victims of a crime were supposed to do that.

She tried to focus.

The man in charge was about six feet and beefy. Barrel-chested. Wide nose, close-set brown eyes. Heavy overhanging brow. He had an intense, almost predatory look. Thinning dark hair. Over fifty. His face was flushed. Angst and energy rose like steam off his big shoulders. Any minute now his impatient finger could jerk the trigger.

Second man. Much Younger. Same height but skinny. Gaunt cheeks. Large ears, a mole on his left jaw. His pupils didn't look right—way too large. His eyes darted this way and that. His tongue ran back and forth under his top lip, his torso rocking.

She cut her gaze back to Brad. He looked like a young version of the first man. But the way he moved, the looks he threw at the man in charge ... Brad was steely. Full of anger. Bristling with arrogance.

Movement outside the front window caught Bailey's attention. She flicked her eyes without moving her head.

John.

He was trying to reach Frank. But a bullet could pierce that glass so easily.

Oh, dear Lord, no. She couldn't lose John.

She glanced at the two men with guns. Both were in profile to the front of the cafe, focused on their hostages. Brad's attention was riveted to the duffel bag.

Bailey's eyes cut again to the window.

Her husband crept forward.

FOURTEEN

John's leg muscles shook. He focused on Frank's still body, screaming at himself not to look inside Java Joint. The terror of what he saw might freeze him.

His head turned.

The sight stabbed him. Three men, two with guns trained on everyone in the café. The Scenes and Beans crew huddled near the counter. Bailey stood alone on the serving side. Looking at him.

John's knees nearly gave way.

Everything within him pulled toward Bailey. Right there—she was *right there*. His arm twitched to punch through the glass, rescue his wife—

Some unseen hand shoved him forward.

He reached Frank. John squeezed between the young officer and the wooden door, breathing hard. He was now out of sight through the windows. His wavering gaze fell on the white thing stuck in Frank's waistband. Looked like an envelope. With the visible letters "ce Edwards."

Vince Edwards? Kanner Lake's chief of police.

With trembling hands John grabbed the envelope and stuffed it in his pants pocket.

He had to get Frank out of there.

Which way? Up the street and around the corner?

No, down to his car.

John grasped Frank's shoulder and turned him onto his back. Three red stains glared from his chest and stomach. *Dear God.* He was already dead.

Rage shot through John. He couldn't save Frank. It was *too late.*

His eyes stung. He would still get Frank out of here. He was not leaving the young man's body to lie in the sun.

John leaned forward, peered over his left shoulder through the window. The two men with guns hadn't moved. He couldn't see the youngest one.

Now or never. Ten seconds, that was all he needed. Ten seconds to drag Frank past those windows ...

Energy burned his veins like a fast-catching fire. *One, two, three—go!*

John scuffled below Frank, grabbed his feet, and tugged with all his might.

Movement through the window. John's head swiveled. The youngest man was pulling something out of a duffel bag. His head jerked up.

Their eyes met. The man's motion stopped.

I'm dead.

The split second stretched out. John didn't slow.

One of the gunmen spotted John and yelled something. The younger man's eyes held John's for a split second. Then he twisted back to the duffel bag.

Air gushed from John's throat. He cleared the last window and jumped out of view.

Keep moving, shouted a voice in his brain. He couldn't stand the sight of Frank's unprotected head dragging along the cement, but what could he do?

He checked back over his shoulder, gauging the distance to his car, his cell phone. The Subaru looked a million miles away.

John's head swam. Dizziness brushed his limbs. He wasn't going to make it. If he collapsed on the sidewalk and one of those gunmen stepped out Java Joint's door ...

Somehow he kept on his feet.

Halfway down the long block he passed the bait and tackle shop—with a deeply recessed entry. John swiveled into its safety and yanked Frank all the way in.

Gulping air, John collapsed beside the still form. He leaned back against the hard brick, hardly daring to believe he'd made it this far.

His vision dimmed.

He'd just stay here a minute until the dizziness passed. He had to get Frank to his car. Call 911. Drive off this street ...

All energy drained away.

No, no. Bailey ... I have to help Bailey ...

John's world faded to black.

FIFTEEN

Bev Trexel saw John disappear past the windows.

She closed her eyes in fleeting relief. When she'd caught sight of John trying to drag away Frank's body—the epitome of heroism—Bev's terror had risen to the point of nausea. She could not imagine Bailey without John. That moment of eye contact between John and the despicable man named Brad still hovered in Bev's head. She'd been so sure Brad was going to shoot.

Bev stood toward the front end of the counter next to Angie, who gasped each breath in a sob. Bev's eyes remained dry—she couldn't muster the ability to cry. But her legs shook. Her whole *body* shook as she tried to hold up both hands. She felt the blood rushing down her arms, into her shoulders, until both limbs wobbled as if made of straw. Her rational mind knew this nightmare was real, screamed that she'd witnessed Frank West being shot to death. But her heart couldn't yet comprehend it.

Bev wanted to look over her shoulder and check on Bailey, standing by herself behind the counter. Had she seen John? But no. It might only draw attention to her, and the mere act of turning her head might upset the little balance to which she clung.

Her eyes fixed on Brad.

From the duffel bag he yanked out a long black sheet. Masking tape ran along its top, half of the tape's width on the fabric.

Sections of the tape above the sheet had stuck together, and Brad ripped them apart. He threw a dark glance at their huddled group. "That one?" He jerked his head toward S-Man.

The thug who had shot Frank turned to S-Man. "Help him hang the sheets. And move fast." His words came clipped and hard. "You." He sneered at Pastor Hank. "Get chairs for them to stand on."

S-Man glared at him, then strode to the duffel bag and took one end of the sheet. Hank hustled toward the nearest table and chairs. Picked up a chair in each hand. Brad pointed to the window closest to the counter. "Put 'em on either side."

Hank obeyed.

"Hurry up!" Frank's killer spat. Tension pulsed from him, beating into Bev's chest.

Alexander. Abigail. Angela. Her three grandchildren, ages fourteen to eight. From nowhere, their faces burned into her mind. *Harlon.* Her husband of over forty years.

Harlon, don't despair. I'll get through this.

She had to—what would the man do without her? He couldn't even wash his own laundry.

"Everybody else line up with her." Frank's shooter pointed toward Bailey. His animal-like gaze swung to Bev and hung there. She cringed. "Move it, move it!"

Line up. So they all could be shot?

Bev's legs moved. Her raised arms collapsed, and she grabbed on to Angie's shoulders. They clung to each other as everyone scuffled around the counter like a flock of frightened birds. Bev registered jumbled flashes of sight and sound as the group fell into a ragged line. Carla's arms around Brittany and Ali. The girls' white faces, Ali's chin trembling. Wilbur, tight-jawed and indignant. Leslie and Jared holding on to Paige, who barely managed to keep on her feet.

Angie scuttled next to Bailey and stopped. Bev pressed in behind her. Backs against the wall, they turned to face their executioners. Carla and the girls crowded next to Bev.

Ted and Brad hung the first sheet, and the café dimmed. Pastor Hank stood watching.

"The next one, go, go, go!" Frank's killer flicked his gaze from the street to his hostages. "You!" He pointed to Pastor Hank. "Get the next sheet."

The gaunt-cheeked man holding a gun on them jittered, eyes cutting right and left. *High on something*, Bev thought. She watched his finger on the trigger, knowing he could pull it any second.

Pastor Hank hurried to grab a second sheet from the duffel bag. Ted and Brad shoved their chairs to the next window.

"Bailey" — Frank's killer gestured — "grab the phone cord out of the wall."

Bev sensed her stiffening. *Bailey*. He knew her name.

The man leaned forward menacingly. *"Pull out the phone cord."*

Bailey jumped, pivoted toward the phone. It sat on the counter near the back wall. Bev watched her trembling fingers shove up the little lever on the cord and slide it out of the phone. She dropped the dangling end on the counter.

"Now turn out the lights back there."

Two large overhead lights stretched above the counter area. "Th-the ..." Bailey could only stutter. "S-switch is at the other end."

Someone down that way hit the control, and the room dimmed more.

Gaunt Cheeks swung about, looking for more lighting controls. He spotted them near the front door and hurried over to flick them off. All lights cut except those over the back hallway.

58

The second window was covered. Brad, Ted, and Hank moved to the first window on the other side of the door. They covered it, then started in on the last one.

Within minutes all glass was blocked. The café fell into a deep, unnatural dusk.

Frank's killer turned a piercing look on Ted. "You S-Man?"

S-Man nodded. His lips were pressed, eyes narrowed. If he was surprised at being known, he didn't show it.

"Get behind the counter with everybody else." The man looked to Hank. "You the preacher or Jared?"

"I'm Pastor Hank." An unblinking calm spread across his face.

The man sneered. "Get back there too. And don't bother prayin', 'cause God done heard our prayers first."

With a defiant expression, S-Man squeezed between Jared and Leslie. Pastor Hank stopped at the end of the lineup, next to Jared.

Brad jumped down from his chair and made for the second duffel bag. Unzipped it. Pulled out a gun that snatched Bev's breath away. She didn't know much about firearms. Only that she'd seen something like this in the ridiculous Rambo-type movies Harlon liked to watch. Some kind of automatic that could kill a lot of people in seconds.

"Let *me* do it." Brad clutched the weapon, lip curled and fire in his eyes.

Angie moaned. Bev's ankles turned to putty. *Oh, Harlon, I'm going to die.*

Frank's killer evaluated Brad, his jaw working. He turned to the drugged, skinny man. "*You* wanted him to come."

Skinny hitched his shoulders. "Let him do it—I don't care."

The thug in charge gave Brad a hard look. "Make it good."

SIXTEEN

For heaven's sake, I can be such a scatterbrain.

Fifty-six-year-old Sarah Wray muttered to herself as she crossed to the storage closet in her office at the back of Simple Pleasures. Directly across the street at Java Joint, all her friends were celebrating, and here she was, late to the party. Not until she'd parked her car in a lot off the back alley did she remember Ted's present, sitting on her desk in the shop. Now that she'd come to fetch it, she saw it wasn't even wrapped. Doggone it all. She'd hurried out of the store last night, forgetting to get the gift ready.

Now look at the time. She'd probably miss seeing Ted sign his contract.

Sighing, she opened the closet door and pulled out the roll of solid navy paper—the "manly" version of gift wrap she used. Female gifts were done in shiny silver. She walked over to her rectangular table and pushed boxes aside. Cut a small piece of the paper and laid Ted's gift in the center. It was a brown leather business card case, with *Ted Dawson, Writer* engraved upon it in regal-looking letters. Quite the needed item for S-Man when his fame as a novelist soared. And no doubt it—

Faint sounds hit Sarah's ears. *Crack, crack, crack.* Her chin came up. What was that?

Other sounds—more raucous. Drawn out.

Screams?

Sarah froze, listening.

Nothing more.

Her eyes roved to the corner shelf, full with boxes of new products. She cocked her head to the right, toward the office door.

All was quiet.

She let out a sigh. *Wonderful.* Now she was late *and* imagining things.

Her pudgy fingers scrambled back to work, wrapping the package. When it was taped, she finished it off with some ribbon. *There.* She bustled back to the closet to put the paper roll away.

Sarah stepped out of the office and hurried through her long shop, past all of the glitzy, colorful items she loved to sell. She focused through the front windows directly across the street at Java Joint—and pulled to a halt.

What had happened to the glass over there? One of the windows was all black.

She took a few steps forward, moving her head to view the café from different angles. Maybe it was just some trick of the morning sun...

But no. The window was solid black.

An odd feeling crept over Sarah. First those sounds she'd decided she hadn't really heard; now this. Either S-Man's gathering was one wild party, or something else was going on.

She surveyed the café, wondering what to do.

In the next moment, a second window blackened.

Sarah leaned forward, squinting. Trying to make out the movements she saw on the other side of the windows. Impossible, with the way the sun's rays hit the glass.

A third window went dark and then—as she watched—the fourth.

Sarah ran a hand through her gray curls. It would be so simple to just cross the street and walk into the café, see what was going on. But something deep inside just wouldn't—

61

The Simple Pleasures windows exploded.

The world erupted with sound. Glass shattered, a *radt-adadt-adadt—guns?* Walls were punched behind her; displays crashed to the floor. Then more breaking glass out on the street—the building next door? Farther away, *radt-adadt-adadt-adadt*, then coming back, closer and closer—

A force hit her left upper arm. Sarah jerked backward. Pain pierced the spot like a burning ice pick. Sarah screamed, lurched sideways, and fell to her knees.

Her wild eyes looked to her shoulder. *Blood!* Oh, dear Lord in heaven, blood, her blood, lots of it.

Radt-adadt-adadt. Up the street glass clattered, thick smacks against building walls.

Sarah's right hand flew to her wound. She drew it back, sticky and red.

The world fell silent.

She screamed again, long and loud until the sound sizzled her ears.

Energy drained from her body. She rolled onto her back, staring at the ceiling. Her arm throbbed and flamed. She couldn't *stand* the pain—it would eat her alive.

Nausea swept through Sarah's stomach.

What had hap—? Where was . . . ? How . . . ?

Shock uncoiled through Sarah's limbs and dragged her into unconsciousness.

SEVENTEEN

The gunfire and crashing glass stopped.

Pastor Hank found himself clutching Jared's arm hard enough to cut off circulation. He loosened his grip. Jared looked over at him, the man's mouth hanging open. All down the line of his friends, Hank heard sobs and moans. He glanced farther to his right, checking on Brittany and Ali. Carla stood between them, the trio huddled and shaking.

Lord, couldn't You at least have kept those two young girls away from this?

Brad strode back into the café, the gun he'd just fired up and down Main Street grasped in one hand. He locked and bolted the door. Victorious revenge blackened his face, turning it hard, almost inhuman.

Somewhere in the distance, a woman screamed.

Brad gave the man in charge a stiff, smug nod. "Glad I came now?"

The man's expression remained like stone. "Finish the windows."

Brad laid his weapon down on a table across the room. Walked to the first duffel bag and snatched up a roll of clear packaging tape. He jumped on the chair he'd left by the far window, tore off sections of the tape, and reinforced the entire top of the black sheet. Then ran tape along both sides and the bottom.

He repeated the procedure on all four windows, working as if racing a time clock.

The crying and groans among the hostage lineup died to shocked silence. Hank slipped a look at Paige. Her face was drained of color. Hank pictured John, somewhere off Main Street, watching a coroner's wagon loading Frank's body.

Bile rose in Hank's throat. He swallowed it down. *How* could this have happened?

Janet. Thank God his wife hadn't come today. She'd gone to help their oldest daughter in Boise, who was fighting mono. Amy had four kids and just couldn't keep up.

"Done." Brad pitched the tape back in the duffel bag.

"Check the other door." Man-in-Charge kept his eyes on the lineup. "Get the hall lights. And phone cord."

Brad threw him a hard look, as if he resented being told what he already knew. He strode down the hall, flicking off the light without slowing. Hurried in and out of the office, then disappeared on his way to the back door. Hank listened to his footsteps take him down the hall and back. He reappeared.

"Locked, like we knew it would be." His shoulders were straight, face defiant. "I say we upend the desk against the door."

Man-in-Charge surveyed him, then nodded. "Mitch, go. I got this covered."

Mitch. The shaky one.

Mitch stuck his weapon into his jacket pocket and ran to help. In seconds papers swished and items clattered in the office. Hyena-like laughter floated from the room. *Mitch.* Hank pictured his arms sweeping Bailey's possessions off her desk onto the floor. In two minutes the men had moved the desk down the hall and out of sight. Wood creaked, and items tumbled in drawers as they turned the desk on its side.

Brad and Mitch returned. Mitch's face flushed red, his lips twitching with excitement. Brad headed for the near-empty duffel bag and picked it up. Mitch planted himself next to Man-in-Charge, pulled his gun out to aim at the group.

"Listen up." Man-in-Charge stepped sideways as Brad approached the counter and laid down the bag. "We want everybody's cell phone. One by one turn off your phones, step forward, and put it in the bag. You first." He gestured to Bailey.

Hank threw her a glance. *Lord, keep her strong.*

Her throat convulsed in a swallow. "I ... my husband ... I don't have it with me."

The man glared at her. "Get over here, right in front of this gun barrel. *Now.*"

EIGHTEEN

The shriek of gunfire and breaking glass roused John. He opened bleary eyes. Saw gray cement. Fear gripped him, but for a split second he couldn't remember where he was.

The gunfire stopped, followed by more bursts. Glass crackled and splintered.

The world fell deathly silent.

A woman screamed.

John blinked, and his vision cleared. Frank West lay on the cement at his feet.

He shuffled to his knees and leaned over Frank, gazing at the young man's pale skin. Instant tears stung John's eyes. Frank was only in his midtwenties. So strong and healthy, so much to live for. He loved being a cop. Last Christmas he and Paige had started dating. John had heard all the details from Bailey, who knew everything about everybody. Frank and Paige seemed so happy.

The area around the bullet hole in Frank's stomach was seeping blood. The other two holes in the chest hadn't bled much. John felt for a pulse in Frank's wrist.

Nothing.

John raised his eyes toward heaven — and his gaze caught on the damage across the street. It looked like a war zone. Windows broken everywhere, chunks of brick and wood knocked from building walls.

The gunfire. It had come from Java Joint.

Bailey. A shuddering gasp wrenched from John's throat. He crawled forward, stopped at the end of the entryway, and stuck his head out. Squinted up the street. No one in sight.

Was *anybody* in Java Joint still alive?

Brain numb, John crawled out to the middle of the sidewalk and peered at the café, expecting to see shattered windows.

They were intact. Which meant the gun had been fired from outside the café.

But they were dark. As if they'd been blacked out?

John swiveled his head up and down his side of Main, checking all other businesses.

No damage.

He reversed back into the entryway and collapsed against the brick wall, trying to reason. The men had come out of Java Joint and shot across the street—just to show their firepower? The gun—it couldn't have been the one used to shoot Frank. He'd be cut to pieces.

Bailey and the others. *Please, God, let them still be alive.*

John's chest constricted. He forced his chin up, took three deep, long breaths. Longing, *needing* to see life, he pushed to his knees and leaned over Frank again. He tried a second time for a wrist pulse to no avail. He groaned and in desperation pressed the palm of his hand against the policeman's chest.

He felt a faint stir.

A *heartbeat?* He pressed harder, holding his breath.

Yes! It was there. Frank was alive. Barely. But he was *alive.*

John had to get him to a hospital—now.

Cell phone. In the Subaru—

The sound of a car engine, coming from the bottom of the street. John staggered to his feet and edged toward the right front of the recessed entry, angling a look left and down. A black pickup truck was turning onto Main from Hanley.

John glanced up toward Java Joint. No movement. He stepped out onto the sidewalk, waving his arms. The driver signaled to him. John jumped back inside the entry.

The truck rumbled past the first block and swerved right onto First Street. John saw its rear bumper as it ground to a stop. The engine cut; a door slammed. Stan Seybert, a muscular logger in his thirties, appeared. He gawked at the broken glass across the street.

John could see a cell phone clipped to the right side of his belt. "Hurry!"

Stan sprinted toward him. Reached the entry and veered inside. "What's going *on*?" He gawked down at Frank.

John gulped air. "He's been shot. Give me your phone."

NINETEEN

Bailey's ankles shook. Was this man going to kill her just because she didn't have a cell phone?

She turned to walk the length of the hostage lineup, prayers running through her head. Her heart pounded, blood whooshing in her ears. Tension vibrated from her friends. She saw clutched hands, trembling limbs. Leslie reached out to touch Bailey's arm as she passed.

"Stop!" The man cried. Leslie's arm recoiled. "*Nobody* else move. And don't talk."

Bailey rounded the counter and stopped. She stared at the man's gun, unable to take another step.

"I said *here*." He pointed to the floor in front of him.

Mitch jumped forward, grabbed her arm and shoved. "Go!"

Bailey stumbled to the man in charge, only half sensing her feet against the floor. He backed up two steps, gun pointed at her chest. "Brad."

Brad strode to her, stopping within inches of her face. He stared down at her, blue eyes as deep and cold as a glacier lake.

What did these people *want*?

"Hold your arms up and out to your sides," Man-in-Charge commanded.

Bailey obeyed.

With efficient movements Brad patted her down like a policeman looking for weapons. Bailey's eyes squeezed shut at the violation, and she swayed. Someone in the line hissed in a breath.

"She's clean." Brad stepped away.

"All right. Get back where you were." Man-in-Charge grazed Bailey with a glance.

Bailey hurried to her place in line, pulled to her friends like a fugitive seeking shelter from a storm.

Man-in-Charge curled his lip. "Anybody else say they don't have a phone, they're coming out here too. We find one on ya, you're dead." He looked to Angie. "You next. Hurry up."

Angie's hands clutched each side of her face. "It's in my purse. Over there." She pointed toward a table in the center of the room.

Brad yanked up the purse, pulled out a phone. He turned it off and threw it in the duffel bag.

They went down the line, each person throwing in a phone except for Wilbur, who didn't carry one. Brittany and Ali carried their phones in their jeans pockets. Bev, Leslie, and Carla had to pull their phones from purses that sat askew on the counter or had been knocked to the floor. Brad lined up all the handbags on the counter when they were done.

Wilbur was ordered around front to be patted down. He stalked to Brad like a stubborn soldier caught by the enemy. Stared straight ahead, his mouth working as he was searched.

Brad smirked at him. "Like your shirt."

Cell phones all taken, Brad zipped up the duffel bag and ran down the hall to throw it in the office. It landed on the floor with a muted clatter. He returned and went to the second bag, pulling out two large guns like the one he'd used outside.

Bailey's fingers clenched, her short nails cutting into her palms. Angie gasped. Ali burst into sobs, quickly muffled in Carla's shoulder.

Mitch grinned and stuck his handgun back in his pocket. "Yeehaw, I like this one much better." He took the large gun from Brad. With Mitch's new weapon trained on the group, Man-in-Charge slipped his handgun in his jacket and took the larger one. From the duffel bag Brad lifted out extra magazines of ammunition, each of the three stuffing them in their pockets.

So many bullets. A shiver ran down Bailey's spine. Did they plan to shoot the entire town?

Leaving the duffel bag unzipped — for easy access to more ammunition? — Brad put it in the far corner, near the computer table.

He grabbed his own gun and pointed it toward them. "All right. We're in business."

The three men stepped into their own straight line, fanned out the length of the counter. All three guns pointed at Bailey and her friends.

Now we die.

Brad's lips curved in a chilling smile. His eyes traveled up and down the line and fell on Brittany with satisfaction. Bailey's limbs flushed cold. She could see the girl tense. Carla's arm tightened around her daughter.

Bailey's mind numbed. Her bleary eyes drifted back to the men, then up to the clock on the opposite wall. Twelve minutes after eight — that was all. Everything had happened — her whole life had changed — in less than twelve minutes.

Man-in-Charge took a deep breath, and his nostrils flared. "Suppose we should introduce ourselves. My name's Kent Wicksell. My oldest son, Mitch. Second son, Brad."

Wicksell. Where had Bailey heard that name?

"You're looking at three desperate men. Nobody listened to reason, so here we are. We want one thing. We get it, you all go free — *if* you do what you're told until then. We don't get it — you die." The corners of his mouth turned down. "It don't get much simpler than that."

TWENTY

Kanner Lake Police Chief Vince Edwards punched off the last call on his cell phone, calculating his next moves. Five minutes ago he'd been reading the paper in his kitchen and enjoying a second cup of coffee on his day off. Now he sprang into action. No time to let his emotions run. No time to mourn for a deputy down or hostages taken.

He grabbed his gun and a backup weapon and ran outside.

A few months ago Vince had earned a national certification in hostage negotiation. Three phases of training in Las Vegas and Scottsdale, each forty hours. Lessons in the psychology of negotiating and the personality types of hostage takers. Acting out scenarios. The final phase included an intense eight-hour drill of being taken hostage himself.

Never had he expected to use the training in his own town.

From his police vehicle Vince grabbed his body armor and slipped into it. By Idaho law the Kevlar vest was with a chief of police at all times. The vest was a level III-A with side panels plus two trauma plates—one each covering the center of mass on the front and back of the body. While the vest alone would stop a bullet, the impact could still inflict serious injuries such as broken ribs. The plates served as protection against those injuries. At a lightweight and comfortable 1.6 pounds, the vest was designed to wear under clothing if needed.

With each second counting, Vince put it on over his shirt and jumped into his vehicle.

Lights flashing, he screeched out of the driveway and headed for downtown, less than a mile away. Vince had already phoned two of his remaining deputies. One was Jim Tentley, a Kanner Lake officer for over six years. Late forties, six feet and stocky, Jim had been out aiming radar on the west side of the Lake. He'd now be flying toward their meeting point—Lakeshore and Hanley, one block down from the beginning of Main.

Vince had also talked to Al Newman, aka Charlie Brown, thanks to his round, bald head. Al had been off duty but was now on his way to block off Main above Java Joint. Vince had given Al the task of calling the fourth officer, Roger Waitman. Crusty, opinionated Roger had been with the Kanner Lake Police almost fifteen years. He was lean but strong, an often humorless, no-nonsense cop. He lived just three blocks from the downtown area and should be at their meeting point by the time Vince arrived.

Dispatch had told Stan Seybert and John Truitt to stay where they were, and someone would come get them. The maneuver was called a "sneak and snatch." A victim down, in line of fire, rescued under temporary cover.

The area would need to be cordoned off for a good five blocks in all directions—and that took a fair amount of people. The Idaho State Police—ISP—were sending officers and three snipers from their Crisis Response Team. The CRT, another term for the often-used SWAT acronym (Special Weapons and Tactics), was based in Coeur d'Alene, with many of its members living between that town and Spirit Lake. CRT response time to Kanner Lake—one hour.

Vince took a circular route toward downtown, since it was unsafe to drive past Main. He hit Lakeshore two blocks to the west, hung a hard left, and carved to a halt opposite the bottom of Hanley.

Roger was already getting out of his vehicle. As Vince slid from the car, Jim pulled up. The three met on the sidewalk in front of the hotel construction site. Jim and Roger both wore Kevlar vests.

"Let's go over this again." Vince launched into details.

Via cell phone he'd talked to Stan and John, who'd told him the location of all cars on their side of Main Street, up to their position at the bait and tackle shop. There were quite a few. Thank God for Kanner Lake's wide sidewalks.

When Vince finished, Jim's face was grim. "Is Frank going to make it?"

From what Vince had heard, it didn't look good. He glanced from one man to the other. "Better be praying."

Roger shook his head. Vince and Jim locked eyes. Vince could feel Jim's adrenaline vibrating the air, mixing with his own.

"Let's go."

He and Jim threw themselves back into their cars. Vince gunned his vehicle forward on Lakeshore past the intersection, then reversed around the corner onto Hanley. He idled, foot on the brake, while Jim followed and lined up with his car single file, stopping within four feet of his front bumper. Al remained on Lakeshore, awaiting the ambulance.

Vince half turned, laid his right arm across the seat. In his peripheral vision he saw Jim doing the same. The sequence that would follow strung out in his mind. In a few minutes he could have John, Stan, and Frank to safety. Or he could get them all killed.

Vince took a deep breath. Into his radio he said, "Ready to reverse?"

"Ready."

Vince's fingers dug into the back of the seat. "On the count of three." His left hand curled around the steering wheel. "One. Two. Three. *Go!*"

He hit the accelerator.

TWENTY-ONE

Sarah Wray awoke to the sound of her own groaning.

Her weighted eyes fought to open, her gaze landing on the lighting tracks along the Simple Pleasures ceiling. Some of the bulbs were gone. *Shattered. Like the windows.*

The nerves in Sarah's left arm writhed with pain. She rolled to her right side and pushed halfway to a sitting position. Her stomach roiled and her head pounded. Broken glass surrounded her. Blood stained the carpet where she had lain.

Telephone.

She had to make it back to her office, call 911. Something terrible had happened at Java Joint. And she'd been *shot*. The *whole town* had been shot.

Could she stand? Her legs felt weak, her gut churning.

She *had* to get on her feet. Couldn't crawl. Too much glass.

"Jesus, help me get up."

Sarah could use only her right arm. The left hung useless, screaming at its wound.

She pulled in two deep breaths. Managed to get on her knees. Then pushed to a tentative, swaying hunch. Dizziness clawed at her. She forced it back, lifted one foot in front of the other. Step by slow step, moaning and praying aloud, she picked her way through the battered store. Soft blankets, glittery bracelets and purses, sets of wine glasses, flower arrangements, and knickknacks—so many on the floor, broken to bits. Her beloved store, tattered and ruined. Sobs rose within her—for her store, for the pain, for whatever was happening in the now ghost-silent town.

She veered into the back wall and bounced off. Shook her head. Closed her eyes against the light and felt the familiar way with her good hand. Into the short hall, right into her office. Across the floor to her desk and phone.

Sarah sank into her chair, fumbled the receiver off its base. Laid it down, forefinger extended, searching for the right buttons. For a moment her mind froze, unable to recall the three digits.

Her finger moved of its own accord. She raised the phone to her right ear.

"911. What is your emergency?"

Words meshed on her tongue. How to describe it?

"This is 911. Caller, are you there?"

"Yes. I . . . somebody's shooting up Kanner Lake. And I think they got me."

TWENTY-TWO

In Java Joint, Leslie sat at a table with Ted and Paige, their arms visible on the tabletop as all the hostages had been commanded. Leslie's insides boiled and seethed, and that's just the way she wanted it. Cut through the outrage and she'd reach her terror. And *that* ran so deep and strong she didn't dare face it.

Wicksell. All too well she knew that name. Had covered the trial not long ago for the *Kanner Lake Times.* She'd recognized the three faces the minute they stormed through the door.

Wound around her anger—prayers. First for Frank, then for herself and the other hostages. *Frank.* Leslie had once been crazy about him, until she started dating Ted. Now Frank and Paige were so much in love. Leslie sneaked a sideways glance at her roommate. Paige pressed back in her chair, eyes downcast, her beautiful features carved from ice. Leslie's heart clutched. She knew her friend all too well. Paige had retreated deep within herself—her ancient method of survival. Nearly two years of slow healing in Kanner Lake, and in two minutes and three gunshots, it had all been torn away.

Dear God, I can't believe Frank is dead.

The attackers had herded everyone out from behind the counter and told them to drag enough of the small, round tables toward the back wall of the café so they all could sit jammed together, at least partially facing the street. The rest of the tables and chairs were pushed against the wall on the right. Which left the center clear for pacing.

Well, Mitch paced. And jerked and sweated. Guy had to be high as a kite, probably on meth. Three steps toward the counter, three steps the other direction. Back and forth, back and forth. Torso twisted so his gun pointed at his hostages. And a twitchy finger near the trigger of a weapon that could blow them all to smithereens in seconds.

At Leslie's table, Ted faced the front door with Paige on his left, Leslie on his right. Leslie had a good view of the counter, where Bad Boy Brad had positioned himself. Behind Leslie sat the corner table that held Java Joint's computer. A glance over her shoulder caught Kent perched in front of the monitor, his gun on the floor to his right, within a second's reach. Lucky Bailey got to sit on his left, between him and Leslie.

Brad had moved their duffel bag of extra ammunition behind the counter.

Leslie focused on Brad. He stood in front of Wilbur's stool, feet apart, gun aimed at their group. A fox in a henhouse.

Frank. Revenge slimed through Leslie. She didn't want to see Kent and his two sons go to prison for this. She wanted to see them *die.*

Brad caught her eye and glared. If his father was stone, this guy was steel. He had an overconfident air about him that read, *Yeah, I'm younger, but I'm meaner and smarter, so don't push me.* His finger, too, edged a trigger. Like he'd pull it just to prove a point.

Leslie looked away.

Oh, for pen and paper. Her reporter's mind catalogued the position of every other hostage in the room. Farthest away, at the table closest to the hall, were Bev, facing her, Angie in the middle, and Jared, with his back to Leslie. Next table, Carla, sitting between Brittany on her left and Ali on her right. Carla held hands with both girls. One thing Leslie knew—if any of the Wicksells touched those girls, mama bear Carla would launch a full-on attack—and get her head blown off in the process. Leslie wouldn't be far behind. She was too close to Ali to sit back and watch something terrible happen to the girl.

Leslie surveyed Brittany. How was she holding up? Only eight months ago her entire life had turned upside down. The only father she'd known was a U.S. senator from Washington, on his way to the White House. Now his political career lay in tatters. Given his history, the media would jump on this story even more when they learned Brittany was among the hostages.

Leslie's gaze moved to the third and closest table—where Wilbur and Pastor Hank sat. Wilbur faced her, but she could see only Pastor Hank's back. Wilbur was studying Meth Mitch with the venom of a cobra.

Ted inched his hand over and laid it on top of Leslie's. Tears bit her eyes. Her wonderful S-Man, trying to comfort.

How can I leave him in two weeks?

She swallowed hard. Hey, who said she'd live till then?

Behind her, Kent cursed. "Come on, what's *taking* him so long?"

Mitch yanked to a stop. "How long's it been since we got here?"

Brad's eyes flicked to the wall clock. "Twenty-five minutes. Dad, let me take over the computer. I know what I'm doing."

"Stay at the counter and shut up! This was *my* job before you decided to tag along."

Brad's eyes narrowed to slits.

Great, can't even get along with each other. Where's that leave us?

Of all things, Kent was waiting for a comment to appear on the current Scenes and Beans blog post. He'd drafted Bailey to show him how it worked. Leslie listened as Bailey popped the comments box up on-screen, then showed him how to close out of it and get back in, checking for a new comment. The man had to be clicking the thing a good three times a minute. Every time he apparently found no change, he cursed louder. Before long he'd bust right out of his skin.

Leslie looked at Ted. If only she could lean against him, feel him hold her. But they were not to move their arms from the tables, were not to talk.

Mitch scratched his cheek and went back to pacing.

Minutes dragged by. The clock ticked. In the hundreds of times Leslie had been in Java Joint, she'd never noticed the faint sound of its second hand. Java Joint usually bustled with talk and laughter, the stutter of chair legs against the floor, the gurgle of the espresso machine. The café's smell was an inviting blend of coffee and pastries and milk. Now the place stank with sweat, some of it her own.

Brad stared at her. The clock ticked. Mitch clomped.

Kent clicked the mouse and cursed.

Clicked and cursed.

Mitch paced.

Brad fingered his weapon.

One of them was going to blow here. Soon.

Mitch jerked to a halt. His dark eyes burned. "It's taking too long."

"Yeah," Brad spat. "I say we shoot another one."

TWENTY-THREE

Vince reverse-rounded the corner from Hanley onto Main and backed straight up the first block. The seconds played out, sights and sounds bombarding his senses. Shops whizzing by, glass shot out of almost every one on his right. His back tires eating up asphalt, the roar of his engine. The distant sound of a siren.

Ambulance.

Any minute the door to Java Joint could burst open, bullets flying down the street. His weapons were ready for a shoot-out, but he didn't want that—not here, not now. Any gunman who survived would only be harder to reach in negotiations, his adrenaline and anger pumping, likely spilling out to his hostages ...

Vince's vehicle hit the intersection of Main and First.

Now.

He cranked the wheel hard, veering backward onto First, passing Stan's truck at an angle, then straightened even with the sidewalk. Stepped on the gas to jump the curb.

His rear tires hit, and the car jounced. Vince's right hand hung tightly to the back of his seat. He shot backward, gripping the wheel, no room for error. His car barely squeezed between buildings and cars parked at the curb. He passed the bait shop, hoping Stan and John were ready with Frank. No time to look. After speeding by he hit his brakes, head whipping front to back to gauge his stop.

He slid to a halt one car length above the bait shop. If the gunmen burst out of Java Joint, they'd have to shoot right through his vehicle to get to the rescue team.

Jim braked in front of Vince's vehicle, his back door lined up with the recessed entry.

Perfect.

Vince's hand wouldn't loose from the steering wheel. He checked over his shoulder. All clear.

Jim leapt from his car, flung open its back door. The edge of the door's frame disappeared into the recessed entry.

Come on, come on!

Stan and John ran forward with Frank, one holding his legs, the other carrying his torso. Jim helped support Frank while Stan dove onto the backseat.

Vince cast another look toward Java Joint. Still clear.

His eyes caught a flash of dark at the café. He jerked. A man?

No. The windows. They were covered in black.

These men had come prepared.

Vince twisted back toward Jim's vehicle.

Stan gripped Frank's shoulders and slid across the seat, pulling the officer with him. John and Stan loaded Frank's legs onto the seat. John jumped in last, crouching on the backseat floor. Jim slammed their door and threw himself behind the wheel. His car surged down the sidewalk and onto the street at First. Vince followed.

They swerved left around the corner onto Hanley and to a stop one block down at Lakeshore. An ambulance stood ready, EMTs pulling out a gurney. Jim waved them over to his car and leapt out, opening the back door for them.

Vince checked his watch. They'd done the sneak and snatch in two minutes.

He sucked in a long breath. Only then did he feel the heavy *pump-pump* of his heart. He lifted his hands from the wheel, fingers stiff from their hard clutch. *Thank You, God.*

He slid out of his car, gave a quick nod to Jim. "Good job."

Jim wiped his forehead. "You too."

John Truitt leaned against the front of Jim's vehicle, out of the EMTs' way. The man looked mighty haggard. Stan stood next to him, a comforting hand on his arm. Vince pointed at them. "Be right with you."

The EMTs lifted Frank onto their gurney and began checking his vitals as they rushed toward the ambulance. Vince jogged over as they started to load him in and took a long—last?—look at Frank's face. The kid was ghostly pale. Emotion flooded Vince, and he steeled himself. Frank was only a few years older than his own son, Tim, who'd died serving in Iraq. Vince studied Frank's wounds. The two bullet holes in his chest had bled little. Could be a good sign. The one in his stomach was a little bloodier, but no apparent hemorrhage. Question was—what was happening on the *inside*?

Gently, he patted his deputy's arm. "Frank, it's Vince. Can you hear me?"

One EMT shook his head.

Vince's gaze met the medical technician's—*Will he make it?*

The EMT lifted his shoulders. "We got vitals. Weak, but they're there."

Vince flexed his jaw. "Take good care of him." His voice sounded gruff.

As soon as the ambulance drove away, another arrived, this one responding to a call from Sarah Wray at Simple Pleasures. Apparently shot in the arm.

Sarah? Vince had thought she was among the hostages. Relief that she was safe dissolved into concern about her wound. He gazed up Hanley, calculating the line of fire from Java Joint.

"See that alley, one block north of Main?" He pointed it out to the ambulance driver. "It runs between the rear of the buildings that front Main and Baxter—the next street over. It's narrow, but you can get in there."

A similar alley ran between the buildings fronting the south side of Main and those on Lakeshore. It dead-ended at Third Street into a long building that stretched the entire block between Main and Lakeshore, then picked up again at the beginning of Fourth. The back door of Java Joint opened onto the first section of that alley—a fact Vince was already calculating.

"Go up and around, come down Hanley, and turn into the alley past Baxter. You're far enough up to be out of harm's way, and once you're in the alley you've got the buildings for protection. Sarah's got a back door into her shop."

"Right." The ambulance driver climbed back into his vehicle.

Vince glanced up and down Lakeshore. ISP officers were arriving, Jim giving them orders for cordoning off streets.

The envelope. Vince hustled to his car, extracted a pair of latex gloves from his kit, and hurried back to John and Stan.

He pulled up before the two men. "I can't say thank you enough. You've given Frank a chance to fight for his life. Especially you, John. You risked your own life."

John lifted a shoulder. "I just ... did what needed to be done."

Vince studied his face. "You're not looking too good. Want someone to drive you to the hospital to get checked out?"

"I'm fine." John waved a hand. "Started some new medicine this morning, that's all. I'll be all right." He swallowed hard, his expression crumbling. "Vince, you got to get them out of there."

Vince gave his shoulder a squeeze. "We will, John. I'll do everything humanly possible; you know that."

John opened his mouth, but no more words came. He managed a nod.

"Can you tell me who all's in there?"

John swallowed. "I couldn't notice everybody in those few seconds I passed the window. But it was supposed to be all the Scenes and Beans bloggers except for Janet Detcher and Jake Tremaine. They're out of town. Plus Bailey said Carla was bringing her daughter and Ali."

Vince's gut twisted. Multiple adults were bad enough. But two teenage girls in such a frightening situation . . .

John reached into his pocket for the envelope, held it out. "Sorry about my fingerprints."

"You had a few other things to worry about." Vince pulled on his gloves and took the envelope from John's fingers. "I need to go read this. An officer will take both of you home. I'm afraid your vehicles are stuck in this cordoned-off area for now."

John dragged a hand across his cheek. "I need to take some medication soon, but . . . can't I come back here and wait? *Bailey's* in there, Vince."

The man's fear pierced Vince, and his mind flashed to his own wife. Nancy was on her nursing shift at Deaconess Hospital in Spokane. If she passed a television running breaking news, if somebody coming on shift had heard a bulletin . . . He needed to call her as soon as possible, tell her he was okay.

He clasped John's shoulder. "You can't be at this location, John. It's now open only to law enforcement and emergency vehicles. I'll set an outer perimeter a few blocks down Lakeshore. You can go there if you like. It'll be the closest you can get."

John nodded. Despite his terror over Bailey, he seemed too weak to argue. Saving Frank's life plus all the stress must have drained the energy right out of him.

Vince called to an officer to take the men home. Then, amid the swarming police and vehicles, a dozen people calling his name, he blocked out all else to focus on the envelope. The message's contents would determine what happened from here. How Vince would negotiate with the three hostage takers. And maybe it would give an inkling as to how long this situation could last.

Taking a deep breath, he pulled out a pocketknife, slid the blade under the envelope flap, and slit it open.

PART TWO
Seige

TWENTY-FOUR

Chief Vince Edwards,

This is Kent Wicksell, father of T.J. Wicksell, who got sent to prison two months ago for SOMETHING HE DIDN'T DO. I got my oldest son, Mitch, with me.

T.J. was in the wrong place at the wrong time. He's never seen a stranger. Ask anyone—they'll tell you how much people like him. He'd never hurt anybody. In fact, he's small for his age. Always has been. Because of that we've always watched out for him. Kids used to beat him up on the playground when he was young. Now T.J.'s in prison BECAUSE OF A LYING PROSECUTOR AND A NO-GOOD DEFENSE LAWYER. Even before the trial was over, he was CONVICTED IN THE MEDIA. You saw all the stories that ran about him and what he supposedly did to Marya Whitbey. Once those stories started running, NO ONE WOULD LISTEN to us.

There is evidence that should have come out in court and never did. We tried and TRIED to talk to the lawyers, but no one would listen. T.J. is in prison for TWENTY-FIVE YEARS. He's only eighteen. AND NOW HE'S BEEN BEAT UP. DO YOU HAVE ANY

89

IDEA HOW SCARED HE IS? HOW SCARED WE ARE
FOR HIM?

We want one thing: T.J. gets out of prison NOW.

Part of getting him out means you have to make
the prosecutor listen to us and the evidence we have
to tell him, and you get that defense lawyer to do
his job—INSTEAD OF SHOWING UP TO COURT
WITH A HANGOVER. And the judge will have to
promise that T.J. gets a new trial so he can prove his
innocence.

We wrote this letter to YOU because we've
read in the papers what you've done for your town
when things went wrong. You help sort things out. If
anybody can make this happen, it's you.

Blame all this on the two lawyers. This is OUR
ONLY CHOICE. We will let our hostages go only when
we get what we want. We will kill anybody we have to
in order to get it. You can see we mean business. So
DON'T take long to answer this letter, or more people
will die.

We have taken everybody's cell phone and
disconnected the phones in Java Joint. The only way
we will talk to you is through the comments on Scenes
and Beans. Write us first and tell us you're ready to
talk. We will answer. The reason for using the blog is
simple. Lots of people read it. WE WANT EVERYONE
ACROSS THE COUNTRY TO LISTEN TO WHAT WE
HAVE TO SAY. Everybody heard about this trial and
my son's supposed guilt. Now they're going to hear
the TRUTH.

We DO NOT CARE what happens to any of the
hostages. We ONLY CARE about T.J. If we don't get
what we want, THE PEOPLE WE HAVE WILL DIE.

TWENTY-FIVE

"I say we shoot another one." Brad's words vibrated in Bailey's ears.

"Don't tell me what to do, either of you!" Kent shoved his chair back from the computer, face flushing purple-red.

Bailey's heart rattled against her ribs. It took every ounce of will she possessed not to shrink from his rage. But something told her she dared not show her fear.

Brad planted his feet apart, blue eyes flaming. "So—what? You gonna stare at that computer all day?"

Kent pushed to his feet, snatched his gun off the floor, and stomped around the other side of the table. "We *planned* it this way, remember?"

Angie whimpered. Mitch whipped his gun in her direction. "Stuff it!" She melted into her chair, drew her hands across her chest.

Brittany's lips trembled. She mashed a hand against her mouth as if to keep herself quiet.

Brad turned a hard look on his father. "Maybe I don't like your plans now that I'm here. We got all these people—"

"So what you want to do?" Kent kept his weapon and eyes on the hostages, his words thrown at his son. "We've been here forty-five minutes. You want to kill somebody every half hour?"

"Why not, we got enough of 'em."

"Fine," Kent spat. "At that rate we run out of people in six and a half hours. Then what?"

"You got a better idea?" Brad's knuckles whitened against his weapon. Bailey's blood ran cold. She pressed back in her chair, prayers streaming through her head. This wasn't going to work. These men were too *crazy*, and with all their ammunition . . .

"Yeah, I got a better idea!" Kent's shout bounced against the walls. He grasped his gun in his right hand, waving it for effect. "We keep with the plan. They'll contact us soon."

"What if they don't, though?" Mitch threw out. "We never thought it would take them this long."

Kent sliced the air with his left hand. "*Then* we start shooting, okay? Tell you what, Brad, I'll let you take the first one, since apparently that's what you came for."

Brad's features twisted. "I came for T.J., and you know it."

Kent snorted. "Then start acting like it."

"Yeah, okay, fine." Mitch wagged his head side to side. "We wait a little longer."

Brad threw him a look. "Now *you* got patience all of a sudden."

"Cork it, Brad. You're not even supposed to *be* here."

"I didn't see you fighting that this morning."

"Yeah, like you —"

Kent cursed and kicked a chair with all his might. It scudded across the floor and slammed into the windowsill. Gasps rose from the hostages. "Both of you shut your traps!" His wide nostrils flared. "I swear, you don't stop arguing right now, I'll put you both outside and do this myself."

Anger pulled at Brad's mouth, but he said no more. He backed up to Wilbur's stool and sat down.

Kent swiveled toward Bailey. "*Don't* just stare at me! Are you checking?"

She dug her fingers into her legs. "I . . . sure." She leaned over to reach for the mouse. Clicked out of the comments box and back in. No change.

Bailey lifted her eyes to Kent. Shook her head.

He pierced her with a look to kill. "Keep checking."

The three men fell silent. Kent stepped back and leaned a hip on one of the tables shoved against the right wall. Mitch and Brad exchanged heated glances, then turned their black stares on the group. Mitch's eyebrows jammed together, and his gaunt face and beady eyes gave him the look of a rat sniffing cheese.

Bailey checked the comments page. Nothing.

She glanced at the clock. Twelve minutes before nine. Was it just an hour ago she'd been making espressos?

Where was John? He would be so worried. And what about Sarah? Bailey was scared to death she'd been in Simple Pleasures when Brad did all the shooting. And Frank. She could hardly bear to think of him. Over and over in her head—the vision of him jerking back at the impact of the bullets, crumpling to the floor…

Kent lifted his chin and gave her a hate-filled look.

She focused on the monitor and clicked the comments. Still nothing.

Down a few tables, a throat cleared. *Wilbur.* Bailey slid her gaze in his direction. He heaved an impatient sigh at Kent. "I have to use the bathroom."

Kent glared at him. "Too bad."

Wilbur mushed his lips and considered Kent as he would a cockroach on the counter. "You got a lot of people trapped in here, and we're all going to need to go sooner or later. You make us all go in our pants, it ain't gonna smell too good."

"Maybe you go when we tell you." Mitch laughed.

Kent ignored his son. "You Wilbur Hucks, ain't you?"

"That's me."

He sniffed. "Think you own this place, huh? Mr. I-duh-ho shirt."

"Naw, he just owns this stool I'm sittin' on." Brad laughed.

Wilbur's eyes narrowed.

Jared raised his hand. "I need to go too."

"Oh, for—" Kent spat a curse. He pushed off the table. "Fine, go. One at a time. Brad, take 'em."

Wilbur hauled himself to his feet. "Key's on the counter." He pointed. Brad picked up the key, walked over to Wibur, and pointed the gun at his chest. "Move." He jerked his chin toward the hall. "Don't forget I'm right behind you, old man."

The look Wilbur gave him could have withered cement. "I ain't gonna forget you sat on my stool."

Mitch guffawed.

Brad gestured with his head. "Go."

Bailey held her breath as they started down the hall. *Please, Wilbur, don't—*

"Hey!" Kent aimed his gun at her. "Check the computer."

Bailey jumped, clicked on the comments. The box popped up. Nothing.

She shook her head at Kent. He clenched his teeth and spewed back curses, calling her vile names. The words withered her spirit. From the corner of her eye, Bailey saw Ali's posture crumble. She swayed over toward Carla. Brittany leaned in too. Carla let go of their hands, put her arms around both of their shoulders. The three huddled together, the girls' heads buried on each side of her neck.

Bailey's eyes stung. Those girls were so young and vulnerable. And Carla so defiant in her protection. Then there was Wilbur and his indignation. Too many personalities here. Too much fear, way too much anger. The entire room was like one big, roiling cauldron, capable of boiling over any minute.

Hurry up, Vince. Please, please hurry.

TWENTY-SIX

Kent and Mitch Wicksell.

Vince read the letter twice, questions and facts swirling in his mind.

First, a detail: two men. John said he'd seen three. Who was the third? The letter was long—obviously written before the men ever reached Java Joint. At the last minute, someone had joined them.

Second, the demand: *T.J. gets out of prison NOW.* Sure, and paint the sky green while you're at it. What was he supposed to do, overturn the nation's court system? Marya Whitbey's murder had been heinous, an unprovoked attack on a twenty-three-year-old mother. The trial had been heavily covered—and Vince didn't question the defendant's guilt for a minute. Too much evidence proved he'd done it.

But Vince could read between the lines of the letter. Kent Wicksell's underlying demand was simply *Listen.* The man had used the word numerous times. Listening was something Vince could do. In fact, negotiation was all about active listening. Vince would have to gain Kent's trust, prove he was willing to hear all Kent had to say about T.J.'s "innocence."

Third: *More people will die.* Emphasis on *more*. When Kent wrote those words, his takeover of Java Joint apparently had been planned out—right down to shooting at least one person upon entry. As it turned out, a cop in uniform had been the obvious target. Then there was the matter of blacked-out windows. The fabric would need to be the right length and width.

These men had planned their attack down to fine detail.

Vince pushed the letter back in the envelope and thrust it in his pocket. Took off his gloves. He had to get to a computer as fast as possible.

First, however—two minutes of crucial coordination of manpower as more ISP officers arrived. Roger Waitman was back on Lakeshore with Jim, now that an ISP officer had taken over his containment post up Main. Vince called everyone together to quickly cover who the hostage takers were and what they wanted. "The command post will be at the police station, two blocks up Main and on the same side of the street as Java Joint." This was close enough to their target without being in a direct line of fire from the café. "Anyone who needs access will use the back entrance off the alley. If the perps go out the back door of Java Joint onto the alley, a building on Third Street blocks direct line of fire to the station. But let me make clear I'll want as few people at that post as possible, and I will say who comes in or out."

Effective negotiation required concentration. Vince did not need distractions.

"This is a deliberate siege with multiple hostages. The three men came prepared, have a lot of firepower and—we'd better assume—plenty of ammunition. We can hope for the best, but experience tells us these kinds of sieges don't often end quickly.

"I will serve as commander and negotiator." Vince spread his hands. "If we were in a major city, we'd have a bigger team and I wouldn't be pulling the double duty. But I need every one of you I can get"—he pointed to the group—"on the streets. I *do not want* our perimeter breached, understand? Jim will coordinate containment and will be second in charge. Roger will stay with me. Al, I'm assigning you to media. Establish a location for them three blocks down Lakeshore, and let them know we'll answer all their questions when we can. But they are *absolutely* to remain there and not breach into the inner perimeter."

"Will do." Al's hand rested on his hip near his gun.

Vince checked his watch. "Three CRT snipers should be here in thirty to forty minutes. Jim, you assign their positions. Put two of them on rooftops with frontal line of sight to Java Joint, and one in the rear."

Vince continued with more instructions. Jim would tell Tactical—CRT members—their assigned "tac channel." The channel would be on a handheld closed-band police radio, giving them direct, private communication with Vince and each other.

"Also, Jim, call Tactical, talk to them about sending more men—"

Vince stopped, frowning. The Coeur d'Alene CRT lacked an APC—armored personnel carrier. With the kind of firepower the Wicksells apparently possessed, he just might need one. An APC could deliver Tactical members safely into a hot zone. His crisis plan for Kanner Lake involved using a fire truck for delivering a team. But after reading Wicksell's note and realizing what kind of siege they faced . . .

Better to make his response team interagency. More resources in less time that way.

He cleared his throat. "Jim, see if the commander can get the APC from Fairchild." Fairchild was the Air Force base in Spokane, under an hour's drive southwest of Kanner Lake. "Take them longer to get here with it, but a better setup in the long run."

Jim nodded. "Agreed."

With a distracted wave Vince ran for his car. Roger followed in his own vehicle. In less than a minute they drove to Fourth Street and into the alley at the back of the station. On the way Vince left a message on Nancy's cell phone, stressing that he was *fine*. She would find the voicemail on her next break.

In his office he whipped off his protective vest and threw it on a chair, spewing instructions. Roger took notes, his thin lips pulled in and narrow shoulders hunched. "I need a background check on Wicksell family members." Vince flicked on his computer and sat down. "And other data—mental health, any known injuries, drug use, places of employment. Photographs. There was a feature article in the *Spokane Review* just after the trial was over—find it. Run down the prosecutor, defense attorney, judge."

He pointed to the empty dry-erase board on his right wall. "There's our situation board."

As they gathered information on the HTs—hostage takers—and as negotiations progressed, all pertinent information would be written on the situation board or tacked to the wall around it.

Vince drummed his fingers as the desktop appeared on his monitor. *Come on, come on.*

What else for Roger?

"Get the floor plan of Java Joint." Some Building Department employee was about to have his Memorial Day weekend interrupted. "And put the telephone provider's central security command on notice. I'll want to move communications off the blog onto a phone soon as possible." When that happened, he'd need a dedicated phone line from his personal number to Java Joint's.

"We need to get the log of events started, and you've got enough to do." The log would contain everything that occurred in the incident, along with the time. "Call Jim and see who he can send up to help."

"Okay. That it?"

Vince reached for the mouse. "Yeah."

Roger hurried off.

Vince clicked on to the Internet, picturing Kent Wicksell. The first hours of a hostage situation were the most volatile. The

HTs could still be running high on adrenaline from their initial attack. Best to keep initial communication short and factual.

He typed in the blog's URL: *www.kannerlake.blogspot.com*. The familiar blue background with the Scenes and Beans logo came up. He scrolled to the bottom of the day's post and clicked on "Comments." The box appeared.

He poised his index fingers over the keys.

Here we go. Lord, help me.

>> Hello, Kent and Mitch. (And I understand you have a third man with you?) This is Vince Edwards. I'm here to listen and help.

TWENTY-SEVEN

Wilbur returned from his bathroom run—still intact. Bailey let out a breath of relief. He settled in his chair, back straight and arms folded over his yellow T-shirt, and Jared got up to go next. Mitch stood glaring at the group, one foot tapping and gun pointed. His ring finger smacked against his weapon. One side of the bottom of his jacket rode up on his jeans, the opposite pocket hanging heavy with ammunition.

Kent leaned against a table, throwing black looks at the clock on the wall behind him. His overhanging brow and the hungry irritation in his eyes reminded Bailey of a beast stalking prey.

She shivered. Checked the blog's comments for the dozenth time.

And there it was—Vince's message.

Thank you, God.

"It's here."

Kent jerked from the table and strode over to sit heavily in the chair next to Bailey. Laid his gun on the floor. He leaned toward the computer, his thick, hairy arm brushing hers. She willed herself not to draw away. "Took his sweet time, didn't he." Raising his chin, he read the words with an expression of disdain.

"What's it say, what's it say?" Now two of Mitch's fingers drummed his gun.

All of the hostages' heads turned, listening.

Kent read the message aloud. Proudly, as if he'd made the Kanner Lake chief of police bow to his power. He elbowed Bailey. "Write him back what I tell you."

>> About time you showed up. You took too long, and we're
   not happy about that. Our fingers were itching to shoot
   somebody else. Good thing you're listening, 'cause we got
   plenty to say. The third man is my second son, Brad.
   You want to help—it's simple. Get T.J. out of prison.

Kent pressed back in his chair. "Send it."

Bailey posted the comment under Kent's name, then typed the verification letters in the appropriate box.

"What are you doing?" Kent leaned closer, suspicion on his face.

He wants to use the blog comments to communicate, but he doesn't even understand how it works?

"I have to type in whatever letters come up on the screen so the comment will go through."

Even as she answered, a part of her refused to believe this unthinkable situation. Sitting here in her own café at gunpoint, calmly talking to Frank's killer about blogging.

"Why?"

"It's the way the system's set up. So we don't get spam comments. But once I log in, since I'm site administrator, I won't have to do it again, even if we post under your name."

Kent frowned. "What's—Never mind, just do it." He shoved both fists on his hips, gaze glued to the monitor.

Bailey posted the comment and refreshed the box. "See—your answer's up now."

Kent grunted.

They waited. Brad brought Jared back from the bathroom and wanted Kent to read Vince's message again.

Kent snorted. "You want me to read everything twice?"

"I was on escort duty, remember?" Brad cocked his head toward Jared. "You want me to do the talking while *you* trek people up and down the hall?"

Kent flexed his jaw and turned back to the computer. Bailey refreshed the comment box. Another message appeared.

>> Sorry I could not answer sooner. But I am here now and will stay available. Together we can work through this. I know you've got a lot of people in there to handle. Would you like to just come out now?

Kent punched his palm with a fist. "Tell him *no*. With three exclamation points."

Bailey obeyed.

>> Okay. Always worth asking.

Kent ran his tongue under his upper lip. Threw a glance at his hostages. He got up, paced away two steps, then paced back. "Tell him who all's in here."

The way he said it. So smug. So arrogant about the lives he held in his hands.

Bailey looked down the tables of hostages and listed them in order of seating, starting from closest to the hallway. Bev. Angie. Jared. Brittany. Carla. Ali. Wilbur. Pastor Hank. Paige. Ted. Leslie. Bailey.

At Kent's insistence, she continually refreshed the comments box. Strange, how her hand almost seemed removed from her body. The rest of her felt frozen. Dead.

An answer appeared.

>> Thank you for telling me who's with you. Is there anyone with any medical problems I need to know about?

Bailey read the words and briefly closed her eyes. *John*. Thank God he hadn't arrived here on time. He could be in real trouble by now.

Mitch gave a jagged laugh. "Yeah, tell him a few beers would be good."

Kent waved a hand at the keyboard. "Type."

>> No other injuries — yet. We're counting on you to keep it
   that way. So stop with the stupid questions.

Brad sighed with impatience. Bailey changed out the comments box until Vince's answer came up.

>> Glad to hear that. And yes, I will work with you to keep it
   that way. We don't want anyone else hurt, you included.

"Yeah, yeah, Mr. Nice Guy." Kent sneered.

>> So work with me, Edwards. Get T.J. out.

>> I plan to work with you, Kent. But you are asking for
   some big things. Tell me this — do you want me to be
   honest with you, or do you want me to lie?

Kent slapped a hand on the table. "What the — "

"What? What's he say?" Mitch shifted from one foot to the other.

Kent read the words aloud.

Brad cussed. "Can a cop tell the truth?"

"Both of you, *shut* up!" Kent's fingers curled into his palms. He hit the keyboard. "Type."

>> Didn't I tell you to stop with the stupid questions? Of
   course I want the truth, or how are we going to get anything done here?

The answer came within a minute.

>> Good. I will be honest. If you and I work together, we
   can get things done. But communicating on the blog is
   not the best idea. It's too slow. Plus anyone can jump in

while you and I are trying to talk. I suggest we switch to
a phone.

Kent read the words aloud.

"No," Brad said. "Uh-uh. The world hears about T.J."

His father ignored him.

>> I TOLD you we use the blog. Everybody heard how "bad"
T.J. is — how "guilty" he is. Now they're going to hear the
truth. We STAY ON THE BLOG.

Bailey's palms were wet. She wiped her hands on her pants.
The acrid smell of Kent's sweat stung her nostrils. He banged a
thumb against the table as he waited.

>> What I'm hearing you say is that you want to tell the
nation your story. What if we find another way to get your
story out? We can use the media. You and I can work
out how they'd give good coverage to your message.
Meantime you and I can talk privately. That way other
people hear only what you want them to hear, not every
bit of our conversation.

Kent read it aloud, then stared at the screen. His breath
sucked in and out.

Brad shook his head. "Tell him *no*. We don't start letting him get
his way already. We decided on the blog long before we got here."

"Yeah, yeah, right." Mitch sniffed.

Kent flicked his fingers at the computer. "Maybe, but this
waiting's annoying. Too slow. I could be stuck here at the computer for hours."

Brad and Mitch exchanged a look.

Bailey sat with shoulders drawn in and chin down. If only
she could melt into the floor. She glanced left. Leslie and Ted
clutched hands. Paige hunched in her chair, still as stone and

spiritless, eyes focused on the tabletop. Her fingers were tightly intertwined. Bailey's heart twisted at her grief. Carla and the girls huddled together. Angie's face blanched. Pastor Hank faced away from Bailey, but she knew he was sending up continual silent prayers. Most of her friends probably were. Although Wilbur looked too irritated to talk to anybody, including God.

Kent smacked Bailey's arm, and she jumped. "Type."

"*Don't* say yes, Dad." Brad pointed at Kent. "You start giving that cop what he wants, he'll think we're weak."

Kent clenched his teeth. "Can't a man just think out loud for a minute?" His eyes drove daggers at his son. "Just hold that gun and leave the talking to me. *Got* it?"

Brad pulled his chin up and glared at his father. Kent seethed back. Bailey fixed her gaze on the keyboard, fear clawing her nerves.

"Now." Kent smacked his knuckles against the table. "You tell that cop this ..."

>> What is the matter with you? Can't you HEAR? I said WE USE THE BLOG. Maybe I WANT other people to see everything you say to me. That ought to keep you honest. You don't like it, maybe another body out in the street will change your mind.

Kent sat back, a satisfied smile curling his lip. "Let's see what he does with that."

TWENTY-EIGHT

Another body . . .

Vince ran a hand through his hair. Not good—Kent Wicksell spoiling for a fight already.

Maybe it was just the man's adrenaline, still running high. Maybe it was pure bravado. But Vince could hardly count on that. One person had already been shot.

Fingers hanging over the keyboard, Vince calculated his response.

Ali and Brittany. Of all the hostages, they haunted him most. He pictured the girls huddled at gunpoint, terrified. Ali Frederick with her long auburn hair and big brown eyes. Last year, she'd been pulled into the events surrounding two murders in Kanner Lake. And her mother had nearly died from cancer after that. Gayle Frederick had responded to chemotherapy and was recently declared cancer free. But the pain of the past fourteen months still showed in Ali's eyes.

And Brittany Hanley—a beautiful girl, with her birth mother, Carla's, black hair and dark eyes. Vince could hardly imagine the toll this new stress would take. Brittany's entire life had been upended eight months ago—and in front of national media.

No teenager should have to face what these two girls did. They had already been through so much . . .

Lord, let them get out of this alive.

Roger's husky voice filtered from the other office. He was running down crucial data, but now Vince needed to know something else—ASAP. Until he got the information, he was going to have to do some stalling.

He hoped Jim would send someone in to help soon.

Negotiation trainers always talked about "crisis negotiation teams." A primary negotiator, a secondary, a team leader, an on-scene commander to make the ultimate decisions, the tactical team leader. Never, never should a negotiator also be commander, Vince had heard many times. For numerous reasons. Good negotiators weren't always good decision makers. An on-scene commander couldn't split his time between commanding and negotiating. A negotiator often needed to stall for time by "passing the buck"—telling the subject he couldn't proceed with some compromise until a commander gave him the go-ahead.

All well and good for big city departments. But Vince was working with a minimum number of people, even with ISP's help. He couldn't pull numerous officers off containment. Fact was, big-city experts had no idea how small towns had to make do.

He stared at Wicksell's last message, then typed his answer.

>> No, Kent, I don't want another body. I have to check
   some things out about this blog, though. I do want a form
   of communication we both can rely on.

Vince posted his message and wiped his forehead. Man, it was hot in here. He reached for the desk phone, held it up with dial tone buzzing as he refreshed the comments box.

>> What do you have to check out?

Vince put the phone back down.

>> Kent, sometimes these comments don't work right. The
   letter verifications often have to be typed in more than

107

once before they'll "take." And sometimes the system goes down for maintenance and then you can't access the blogs at all. I need to call Google, make sure nothing's going to be shut down on us.

Vince posted the comment, then called Jim at the Lakeshore site. "How's it looking down there?"

"I'm handling it." Jim sounded distracted. "Al reports we've got a few volunteer firemen gathering at the media site, wondering what they can do. Is it okay if one of them comes up and helps Roger?"

"Yeah. Actually, we need two people. Roger needs help now, and if I can move off this blog, I'm going to need a scribe." The scribe would take notes on communications over the telephone. "If Justin Black's down there, he'd be my first choice." In his younger days Justin had been on a SWAT team in Nevada and done some negotiating.

"He's not here, but I'll try to reach him. How about Larry to help Roger?"

Larry Emmet was sixty-seven, a retired teacher and avid outdoorsman who exuded energy. "Fine. Send them both over as soon as you can."

Vince hung up the phone and clicked the mouse.

>> I don't believe you, Edwards! I'm sick of you trying to get me off this blog!!

Vince's throat ran dry. So much anger. Gave him a bad feeling in his gut.

Roger appeared. "Found the *Spokane Review* article for you online. I'll let you read it, then I'll tack it up." He laid it on the desk. "The judge is in Spokane. I'm trying to reach his cell phone. Also working on the prosecutor and defense attorney."

Vince glanced at the article. He'd get to it as soon as he could. "Thanks. While you're in here, would you get me some water? And call John Truitt immediately—ask if there's an easy way to hide this blog from the public. If not, we're going to have to work with Google."

"Right-o." Roger left the office.

There was another issue, one Vince hoped he wouldn't have to mention to Kent. Blogs were a form of national public communications. If one was being used in a crime, the FBI would become involved. Jurisdiction could get sticky. Vince didn't need to be slowed down by fights over who did what.

Roger brought Vince a cup of water and hurried back to his phone.

Vince guzzled a drink, then focused on the keyboard.

>> Kent, most of the time the blogs are fine. But you can't always rely on them. What if I'm about to tell you something about T.J., and suddenly everything goes blank? Since you want to use this blog, I have to make sure it will be reliable for us. I am making some phone calls right now. Please give me a minute to do that. I'll get back to you as soon as possible.

Lying in negotiations was a real gamble. Vince wasn't happy he'd resorted to it so soon. Sometimes a negotiator had to stretch the truth. But he'd doggone well better not be caught, or he'd lose all credibility with Kent.

Within minutes Roger hustled back, a pad of paper in his hands. "First of all, no surprise—John wants to come down here and help. He does know all about this blog. Says he's the one who puts up a lot of the posts. Even though it looks like they're posted at 7:00 a.m., he actually puts them up the night before from home."

Vince was already shaking his head. "No, can't have him here. He's too close to the situation. Just ... thank him and have him stand by his phone. But what'd he tell you?"

"He gave me the user name and password. Here." Roger tore off the top piece of paper from his notepad and laid it on the desk. "I'll put it on the board too. He also said taking the blog private is easy, but he questioned whether you could do it without them knowing. You go to "Setting," then "Permissions" to make it private for just blog authors. First you'd have to sign in under Bailey's user name and password so you wouldn't be blocked. The question is what it does to the blog. Will some message about the new restriction come up that they'll see on their end? John didn't know."

Not what he wanted to hear. Vince rubbed his forehead. "Okay, call Google. If we can't go private the normal way, maybe they can do it on their end. But stress that I need it done without the other party knowing about it. And I need their answer soon as you can get it."

Which may not be very fast, thought Vince as Roger walked to the situation board and started writing. It was Saturday. Techs worked 24/7, but online, not by phone. An online answer could take days, and besides, no techie would have the authority to take some public blog private. They'd need a decision maker in the company.

Vince positioned his forefingers over the keys. One important rule in negotiating: Never give something without getting something back. If he agreed to use the blog, he wanted a concession in return. And it wouldn't be a small one. But first he needed some time.

>> Kent, we're having trouble contacting Google to make
   sure they'll take care of us. It's not helping that this is
   Saturday. I will keep trying.

The answer shot back.

>> Stop talking about it and just do it! You've got five
   minutes.

Five minutes. Hardly. But Vince couldn't afford to be silent for long. Talking—about anything—was good. As long as they were talking, Kent's attention was on him, not on harming the hostages.

But for now, he'd take the five minutes. It was important to learn a little more about the man he was dealing with.

Vince picked up the *Spokane Review* article.

TWENTY-NINE

Bailey listened to the clock tick.

Kent waited for Vince's response impatiently, scratching his arm, tapping a foot. He was beginning to mirror Mitch. Bailey clasped her hands in her lap, nerves pinging. She felt Kent looking at her, as if he sought distraction. She slid him a glance.

He smirked. "Bet you never thought your blog would be used for such a great purpose, huh?"

She made no response.

"Make you proud?"

Bailey licked her lips. "You want me to be proud that you've used Scenes and Beans to take my friends hostage?" Her voice wavered, and she worked to steady it. "To shoot Frank?"

Kent shrugged. "He was a cop."

"He was *twenty-six years old*."

"Yeah? If you're so worried about him, why aren't you worried about a kid who's only *eighteen* in prison with a bunch of grown *men*? A kid who's found guilty of murder, when he's *innocent*? And now he's been *beat up*."

Wicksell. The name suddenly triggered. That awful murder case in Hayden … *This* was the family of that cold-blooded killer.

Dear Lord, help us all.

Bailey forced herself not to look away. "Yes. That would worry me."

"Then *be* worried." Vindictiveness twisted Kent's mouth. "We chose Kanner Lake because of *you*, you know."

Because of me? Bailey stared him, coldness seeping through her body.

"That's right. When we heard about T.J. getting beat up, that was it. Mr. Smart One over there" — he pointed at Brad, tone tinged with sarcasm — "says he's got an idea. Takes me down to the library so we can read your ... posts — ain't that what you call 'em? There was one said you'd be having a party today 'cause of the writer." He threw a look at S-Man. "Even gave us the time. Seven thirty."

Bailey's veins iced over. For a moment she couldn't speak. "You planned this — today — because you *knew* we'd all be here?"

"Yup."

Bailey's hands tightened in her lap. *Frank.* His body crumpling. The way he'd been dragged like some sack across the café, shoved out the door. And *she* was to blame? The thought turned her heart inside out. Now others might die. Who would be next? Pastor Hank? Jared? Carla?

Brittany or Ali?

Bailey slumped away from Kent Wicksell and covered her eyes with one hand. Hot tears began to fall.

"Don't listen to him, Bailey." Leslie's voice trembled with anger. "This is nobody's fault but theirs."

"Oh, Know-It-All Reporter finally speaks up." Kent's chair squeaked. "And I'll just bet you know everything about my son's case too, don't you? Musta wrote a hundred articles about how *guilty* he is."

"I don't give my opinion in the news; I just report it."

"Yeah? And what did you 'report'?"

"What I saw in the courtroom."

"Which means the same lies everybody else heard." Kent shoved to his feet. "T.J. *didn't* kill that girl. Your favorite cop

Vince Edwards gets him out of prison, you all get to go home. If he don't ... too bad for you."

"If that's—"

"Shut *up!*" Kent jerked his gun from the floor, strode two steps to Leslie and shook her chair furiously with one hand. "Turn back around! I don't need any lip from you."

Leslie melted into Ted. He put an arm around her shoulders.

Bailey hitched a breath. Her tears wouldn't stop.

Kent clomped back to his chair and sat down hard. Set his gun on the floor. "*Where* is that stupid cop?" He grabbed the mouse, started clicking.

"He's making us wait." Mitch was back to pacing. "Thinks if he takes too long answering, you'll get tired and say okay to a telephone."

"Shut up your cryin'!" Kent slapped the table. Bailey jumped, fought to stifle her tears. Pulled in a long, stuttering breath and sat up.

Kent clicked on the comments box. "There! Finally."

Bailey focused her burning eyes on the screen.

>> What's going on here? Kent and Vince, you two lost or
    something? — Fred Meyer

Kent read it aloud and cursed. "It's not even him."

"Bet it is." Brad pushed off Wilbur's stool and stood. His gun aimed straight at Pastor Hank. "Posing as someone else to prove his point about interruptions."

"I'll handle this, Brad. *Back* off!" Kent glared at the monitor, his broad chest expanding as he breathed.

"Type this — no, wait." He leaned back to gaze at the tables of hostages. "Any other good typists in here — raise your hand."

Jared, Bev, Angie, Hank, Leslie, Ted, and Carla raised their hands.

"Well, now, that's quite a bunch." Kent focused on Bailey. "Evidently you're replaceable. So here's the deal, now that five minutes is up. *You* talk to Edwards. Tell him I've got T.J.'s story written out for you to post." He patted the left pocket of his jacket. "Tell him I want the world to see it. *That's* why we keep using this blog. Edwards answers right quick and agrees—you get to live. He don't—I got plenty more typists."

He leaned back, folded his arms. "If I were you, I'd make it good."

THIRTY

Spokane Review, April 13, 2008

ONE CRIME, TWO CONVICTIONS

By Robert Maxey

By mere appearance, no one would think of eighteen-year-old T.J. Wicksell as violent. His short blond hair — "My parents don't like hippies," he's quoted as saying — frames rounded cheeks dusted with freckles and a large mouth with an easy smile. T.J. stands only five-foot-seven, with a slight build. With his light features, he looks nothing like his brown-haired, dark-eyed father, Kent Wicksell, fifty-two. He favors his mother, Lenora Wicksell. Like her, he has a friendly face. A face you can trust, one might think. In fact, many people have. Friends and teachers alike are apt to mention T.J.'s "charm." How he could talk to anybody.

But appearance can be misleading. In the last few weeks the world has learned the truth about T.J. Wicksell: he is a cold-blooded, sociopathic killer.

Testimony in his trial, which ended Friday, laid out the grim details. In late afternoon on Saturday, October 13, 2007, T.J. drove his beat-up Chevy down Highway 95 into Hayden. The Wicksells live on a five-acre parcel cut from the forest to the east of 95, four miles north of town. The drive was typical for T.J., who often made the trip to the convenience store at the edge of Hayden city limits.

"He'd be in here two, maybe three times a week," store owner Ralph Kranck said. "Buying milk, bread, things like that. He'd always talk to me and anybody else in the store. Made me laugh. I always thought he was such a nice kid."

Which is why Kranck thought nothing of the conversation T.J. struck up with Marya Whitbey the first time he saw her in the store. As well as Kranck can remember, it was June or July. Marya was another regular customer, a well-liked twenty-three-year-old single mother with a little girl named Keisha, eighteen months. Marya, with bitter childhood memories of moving from foster home to foster home, was known in the community for her determination to better her life—for herself and her child. She'd been on her own since graduating high school, going to work in a bank and saving her money for future nursing school. Neighbors and friends considered her a "wonderful" mother, attentive and patient with her highly active daughter. Kranck had privately thought she'd be a good match for his son—if he could ever "get the kid back home to Hayden for a look at her."

As Kranck recalls, T.J. first asked Marya how old her daughter was. He teased with the little girl, who giggled at his tickling fingers and peeked out at him from behind her mother's legs. T.J. then asked Marya's name ... where she worked ... did she come to the store often? Funny, he said, how he'd never seen her before. Marya answered his questions, mentioning she'd walked from her apartment just a few blocks down. She asked him about his family, what he did. "I work at my dad's auto wreckage place," he told her. "Up the highway. You need any car part, come see us."

"Wish I could, but I don't have a car. Someday."

After that, Kranck says, T.J. and Marya spoke whenever they met in the store. Sometimes when she wasn't there, T.J. would ask if Kranck had seen her. "I got the feeling he liked her, but he was never pushy with her or anything like that," Kranck noted. "I never saw the slightest reason for concern."

On that fateful day in October, T.J. and Marya ran into each other once again. They talked, and T.J. teased with Keisha until Marya said she needed to finish her shopping. She ended up with a heavier bag than usual since she'd bought a gallon of milk. T.J. picked up some lasagna noodles and sauce.

Kranck checked Marya out first, then T.J. It was nippy outside.

"Let me drive you home," T.J. offered. "It's too cold, and you have a heavy bag plus Keisha."

Marya looked to Kranck, as if questioning whether she should. He nodded. "Let T.J. take you. He's right; it's cold."

During the trial, when Kranck testified regarding his statement, his voice caught. A moment passed before he could go on.

"I'll regret those words till the day I die," he told the court.

Kranck watched them leave. T.J. was a gentleman, carrying Marya's bag and opening his passenger door for her. She held Keisha in her lap.

That was the last time Kranck would see Marya.

What happened next is now public record. But while the facts are known, understanding is still slow to come for many. T.J. was an easygoing young man with no priors, although he'd been in numerous fights at school when he was younger. Kranck saw nothing in his behavior that day to cause concern. Yet T.J. Wicksell took Marya Whitbey the few blocks to her apartment, drove away, then soon returned. When she let him in, he stabbed her sixteen times and left her eighteen-month-old daughter to toddle through her blood. The body was discovered an hour later by neighbors alerted by the little girl's cries.

Only after that gruesome discovery would Fred Banst, a car mechanic who lives in the building, realize he should have listened to his gut instincts when he saw a young man running out the front door of the building and down the driveway toward the back parking lot. Charles Griffin, a retiree in his seventies, pulled into a parking space next to T.J.'s Chevy just in time to get a look at T.J. as he jumped into the car. Griffin saw what appeared to be blood smears on the front of T.J.'s shirt. After Marya's body was discovered, Griffin and Banst gave descriptions of the running young man to the police, and a composite was drawn of the suspect. That drawing was a ringer for T.J.'s "friendly" face.

The knife left at the scene, taken from Marya's own kitchen, bore T.J.'s fingerprints.

Friday's conviction of second-degree murder for T.J. Wicksell came as no surprise to those who followed the case. Although the exact motive for the crime remains unknown, the prosecutor presented the likelihood that T.J. had made sexual advances that were rebuffed. But his family's conviction is far different. They still insist he's innocent. Sociopath? They scoff at the word.

Spokane psychiatrist Dr. Patrick Johnson notes that while sociopaths may appear charming, they typically have a difficult time sustaining relationships and show no remorse for their actions. Some can be aggressive, even hostile. Yet only a small percentage fall into violent, criminal behavior. On the surface, they can seem quite trustworthy and are often good conversationalists. In short, they can fool many.

In recent criminal history, the name Scott Peterson comes to mind.

Like Peterson's parents, who to this day declare Scott's innocence, T.J. Wicksell's father insists he could "never do what the prosecutor said he did." The rest of the family fervently agrees. The system set up T.J., they say.

"I've been protecting T.J. since he was four years old and got beat up by a bigger kid," his older brother Brad told reporters during the trial. "I taught him how to fight back. Other than protecting himself, he's never hurt anybody."

"A week ago Brad said we've protected T.J. since he was young," a red-eyed but defiant Kent Wicksell said on the steps of the courthouse after the verdict. "We ain't done yet. T.J.'s innocent, and we're going to make the world hear that. Hear me, out there? He *didn't do it.* We'll show everybody that—if it's the last thing we do."

"How can parents," prosecutor Mick Wiley wondered aloud, "be so clouded in their vision of the truth?"

Indeed, that is the question many are asking. And it is a question for society at large. We are left to wonder—if family members could spot sociopathic tendencies early on, could such later violent acts be avoided?

Dr. Johnson points out that the most charming of sociopaths often fool their families even after they explode in violence. "When outward behavior masks this personality defect, those closest to the subject simply cannot see what is there. Day to day these people see only what the subject wants them to see. It will take a high degree of evidence to change their thinking." Beyond those factors, he added, "We have to recognize the close ties between parent and child. Whereas someone outside the family may be able to decipher facts more objectively, a father or mother—or even sibling—cannot so easily be objective. Familial love clouds many a rational mind."

A teary-eyed T.J. Wicksell was escorted in handcuffs from the courtroom to begin his sentence of twenty-five years in prison. His family, shaken and despairing, drove off to their own lifelong sentence—believing in an innocence that never was.

THIRTY-ONE

"We'll show everybody that—if it's the last thing we do ..."

Vince set the article on his desk.

Roger's voice filtered into his ears. The man was still on the phone in the other office. Vince strained to listen. Sounded like he was trying to get through to someone at Google.

Maybe Vince could stall Wicksell a little longer.

He picked up his water and downed what remained. As he set down the cup, his cell phone rang. He checked the ID. *Nancy.* He flipped it open.

"Hi, honey. You got my message."

"Yes." Her voice sounded tight. Vince's heart panged. Nancy was a strong woman, but the last couple of years had taken their toll. First Tim's death, then all that had occurred in Kanner Lake. "Vince, tell me you're safe."

"I'm very safe. My job's to talk them out of there."

No point in telling her about the sneak and snatch. Later.

"I can hear it in your voice already—the load is all on you." Nancy's words cracked. "And I'm just heartbroken over Frank ..."

Vince listened to her ragged breathing. Sudden rage at Kent Wicksell shot through him. The man wanted to protect his own son—and didn't care who he hurt in the process. "Me too."

"Where'd they take him?"

"KMC." Kootenai Medical Center in Coeur d'Alene. "Sarah Wray too."

"Let me know when you hear anything about them, okay?"

"I will."

"I love you, Vince."

"Love you too."

He laid down his cell and grabbed the mouse. Clicked the comments box. Two new messages had been posted. One from an outsider—exactly what he feared. And one from Java Joint.

>> Vince, it's Bailey. Kent told me to talk to you. Where are you? He's not patient at all in waiting for your answer. He has the story of what happened the night of Marya's murder—in T.J.'s own words. He wants me to type this story into a post so everyone can read what really happened. You need to say yes to this, or he says I will die. He doesn't care—there are other typists in here, so I'm expendable. Please answer now.

Air seeped from Vince's lungs. Bailey Truitt—one of the kindest women he knew.

He typed quickly.

>> I'm here, Kent. We're still trying to get through to Google, but in the meantime we can continue to talk here. No need to make threats. I'd rather concentrate on helping you. But how do we do this? If you want Bailey to type a document, that's going to take time. In the meantime you and I won't be able to communicate. Is this what you want?

He sent the comment and almost immediately received a response.

>> Yeah. You have enough to do. Go find that lowlife prosecutor and the judge who put my son in prison!

Vince hoped they could do that—and soon.

>> I will agree to working on finding the judge and prosecutor while Bailey types, but I expect something from you in return. This is a two-way street. I do something for you, you do something for me.

Roger stuck his head in the door. "I've got some calls in to Google. Waiting to hear back. Meantime, Jim says Frank's in surgery. He's going to be in there awhile—there's a lot to repair. But he might make it."

Vince soaked in the news. "Oh, that's wonderful! I didn't think he had much of a chance."

"I know. It's still touch and go, but ..." Roger winced. "Also, Sarah's had the bullet removed from her arm. She's sedated but okay. Her husband's with her."

"Okay, good." A thought struck Vince. "Did somebody alert Frank's parents?"

"Did that first thing. Just called them back with this news. They're already on their way to the airport."

Frank had grown up in the area, but his parents had recently moved to Seattle because of a transfer in his father's employment.

Vince shook his head. "Glad you remembered. I should have."

A shrug. "You got enough on your mind." Roger rapped the threshold with his fingers and withdrew.

Vince checked the comments box.

>> What makes you think you're in a position to ask for ANYTHING?

Vince stared at the words. If Wicksell didn't start showing a willingness to negotiate, the situation could go south in a hurry.

>> Kent, you want me to help get the story out about T.J. I said I would. But you've got to work with me. Also,

you need to be mindful of something. While you are telling the nation about your son's innocence, the media
are already putting out word that you've taken a dozen
people hostage and shot a police officer. Can you see
how this makes it hard for people to believe you? It would
help a lot if they can see you're working with me as I try
to help you.

Vince read over his words twice. Clicked *submit*.

He waited for a reply, muscles tense. *Come on, Wicksell, give
me something.*

What if the man flat out wouldn't listen to logic? He already
refused to believe the truth about his son.

Vince refreshed the comments box. No answer.

Tried fifteen seconds later. Nothing.

A minute ticked by. He kept trying.

Two minutes.

Three.

Maybe they weren't checking comments. Maybe Bailey was
typing T.J.'s story.

Maybe not.

Vince broke out in fresh sweat.

THIRTY-TWO

Bailey's heart flailed against her chest like the wings of a trapped bird.

She sat at the computer, eyes glued to the monitor, hands clutched in her lap. Kent stalked back and forth along the tables shoved against the right wall, kicking at one, shoving a chair at another. He clutched his gun in his left hand. Fear of being trapped in his own game rolled off him in waves.

This man was deadly enough in control. But if he felt cornered, saw no way to get what he wanted, Bailey *knew* he'd gun down every hostage in that room. It was in the way he moved, every expression on his face.

Bailey sensed the rising tension of the other hostages. Brittany and Ali muffled sobs, Leslie shifted in her chair, someone farther down coughed. Mitch and Brad pointed their high-powered guns at the group with intensity, as if itching to pull the triggers.

Brad stood before Wilbur's stool, feet planted firmly apart, his expression crimped with anger. "*Don't* do it; don't give in to anything! He'll just—"

Kent threw his gun down on a table, picked up a chair, and flung it across the floor. It landed with a loud clatter and slid within three feet of his oldest son.

Mitch cursed and jumped sideways. His face flushed. "Good, Dad, hit me next time."

Kent stomped toward him, finger raised and shaking. "I don't want to hear nothin' else out of either of you!" He glowered at Brad. "Just keep your opinions to yourself and let me *think*!"

Brad and Mitch fell into a sullen silence. Minutes strained by. Kent stomped around, heels hard against the floor. Bailey stole a glance at her friends. Angie clutched her palms together in a sign of prayer. Brad saw her and laughed with derision.

Kent whipped toward him, hands clenched. "I swear, Brad, I'm going to throw you out that back door—"

"I wasn't laughing at *you*." Brad jerked his gun. Bailey cringed.

"Fine, don't laugh at anybody. Just shut up!"

"I'm tired of you telling me to shut up!"

"You weren't here, you wouldn't be hearing it." Kent's voice lowered to cold rage. "I let you come along, but I'm still in charge. Got that?"

"Fine, Dad, you handle it. Mitch and I'll just stand here aiming our guns all day while you pace around and talk to yourself. Why don't you just tell that cop where to stick it?"

"Because he's *right*." Kent spat the word. "Everyone out there"—he waved his arm toward the covered windows—"is going to be watching. And they'll want to see *something* from us."

Bailey gave her head the slightest shake. Didn't they think of this before?

"Yeah, well, make it something later. Like I said, too soon and you tip your hand."

"Why don't you just ask him what he wants?" Mitch's torso rocked. "Ain't no skin off your nose to go that far. See whether you want to play along or not."

"If I may." Jared Moore dared to raise a hand, his voice calm. Kent and Brad glared at him.

Mitch stretched his neck right, left. "You got to go to the bathroom again?"

Jared kept a steady gaze on Kent, signaling that he recognized him as the man in charge.

Kent puffed out air. "What?"

Jared cleared his throat. "I know the media, how they think. We got two sides here, both needing something. You want people to hear your story. Reporters *want* that story. Every reporter wants to get it first. But once your story's in that reporter's hands, it's out of your control. He or she can put his own spin on it. He can make you look bad or he can make you look good. Instead of worrying about this blog, I suggest you choose one or two reporters to feed information to. Give them T.J.'s document. Tell them they'll keep hearing first as long as they represent your story well. Ask Chief Edwards to set that up for you, and in return you'll talk to him about doing 'something for him,' like he says. That way you'll move forward in a positive manner without relinquishing control, *and* you'll have better access to the media."

Jared fell silent. Mitch and Brad considered him, then cut their eyes to Kent.

"Who you got in mind?" Kent surveyed Jared with suspicion. "And don't you dare say Robert Maxey from the *Spokane Review.*"

Brad and Mitch scoffed.

Jared tapped a finger against the table. "I was thinking television, not newspaper. Faster dissemination that way. I'd say Jeremy Cole from Channel 2 and Teresa Wright, the Channel 4 evening anchor. That way you have two stations in case one of them doesn't work for you."

Kent sniffed. "How would I get to 'em?"

"Email them. Chief Edwards could get their addresses."

Kent considered him for another moment, then sneered. "Well, thank you for your idea, Mr. Reporterman. But *I'll* make the decisions in here."

His eyes swung to Brad.

He snatched up his gun and stood staring at a blacked-out window. Mitch and Brad exchanged glances.

Fresh fear stabbed Bailey. To watch Kent Wicksell fight with himself, to know that any one of them could be gunned down just to prove he was in control ...

Kent jerked around and stared at the computer. Then filled his lungs, nostrils flaring. He strode back to the computer like a man on a new mission. Smacked a palm against the table. "Type."

>> You want something, cop? Fine, here's what I'll give you. I'll move off the blog, and me and you can use the phone — on these conditions. First you get me the email addresses of Jeremy Cole at Channel 2 and Teresa Wright at Channel 4. I will send T.J.'s story only to them, IF they will read the ENTIRE THING on TV. And they have to make us LOOK GOOD to people. Long as they do that, we'll stay on the phone.

Bailey posted the comment, keeping her face expressionless. But a tinge of hope blended with her fright. Kent Wicksell's need to be in charge made him unpredictable, but it was also his weak spot. Jared had seen that.

Brad smacked his tongue against his teeth. "Terrific. Only I don't see no TV in here. How we going to know what they're doing?"

"You think I haven't thought of that?" Kent shot back. He turned his narrowed eyes on Bailey. "You got a cable outlet in here?"

She shook her head.

He cursed under his breath. "Well, then, a snowy picture will have to do." He pressed his knuckles into her shoulder. "Tell him we want a TV."

A TV? The hope withered. That meant someone had to bring it. Bailey imagined someone from the outside world stepping into this nightmare. He'd probably either become a hostage too or be shot as he tried to leave.

"*Do* it."

Heart sinking, Bailey placed her fingers on the keys.

>> We want a TV brought in so we can watch the news.

"Hey, Dad." Brad leaned one elbow on the counter, a smirk on his face. "I got an idea. Tell 'em you want that man who dragged the cop away to deliver it."

THIRTY-THREE

>> I'll move off the blog . . .

Satisfaction trickled through Vince as he finished reading the message. *Yes.* Finally Wicksell was showing a willingness to compromise.

What had happened to change his mind?

Never let your guard down. The words of an expert from Vince's training whispered in his head. A volatile HT could turn negative just as quickly.

Vince's brain churned logistics. He could agree to contacting the reporters. No doubt they would love being handed semi-exclusive stories, even if it was their day off. And thanks to the Patriot Act, he could better control what they said. Established after 9/11, the Patriot Act gave law enforcement greater latitude in instructing the media during terrorist acts—and this would be considered as such.

But one thing remained out of Vince's control—how Wicksell, driven by his own warped perceptions, might choose to interpret anything a reporter did or said.

Still, this was something to work with.

>> Kent, I will agree to your compromise — moving off
   the blog in return for getting you these two reporters.
   I will try to contact them, but please realize it may take

awhile. As soon as I get their email addresses, I'll let
you know.

When he posted the comment, he saw a new message from
Wicksell.

>> We want a TV brought in so we can watch the news.

Vince puckered his chin. No surprise, but fulfilling the
request would be a dangerous procedure. Vince would need help
from Tactical, and he and Wicksell would have a lot of negotiating to do beforehand.

You want a TV, Wicksell, I'm getting something else in return.
Something big.

He already knew what to ask for.

>> I understand your request for a TV. Let me see what I can
do.

He posted the comment, then turned toward the door. "Roger!
You available?"

"Coming!"

When Roger appeared, Vince gave him the names of the two
reporters and why they were needed. "Also, call the phone company now and get that dedicated line to Java Joint set up."

Roger listened, jotting notes, then hurried away.

The station phone rang. "I'll get it," Roger called over his
shoulder.

A minute later Vince heard the rear door of the station open.
He stepped into the hall to see an ISP officer escorting in Justin
and Larry.

Vince shook hands with them both. "Thanks for coming. We
really need your help."

"No problem, where do you want us?" Larry dug a leathered
hand into his scalp.

"Roger can use you to post information on the situation board in my office as he gathers it, and also to help keep the log. He's in there." Vince pointed to the closest office. Larry gave a quick nod and headed off. "Justin, I need you with me."

In his late fifties, Justin was over six-two and hard-muscled from working out, with an angular face and dark brown eyes. His experience as a negotiator would provide Vince with a second set of ears and expertise as he communicated with Wicksell.

"Okay. Whatever I can do."

Justin spoke in a level tone, but the words hardened at the edges. For a surreal moment Vince stood outside himself, surveying the scene. Hearing the voices, watching the movements, all carried out in this new, grim normality. *Weighted*, that was the word. Everything felt weighted.

Justin turned to the ISP officer, a salt-and-pepper-haired man who looked to be in his forties. "Thanks for bringing me in."

"No problem." The officer looked to Vince. "Anything you need me to run back?"

"Not right now. Thanks."

The officer exited the station. Vince motioned Justin into his office. "I'll print the blog conversation so you can see where we are."

"All right." Justin pulled a chair up to the other side of Vince's desk. As the printer spat paper, Vince plucked up the sheets and handed them to him. Justin read them swiftly, his lips pressed. "This where we are now, with your answer about the TV?" He tapped the papers.

"Yeah. I'm waiting for Roger to get through to the reporters. Once I manage to move Kent to the telephone and we can tape the communications, you can be my note-taker and help me with ideas." Even though the digital taping system could feed into a computer, it would be much quicker to refresh memory from notes than to search for specific information in a down-loaded file.

Roger leaned in the office door, a phone to his ear. He pointed to it, mouthing, "Prosecutor Mick Wiley."

Vince looked back to Justin. "I need to take this. You know how to check the blog for comments, in case Wicksell says something?"

"Sure. I always read the blog posts."

"Okay. Let me know if anything comes up."

Justin came around the desk to sit at the computer. Vince picked up the receiver for the station line and walked a few steps toward the front window. Staring at an empty and silent Main Street, he hit the *talk* button and greeted the prosecutor who'd sent T.J. Wicksell to prison.

THIRTY-FOUR

"That man who dragged the cop away..."

Brad's words turned every vein in Bailey's body to ice.

Kent hulked nearby, gun in his left hand, scratching his neck with the other. His expression indicated he was considering the idea.

Mitch jerked his chin. "He's gotta be a friend of these people. Probably won't try to pull a fast one like some cop."

"Exactly." Brad sniffed.

Bailey looked down at her lap. She couldn't move. Couldn't breathe.

Kent's clothes rustled. She could feel his cool gaze on her.

"Who is he?" He leaned down toward her.

She refused to answer, even as she knew her silence would give her away.

Mitch pulled in air with a whistle. "Obviously somebody she likes pretty well. Her husband?"

"Mm." Kent sounded pleased with the thought. "That true?" He eyed her coldly.

She managed the barest of nods.

"Hey, man, that's perfect." Brad gave a low chuckle.

"Yeah." Kent pressed his knuckles into Bailey's upper arm. She cringed. "Tell Edwards we want your husband to bring the TV and nobody else."

Bailey was afraid of heights. Put her near the edge of a cliff, on a high bridge, and the panicky sensation was always the same. Like an unhinged trap door, the bottom of her stomach would just ... drop away. A sickening feeling, dizzying. The same reaction could come just from watching someone else sidle too close to an abyss, particularly if it was someone she loved.

This was what she felt now, with Kent's hot breath on her, his fingers digging into her skin. The thought of summoning John *here* perched her on a crumbling mountaintop, no end to the drop in sight.

"Hey!"

Kent hit her shoulder. The punch landed so fast she didn't even see it coming. Pain shot through her muscle. Bailey heard her friends gasp.

Fine. He could hit her again. Kill her if he wanted. She was *not* luring her husband into this death haven.

Slowly she raised her head and dared look him in the eye. "No."

Anger twisted his features. "Don't tell me no. *Do* it!"

Bailey shook. Try as she might, she couldn't bear to look into his heartless face any longer. She lowered her head and focused on the keyboard, heart thumping.

"No."

Silence. Bailey squeezed her eyes shut, steeling herself for whatever came next. A strange aura settled over her—not calm, surely not peace.

Acceptance.

She sensed a motion from Kent. Then—firm footsteps. Coming from Brad's direction. They stopped.

Sudden rustling. A moan. Someone wailed.

Angie?

Bailey's eyes flew open.

The barrel of Brad's automatic weapon dug against Bev's left temple. She sat frozen, head tilted away from the killing machine, eyes round, mouth hanging open. Both hands clawed the tabletop.

Kent sank his fingers into Bailey's shoulder. "Do it or he shoots."

THIRTY-FIVE

"Mick, Chief Edwards here." Vince wandered the office, unable to keep still. He pictured Mick the last time he'd seen him in a courtroom.

At five-seven, Mick Wiley could only be described as round. Round face, rotund body, big round green eyes. He looked like a teddy bear—until he opened his mouth. His booming voice echoed off courtroom walls and straightened tired jurors' spines. Mick had won a lot of convictions, and he was proud of every one. Especially, according to the papers, T.J. Wicksell's, because of the heinousness of the crime.

"Vince, sorry it took so long to get back to you. I was out on the lake without my cell phone. I hear you got yourself a situation with the Wicksells. Can't say I'm surprised, knowing that family."

"You deal with any of them during the trial?"

Mick snorted. "Oh yeah. Big brother Mitch is a meth head. And daddy Kent's a roaring locomotive. Guy was in my face every time I turned around. Complaining about the defense attorney, insisting his son was innocent. Had to kick him out of my office twice. After that I refused to see him."

"We tried and tried to talk to the lawyers, but no one would listen." Kent's words in his letter.

Vince knew Mick's case had been airtight. He'd put forth evidence; the jury had convicted. End of story. There was little Mick could say to placate Kent Wicksell—yet that was exactly what Vince was asking him to do.

"Kent accused the defense attorney of showing up in court with a hangover. You know anything about that?"

Mick snorted. "Get real. We had reporters in there every day, hanging on every word. You think one of them wouldn't mention some bumbling attorney? T.J. got fair representation. He just happened to be guilty."

Larry hurried into the office, notepaper in hand, and made a beeline for the situation board. He picked up the fine-tipped marker lying on the ledge beneath the board and started writing, head jerking up and down as he consulted the paper.

"No questioning that. But I need to give Kent something. Of course I'm trying to talk him out of there, but his level of anger tells me that won't happen anytime soon."

"What can I do to help? Roger said he's demanding we cut T.J. loose. That's not about to happen."

"No. But Wicksell needs to see me talking to you. Like I'm trying to free his son. Will you be willing to listen to his so-called evidence?"

"Sure, sure, we have to do something. You talked to Lester?"

Mick's tone dipped. Lester Tranning—T.J.'s defense attorney. The two men's animosity toward each other was legendary. According to courthouse talk, it started years ago over some case Mick won, with Lester publicly accusing him of underhanded lawyering. During T.J.'s case their hostility had only given the media more titillating stories.

Vince would have his hands full trying to work with them in the same room.

"We're trying to reach him. Judge Hadkin too. I'd like to get the three of you down here to talk this thing over while I communicate with Wicksell. I'll want to keep it quiet because I don't want to tell him you're here until I can get the best negotiating advantage from the information."

Larry began taping photos of the Wicksell men to the situation board.

"Yeah, got it." Mick paused. "Okay. I can be there in forty-five minutes."

Mick was driving from the Coeur d'Alene area. "Great. Thanks." Vince gave him Jim's cell number to call for instructions on being escorted into the inner perimeter. He didn't want the attorneys meeting at Al's media site, where reporters would recognize them.

Vince hung up and strode to the situation board to study photos of the three Wicksells. He gazed into Kent's eyes, trying to get more of a feeling for the man. Then read through birth dates, contact information, and other pertinent data. *Kent's wife—Lenora, 51.* He might want to talk to her at some point. Priors: Kent—armed burglary, 1988. That would be a year before T.J. was born. Brad—two assaults against girlfriends. Mitch—drug possession and sales.

"You make copies of these photos for Tactical?" Vince asked Larry.

"Got a set ready."

"Thanks." Vince veered toward his desk. He needed to give Jim a heads-up about the attorneys and judge. Justin still focused on the monitor, clicking the mouse.

"Anything?" Vince reached for the phone.

"Nada."

Two minutes later as Vince hung up from the call, Roger hustled into the office. "I checked with Al first about reporters Jeremy Cole and Teresa Wright, in case they're already at the media site. No such luck. I called their stations—both are off today. Called their cells and left messages."

"Good. They should call back before long." Reporters stayed close to their phones.

Roger's cell rang. He checked the ID, his face lighting with recognition. Held the phone out to Vince. "Lester Tranning."

As Vince took the call, Roger moved to Larry and handed him more paper. The reporters' names and phone numbers went up on the board.

"Vince, I heard what's going on. What can I do?" Unlike the dichotomy between Mick's voice and body, Lester's nasally tone had always struck Vince as fitting for his tall, lean frame.

"Tell me about Kent Wicksell."

"He's bad news, that's what. Kept accusing me of not doing enough for T.J. I finally stopped taking his calls. One day he barreled into my office when I was in the middle of a meeting. I had to call an officer to escort him out. Hate to tell you, but I'm not all that surprised to hear what he's done."

Vince asked Lester if he could come to the station to meet with Mick and—if they could get ahold of him—the judge. Lester said he could be there within an hour.

"Judge Hadkin can be a big help, but don't count on much from Wiley." Lester's pitch turned sour. "That guy'll bend over backward to protect a conviction—a dozen hostages or not."

Vince repressed a sigh. Dealing with these two attorneys was not going to be fun. Even so, faint hope swirled in his chest. At least both attorneys were available. A small miracle in itself on Memorial Day weekend.

"Vince." Justin looked up from the computer, his expression grim. "You'd better come look at this message."

THIRTY-SIX

John Truitt slumped at the desk in his compact home office — a bedroom refurbished after their youngest daughter had moved out. His right hand ached from clicking the mouse, but he kept at it, seeking yet dreading the next message from the captors. That ache was mere dust beneath his feet compared to the one in his heart. It was a tangible pain that more than once had nearly knocked him from his chair.

He'd stumbled upon the talks between Kent and Vince by accident. Devastated upon his arrival home, he found himself at the computer, desperate to see Scenes and Beans, his closest connection to Bailey. Something had led him to check the comments.

Bailey. Her beautiful face shimmered before him. Her shoulder-length red-gold hair, the warm brown eyes. His wife had the biggest heart of anyone he'd ever known.

Even now, after seeing the men inside Java Joint, after dragging Frank down the street, John could not fully grasp what had happened. His mind trailed random thoughts, screaming it was all a nightmare, running snippets of psalms for protection — psalms John didn't even know he'd memorized. Tears flowed, then stopped, flowed, then stopped, his vision now blurry and his eyes burning.

He who dwells in the shelter of the Most High will rest in the shadow of the Almighty. I will say of the Lord, "He is my refuge and my fortress, my God, in whom I trust ..."

He needed sleep. The frailty caused by his epilepsy required hours of rest every day, timed around his medication schedule. But no way could he sleep now.

Hear, O Lord, my cry for mercy. O sovereign Lord, my strong deliverer, who shields my head in the day of battle—do not grant the wicked their desires, O Lord; do not let their plans succeed ...

The phone jangled, sending electrical current through his nerves. He snatched up the receiver. "John here."

"John, it's Helen Communs."

The familiar voice washed over him like warm rain. Helen, a woman in her early seventies, known for her strong faith and prayers for others amid her own suffering from arthritis. "Hi, Helen."

"Is anyone with you?"

No stupid questions—*Are you all right?* No platitudes or prying for information. That was Helen.

"No. But I really ... don't want company right now."

Silence. He could feel her empathy thrumming over the line. "You remembering to take your medication?"

Something his mother would ask, if she were still alive. "Yes."

"All right then." Her voice caught, then evened out. "I wanted to tell you we've got quite a gathering at the church. People just keep arriving. Old folks like me, mothers with children. We've even got someone down at the nursery, watching the little ones so their moms can pray. Other people are leaving work. Seems like all those with shops on Main Street are here, plus many others who just walked out of work. Bailey and all the others with her—they're covered in prayer, John. Downright drippin' in it. I want you to know that. *Grab on* to that and don't let go."

How he wanted to. But all John could picture were the holes in Frank's chest, the weapons in the three men's hands ...

His throat squeezed. "They're killers, Helen. They don't care who they hurt."

"Listen to me, John Truitt." Helen's words trembled, but she spoke almost defiantly, as if her words aimed straight at the devil, who just might be listening. "Our God's a whole lot bigger than any murderer on this earth. *He's* the God who will answer."

Yes, God answered prayer. John knew that. But sometimes the answers came after all hell broke loose. *Why?* Why Bailey? His most precious, beloved wife?

"Helen, in the past two years, just *look* at all the tragedy that's hit this town. I just can't ... I don't ..."

"I don't understand it either, John." Helen's voice was gentle. "Who can, this side of heaven? But let me tell you what I can see—what's come out of it. I see more people in our church than ever before. I see a blog—my goodness, I didn't even know what that was before!—started by your own wife, that half the country reads. It's full of funny stories, sure, but it's also full of God's truth. How many letters has Bailey received from readers, saying they first started thinking about God after reading those posts, and after hearing how this town prayed through its tragedies? Time after time the country has seen Kanner Lake down on its knees—and God raising us right back up. We're a living, breathing witness to the power of God, John. And we will be again, this time."

She stopped abruptly, as if afraid she'd begun to preach.

Sudden anger swelled. "If that's what it takes to be a witness, I'm *tired* of it."

"Yes. We all are. And you ... I can only imagine—" Helen cut off the words. "John, I can't tell you why. I don't *know* why. I just know God. I know he's merciful and trustworthy, even in the worst of times. Whatever, *whatever* happens—God *is*. Even now. And I'm praying that this ... *thing* will end soon, and safely. I'll stomp up and down these aisles and shout the prayers in Jesus' name if I have to." She emitted a raw little laugh. "Not that I think I have to shout for him to hear me. But it might make me feel better."

John leaned his left elbow on the desk, forehead pressed against his palm. His eyes closed. Somebody turned the heat down in his soul, the anger at God bubbling one last time, then settling. Maybe he was just too tired to feel it any longer. "Thank you, Helen. Thank you and all the folks down there with you. Please tell them I said that."

"I will." Helen sighed. "Lord bless you, John. If you need to get word to us, Lyda Hill says to call her cell phone. Crazy old woman. I never saw anybody so thrilled about a new little piece of plastic." Helen gave him the number, and he wrote it down.

John hung up, strangely calm. *Give me a minute. It'll pass.*

His bleary gaze refastened upon the computer screen. And from nowhere—God?—more lines from the Psalms flowed through his head.

O Lord, the God who saves me, day and night I cry out before you. May my prayer come before you, turn your ear to my cry . . .

He reached for the mouse, clicked to renew the comments.

. . . For my soul is full of trouble and my life (Bailey's!) *draws near the grave . . .*

The new comments box appeared.

>> Vince, this is Bailey . . .

John read the words—and all soothing psalms whisked away.

THIRTY-SEVEN

>> Vince, this is Bailey. About that TV — now they're demand-
ing that John be the one to bring it. No one else.
>> Brad held a gun to Bev's head, and they made me type
this. Because I was telling Kent I wouldn't do it.

The words punched Vince in the gut. He straightened and gazed out the front window. Had Kent now pulled that barrel away from the head of a retired teacher who'd never done him harm?

Roger moved to Justin's side and frowned at the monitor.

"What's happening?" Larry set the marker down on the situation board's ledge and came over.

Vince pushed both hands on his hips, anxiety descending over him like a cold fog. He didn't want to have to go tactical, but these kinds of threats . . .

Justin clicked the mouse. "Vince, look. A new one."

He jerked his head to the screen.

>> Bailey again. Kent says to tell you Brad moved his gun
away from Bev.

Roger grimaced. "Yeah, for how long?"

Vince buffed his jaw. "Let me sit down there, Justin."

They changed places.

John Truitt. Why demand he make the delivery?

The station line rang. "I'll get that in the other office." Roger trotted out, followed by Larry.

Vince poised his fingers over the keys. No way could he allow John to take in a television. But he couldn't say so — not yet. Not when a mere moment ago, Bev had felt the cold steel of a gun against her head.

The second phone line rang, once, twice, three times. Justin picked it up. "Kanner Lake Police Station." He listened a moment. "Yes, he's here. Hang on." He turned to Vince. "Jeremy Cole from Channel 2."

Vince focused on the monitor. "Give me one minute. Get his email address for me."

As Justin got back on the phone, Vince typed.

>> Kent, you make it more difficult for me to help when you threaten hostages. How about if we just forget about them for now and concentrate on setting up what we have agreed to do?

Vince read the comment over and posted it. The answer came in under sixty seconds.

>> I won't threaten any more hostages if they'll just do what they're told.

Great. But what crazy thing might he ask them to do?

>> Glad to hear it.
>> Kent, one of the reporters just called. I need to talk to him now. It will take a few minutes. This all right with you?

Vince looked to Justin. "Just another second."

He clicked the comments box impatiently, thinking about Kent's agreement to move to a telephone. Good choice for his sake. The comments the man was posting on the blog wouldn't exactly win the hearts of Scenes and Beans readers across the country.

>> Yeah, talk to the reporter. But make it quick.

Roger stepped into the doorway. "That was John Truitt on the line. He's reading the blog comments. He says he'll take the TV in."

Vince blew out air. *Poor John.*

How long before the media caught on to the comments? Bound to happen anytime.

"Call him back, tell him I can't let a private citizen go into a hostage situation. If we get them that TV, an officer has to deliver it."

Roger nodded.

"And listen, we're coming close to getting on the phone. Is the dedicated line set up?"

"Ready to go—onto your private line. All we got to do is set up the taping system."

"Great. Thanks."

Roger left. Vince held his hand out to Justin for the phone.

"Jeremy, thanks for calling." Vince knew this reporter, as he did all the other locals. With the rash of incidents in Kanner Lake in the last two years, he'd met more reporters than he had in the entire previous decade. Jeremy was in his midforties, with dark hair and a wide smile that had raised him to popularity.

Vince explained the situation. "I have no idea how long this document is. Now they're wanting a TV to watch the coverage. Will your station be willing to hold running the thing until that delivery is made?"

"I'm sure we can work that out. It's going to take a bit of time to set things up anyway. In the meantime we've already started covering the story."

Vince could detect stirred excitement in the reporter's voice. "Good. Now understand these men will be watching your coverage. I need you to tell your viewers the basic facts without looking or sounding negative or even the least bit judgmental about what the Wicksells have done. Remember these men are volatile, and it won't take much for Kent Wicksell to be sorry he chose you to read the document. Can you agree to that?"

"Yes. I understand lives are at stake."

"All right then. I don't know how long this will take. Somebody in that café's going to have to type the document. They will send it to me, and I will forward it to you. Meanwhile, Wicksell and I have a lot of details to negotiate regarding the delivery of the TV. But keep checking your email and stay close to your phone."

Jeremy agreed.

By the time Vince hung up, Roger stood near his desk. "Jim called. ISP helicopter's available when you want it. And the CRT team has arrived. Jack Little's the commander. They've got their mobile command post, a van, and the APC from Fairchild. And they got techs to mount three cameras where the snipers are positioned."

From CRT's mobile post, packed with communications equipment, Commander Little could watch monitors showing footage from each compact camera.

"How many new men?"

"Seven."

Vince's thoughts raced. "Tell them to set up their command post on Lakeshore, just around the corner from Second Street. Move the APC and van there too. Jack needs to get up here immediately for a briefing. Also, the ISP helicopter team needs a heads-up. If I get the breakthrough in negotiations I'm hoping for, we'll need them over here, pronto."

Media. One of the hundred details . . .

"Roger, have Larry help you call the local TV stations. Tell them to keep their copters on the ground. I want our airspace open only to emergency and police aircraft."

"Right. Okay. On that—"

The station phone rang.

Justin picked it up, identified the caller, and muffled the mouthpiece with his hand. "Teresa Wright, Channel 4."

"Oh. Good." Vince took the receiver. "Roger, call Jeremy Cole back. Ask him to tell his station about keeping their helicopter away. I'll cover it with Teresa. You and Larry can catch the other stations."

Roger nodded and hurried off.

Vince rubbed his eyes as he put the phone to his ear. "Teresa, thanks for calling ..."

Their conversation was brief, Vince's brain running ahead with details and possible scenarios. Like Jeremy, Teresa agreed to hold the footage until Vince gave the go-ahead.

Vince hung up and stared at the wall, ticking off items. CRT team. Helicopter. Air traffic. Reporters.

Google. They'd never called back.

Didn't matter now. Not as long as he succeeded in moving Wicksell off the blog.

Vince returned to the keyboard.

>> Kent, good news. I've talked to BOTH reporters. They are willing to read your document. I know it will take Bailey some time to type it. I suggest you and I move to the phone now. That way we can continue to communicate about the TV while she works. As soon as the document is typed, email it to me and I will forward it to the two reporters. Agreed?

Come on, Wicksell, let's get off this computer.
Wicksell's answer shot back.

>> I'll call you. What number do you want to use?

"All *right*." Vince ran a hand across his jaw.

He looked to Justin. "Ask Roger to get you the headphones. Wicksell's agreed."

"One for our side." Justin pushed back his chair.

>> Kent, we will have a "dedicated phone line." That way no one else will be able to call the regular Java Joint number and interrupt us. All you need to do is push the talk button on your phone, and mine will automatically ring—no need for dialing.

Justin returned with the headphones and a tablet of paper for note taking. He would also use the paper to write suggestion notes to Vince during communications. Roger set up the digital recorder.

A minute later, Vince's line rang.

THIRTY-EIGHT

Lenora Wicksell scrubbed the kitchen baseboards with all her might.

Her knees hurt from the hard floor. Her back hurt. Her arm muscles ached from the constant motion. The pain was good, *good*. Something to focus on, something to wrap her mind around, because if she dwelt on the fear and grief, she would lie down on the cracked linoleum right now and die.

She hadn't cleaned in weeks. No energy. And who cared? Ever since the Day of the Verdict, she had merely lived one moment to the next, reminding herself to eat, to breathe. Sleep—what was that?

Dirty water ran from the brush to the floor. Lenora wiped it away with a soggy white cloth. She dipped the bristles into a bucket of now-dingy water and scrubbed some more.

Laughter and applause wafted from the TV in the den. Some silly infomercial about skin care. Those people lived in another world. Another *planet*. Lenora gritted her teeth at the stupid claims and constant clapping. But she would not turn off Channel 2. Any time now she might hear some news.

It'll work, Lenora, and it won't take long.

They'd left over two hours ago. Wasn't that long enough?

Lenora sat back on her haunches, remembering the feel of Kent's arms around her. His familiar smell. Fresh pain stabbed through her. *How* could she have let them go when she knew they wouldn't be coming back? Kent, Mitch, and Brad — now she'd have to visit them *all* in prison.

But T.J. would be home.

She didn't know how, exactly. They wouldn't just let him out like nothing happened. But when the world heard his story, when caring people around the country bombarded the judge to *do* something, relook at evidence ...

The voices of many could make all the difference for one.

T.J. Every day the thought of her innocent young son in prison with all those horrible men had turned her inside out. Then to hear that he'd been beat up. She'd curled into a fetal position in bed for a solid day — until Kent told her what he and Mitch planned to do. She pictured T.J. falling under punches, being kicked and bloodied — and felt every blow in her own body. That's what a mother did. That's all a mother knew.

How well she remembered T.J. at age five, proudly giving her a bunch of wildflowers he'd picked in the field. At age eleven, parked in front of the oven, wanting to be the first to get at the chocolate chip cookies she was baking. At fourteen he'd gone crazy over the used dirt bike Kent bought him. She'd been scared to death he would break all his bones with such wild riding. Last year at this time he was just graduating from high school. As he accepted his diploma, he'd shot her that lopsided grin of his —

Stop it. Stop thinking.

Lenora shuffled forward on her knees, wincing, and redipped the brush. Even now two days' worth of dishes cluttered the sink and countertops. But that was far too easy a job for a morning like this.

"... special report from Kanner Lake." The words hurled into her ears.

Lenora dropped the brush and cloth, struggled to her feet. Hunched over, one hand at her lower back, she shuffled into the den, holding her breath.

Kent's face filled the TV screen.

An old mug shot. How unfair. Made him look like such a criminal.

Mitch's face. And Brad's. A grim-faced reporter spoke of a dozen hostages, including two teenage girls ...

Lenora covered her mouth with both hands.

A policeman — shot three times. Clinging to life as he underwent surgery.

Oh, God, let him live, please! If Kent killed a cop ...

The camera shifted to a street milling with people. Policemen, townspeople, other reporters, cameras. Yellow crime-scene tape stretched across the pavement, a state officer standing guard.

Lenora sank onto the frayed, rough edge of her couch, eyes glued to the screen.

The reporter interviewed a man. Stan somebody. He talked about how the cop was rescued, all the shot-out windows on Main Street, how terrified and angry he felt. "I know everybody in Java Joint right now. They're all my *friends*. They don't *deserve* this."

Neither did T.J.

Footage changed to shots of T.J. at trial. Lenora's own image as she came out of court, head down and holding a hand against the cameras. A picture of Marya Whitbey, smiling with her daughter.

Anger spiraled through Lenora. *How about my son beaten up, stitches in his face, his head wrapped. Why don't you show* that?

The kitchen phone rang.

Lenora swiveled toward the sound. She froze.

A second ring.

Kent?

He'd said he wouldn't be able to call her. But maybe ...

She pushed upright and hurried to answer.

THIRTY-NINE

Here goes.

Vince plucked up the receiver. "Hello, Kent."

"Hi."

The voice had a gruff rawness to it.

"Kent, good to finally talk to you. Things can go much faster this way."

"Let's hope so. We're getting antsy in here."

"You have someone typing the document?"

"Bailey. So what are you doing for my boy? You talked to the lawyers?"

"Yes. T.J.'s defense attorney and the prosecutor both say they're willing to listen to whatever you have to say about the case."

Wicksell snorted. "Lester Tranning's not worth his weight in hog slop. We need a new lawyer."

"We can discuss that later, but for now he's the one most familiar with the case."

"Yeah, yeah. Where's our TV? It's got to be one with rabbit ears, since we ain't got cable in here. And we want that man John to bring it."

Vince drew out a pause. First objective—take John Truitt out of the equation.

"Edwards?"

"I'm here. Just trying to figure out how to make this work. I can find you a TV—with rabbit ears—provided you do something

154

for me in return. But I can't allow a private citizen to bring it to you."

"What do you mean, can't allow it? You the head honcho, ain'tcha?"

"Yes. And because of that I'm sworn to protect people in this town. That ties my hands as far as sending in a private citizen. But I want to be sure I understand. You want the TV in order to watch news coverage, correct? Does it really matter who delivers it?"

"You think I want some cop coming in here?"

"You just want to make sure the delivery goes safely?"

"Yeah. And a cop don't fit that picture."

"Whoever brings you the television will be unarmed. What's any unarmed man going to do against the three of you with all your weapons?"

Kent pulled in a loud breath, blew it out. "So how soon do we get it?"

Was that a concession?

"Soon as you and I agree on what you're going to do for me in return."

"I ain't doin' *nothin'* for you, Edwards. Who do you think holds the cards here?"

"I don't think of it as anyone holding cards, Kent. You want something; I want something. Either we work out some deals, or we get nowhere. Now are you willing to work with me?"

"What do you want?"

Vince heard the rear entrance of the station open, followed by a deep voice. *Jack Little, CRT commander.* The man soon appeared in the doorway. Jack stood a stocky six feet, with a square face and flat-topped brown hair. Creases around his eyes. He looked every inch the ex-military man he was. Vince pointed to the situation board. Jack walked over to study it, one ear cocked toward the phone conversation.

"I want to make a fair exchange."

"Oh yeah? What you callin' fair?"

During Vince's negotiator course, trainer Ed Marck had related an incident in Miami involving an HT with the appropriate name of Silas Wretch. He broke out of prison, where he was serving time for double homicide, and took five people hostage in a convenience store. Demands: $10,000 and a plane ticket to Mexico. With all the food in the store, after eight hours Wretch got a hankering for sweet-and-sour pork. The negotiator proposed a deal: delivery of Chinese food in exchange for the release of a female hostage. Wretch said okay. The food was delivered; the woman was freed. Only then did Wretch ask why the negotiator had wanted only one hostage. "There's two women in here," he said. "I'd have let 'em both out if you'd asked."

Vince leaned an elbow on his desk, hearing Ed Marck's punch line: "*Don't* attach a number."

But every incident was unique. In this one, two certain hostages were the most vulnerable. In his gut Vince knew asking for them alone was pushing it.

"Here's fair, Kent. The television goes in; the two teenage girls come out."

Jack turned from the situation board, eyebrows raised.

Kent gave a raw laugh. "No deal."

"I'd like you to think about it. You've asked for some big things in regard to your son. Those things are going to take some time. It'll be easier for you in the meantime if everybody in there keeps his cool. That's least likely for two young girls."

"What I asked for don't need to take long. Take a key, stick it in the lock, and open T.J.'s prison cell. Sounds pretty simple to me."

"You and I both know it's not that simple."

Kent made a noise in his throat. "Maybe I'll send the old codger out. Guy's got a mouth on him. I got an MP5 pointed at him, and he's all bent out of shape 'cause Brad's sittin' on his stool."

MP5. Vince wrote it down, as did Justin.

Vince chuckled. "Yeah, Wilbur's a tough old guy. Talks a lot but not going to give you any real trouble."

"Tell you what, Edwards, I'll let him go. We don't need him anyway. Hey!" The phone muffled, as if Wicksell pulled it aside. "You done typin' over there?" A pause. "Get with it—we ain't got all day!" Kent's voice grew clearer. "Okay, I'm back."

"Well, I appreciate the thought about Wilbur, but I'm still asking you for the girls."

Wicksell swore. "Why they such a big thing to you?"

"Kent, look. T.J.'s just eighteen, right?"

"You know it."

"I know how bad you feel because such a terrible thing has happened to T.J. at his young age. You said he's scared in prison. Kent, those girls are just a year or two younger than your own son. Now they're in a very frightening situation. Do you really want to draw that out for them? These are girls who could have gone to school with T.J., had they lived in the same town. Maybe Ali's even met him at some school ball game."

Larry hustled into the office carrying two sets of building plans and two long pieces of curled brown newsprint paper. He headed for Jack, and they spoke quietly, Larry giving him one set of plans and one curled newsprint. Larry dropped the second set of plans to the floor and uncurled his own newsprint sheet to reveal photos and names of all the hostages taped to it in neat rows. He thumbtacked the large sheet to the wall. Vince's eyes honed in on Brittany's and Ali's pictures, next to each other on the top row.

"Don't tell me you know how I feel." Wicksell's tone crackled with the heat of a slow burn. "You don't know nothin'. *Nobody* can know."

Know. Had he used that word? He shouldn't have. Even though it happened to be true.

"I agree with you—nobody can know exactly what you've been through. I feel the same way a lot of times—nobody can know what *I've* been through. I've lost a son too, Kent. And he was only three years older than T.J."

Wicksell was silent for a moment. "What happened?"

Larry tacked up a set of building plans beside the hostage photos.

"He died in Iraq in 2005. Killed by a terrorist's bomb. I'm his father—but I couldn't stop that from happening. I couldn't save him. It was a total injustice. And Kent, thing is—you have hope with T.J. He's still got a life ahead of him. But Tim's gone forever. So when I say *know*, that's what I mean."

Wicksell grunted. "That's tough."

"Yeah."

A pause. "You get him back here for the funeral?"

The flag-draped coffin flashed in Vince's head. "We did." *What was left of him.*

Justin looked up, and their eyes locked. He and his wife had attended the funeral. Along with the rest of the town. Vince did not look at Jack and Larry, but he could feel their empathy.

"So, Edwards"—Wicksell's voice hardened—"*you* of all people ought to understand what I'm fighting for. How determined I am."

"I understand you're determined. And I'm determined to help."

Wicksell inhaled a long breath. Blew it out. Vince could almost hear the wheels turning in his mind. "So. You want them two girls." It wasn't a question.

"I do."

"That all?"

Hope raised its head. "You want to send out more?"

"Not on your life. It was a test. I don't like when people start dealing one thing, then add on another, know what I mean? Makes me not trust 'em."

"I hear you."

"You got a decent-size TV? We got three people need to watch it, and we're kind of scattered out in here."

Scattered out. Vince jotted the information, followed by a question mark.

"How about at least a twenty-four-inch? That should do it, as long as the three of you are watching from somewhere in the front part of the café."

"Yeah, we're all up front."

Up front. Vince wrote it down. He was beginning to picture the scene. The hostages in one part of the main room. The Wicksells at three different stations, guarding them.

Larry and Jack stood with backs to the board, their full attention on Vince. Larry's hands hung waist-high, lacing and unlacing. Jack's legs were spread a foot apart, one hand trailing the newsprint and building plans.

"All right, Kent. Sounds like a plan. If you'll agree to release the girls, I'll hunt down a TV fast as I can. Meanwhile, we'll have to agree on logistics regarding the exchange. But I'm sure we can work those details out."

"Depends on what kinda details you're talking about."

"It's best if there are no surprises. So I'd want to work out how the TV is brought to your door. Who opens the door. At what point the girls come outside. That kind of thing. That part shouldn't be a problem."

"Maybe. Don't go gettin' too cocky."

"I don't feel cocky. I'm just telling you we've agreed on the hardest part."

"Yeah. Well. It's a pleasure doin' business with ya, Edwards."

Justin made a fist against the desk in victory.

Let it be so. Vince's gaze wandered to Brittany's and Ali's photos on the wall. They smiled back at him. "Glad it's working out, Kent."

Wicksell cleared his throat. "Oh yeah. Forgot to ask one question."

"Okay."

"About them girls?"

"I'm listening."

"You want 'em dead or alive?"

FORTY

"Maybe I'll send the old codger out ..."

The words echoed in Carla Radling's head. *No, not Wilbur!* she wanted to scream. *Let the girls go!*

The air in Java Joint had grown nearly suffocating. Stale and dark. Heavy with sweat and fear and dread. Perspiration itched the back of Carla's neck. Kent slumped at a table shoved toward the front of the café, thick legs spread, the phone pressed to his ear. His massive gun lay on the table within a split second's reach. Mitch jerked and paced before the hostages, his nervous energy crackling. Brad sat like a king on Wilbur's stool, one foot on the circular rest and the other on the floor. Both he and Mitch kept their weapons on the hostages.

I still can't believe this.

Funny, how the mind handled shock. You'd think the body would fold in on itself from sheer terror. That the world would just stop. Yet here Carla and her friends sat, still breathing. Wilbur soundlessly thumped his thumb against the table he shared with Pastor Hank. S-Man and Leslie clutched hands even in the heat. Bev's hard gaze stabbed Mitch, as if he were a recalcitrant student in one of her English classes. Paige's back was to Carla—but she had hardly moved.

Poor Paige. Poor Frank.

Bailey continued to type.

Carla tried to pray. Ever since her life had turned upside down last September, she'd been learning how to talk to God. How to ask for forgiveness, let him wash away the guilt of her past. It had worked too. She'd begun to forge a relationship with the daughter she'd thought was long dead, had felt God's strength uphold her when she possessed none of her own. And Scott Cambry—her estranged teenage love and Brittany's birth father—even he had forgiven her. Now divorced with two kids of his own, Scott had traveled from his Washington home a number of times to visit Carla. He had his own hurts to deal with, but as soon as they first saw each other after all the years, something sparked. The love they had felt sixteen years ago had not vanished but lay buried beneath pain and lies and shamed confession. With time, maybe, just maybe, they could dig it out.

Time. Had it now run out for them? Had God brought Carla this far to have her die at the hands of these crazed men?

It's okay, God. Take me. Just please, please, get my girls out safely.

Carla glanced at Brittany. Her dark eyes looked back, reflecting shock and ... something else. Defeat? The thought pierced Carla. She squeezed Brittany's hand, their eyes still locked, the message flowing from mother to daughter—*I will get you out of here.* Amazing, the bond they had. Forged from the womb, unbroken by almost sixteen years of separation. Carla knew Brittany received her words.

Tears sprang to the girl's eyes. Carla's heart cracked. She knew Brittany's tears weren't for her. They were for fear of losing *her.* She shook her head in small but fierce movements. *No, Brittany, we* won't *lose each other. Not now. Not when we've just begun.*

Ali pulled in a ragged breath. Carla saw the reddish-brown bangs hanging in her eyes, her cheeks pale and streaked. "It's okay," Carla mouthed. "It's okay."

"So you want them two girls?" Kent said into the phone.

Carla's head jerked. *What?*

Brittany stiffened, and Ali's breath caught. Carla reached for their hands.

Yes, God. Please!

Carla leaned forward, hanging on Kent's every word. But now he talked about a TV size of all *stupid, ridiculous things ...*

Kent drew the sides of his mouth down, shifted in his chair. A darkness etched his face.

"About them girls ... you want them dead or alive?"

Carla went numb. For a moment she lifted outside her body, watched herself and the two precious girls turn white.

Someone moaned. Leslie? Brad threw his father a half-amused look. Bailey's typing stopped.

Kent gave a low chuckle. "Just a joke, Edwards. Seein' if I can rattle your cage."

Carla's shoulders sagged with relief, only to tense once more. *Rattle your cage*? Like this was a *joke*?

Oh, for just *one* of those men to let their guard down. Look the other way for a mere *second*. In fast forward, Carla pictured herself snatching away a gun, cutting Kent Wicksell in *half* with bullets ...

He paused, listening, head cocked to one side. So sure of himself. Carla fixed him with a withering stare.

"Yeah, yeah." He flexed his back. "So how we gonna do this?" He whipped his head toward Bailey. "Hey! Type!"

Bailey jumped. The clacking resumed.

For the next half hour Kent argued with Vince Edwards about "the exchange." Carla's nerves pinged with each passing second. Somewhere during that time Bailey finished typing. The hostages barely moved. Now and then Brad barked some suggestion. Kent ignored him.

First Kent returned to insisting that John Truitt bring the TV. Apparently Chief Edwards wouldn't budge on that point.

Kent grew more agitated. Carla trembled. What if Vince pushed too far and the whole deal fell through? Rage and helplessness and sodden, clinging *hope* tornadoed through her. She pictured the girls outside, running to safety, pictured them with Ali's parents. Brittany returning to the parents who'd raised her. The hugging, the crying, the leg-weakening, nauseating *relief.* Now that the possibility hovered before them, they couldn't let it go. Losing it would crush her and the girls.

God, please!

Brittany's head lowered until her chin nearly touched her chest. She shut her eyes, as if closing herself off from the scene, unable to take any more. Ali hugged herself, slightly rocking, gaze fixed upon the table. Carla glanced over to Leslie. Saw her mouth, "I'm praying."

Carla tried to nod, but her head wouldn't move.

"Edwards, you listen to me, or this whole deal's off!" Kent pushed to his feet, paced three steps. He faced the wall, beefy shoulders bent forward, fingers gripping the phone. "I ain't lettin' anybody else in here, period!"

His barrel chest rose and fell as he listened.

"You mean leave it outside the door?"

Brad snorted.

Kent ran the back of a hand across his forehead. "Don't think any of the three of us is opening the door to get it. We're likely to get shot. Tell you what, somebody takes out one of us, the other two shoot every hostage in this place, got that?"

Fresh tears rolled down Brittany's cheeks. Carla squeezed her hand, wishing she could take her daughter in both arms and hold her tight. It was so *unfair*, what these men were doing to her daughter. Forget cutting them in half with bullets; she'd rip all *three of them* apart with her bare hands, one limb at a time.

"Yeah," Kent said, "so he knocks."

"Uh-huh."

"Then we send 'em out."

"No, *I* choose who comes out and gets it."

Wilbur moved his stiff torso around and gave Carla a look over his shoulder. He firmed his mouth and nodded as if to say, *It'll happen.*

But what if it did—at the expense of John Truitt? Carla looked at Bailey, who sat unmoving at the computer. Her face looked as frightened as Carla felt. She was scared to death for her husband.

Kent kept arguing. Logical one minute, yelling the next. Two things Carla realized. He wanted what he wanted. But he would not appear weak to get it.

Sweat ran under Carla's clothes. Brittany's and Ali's faces glistened with perspiration. It was so *hot* in the room, with everything closed up. The black sheets over the windows only absorbed more sunshine. What she would give for some fresh air, a drink of water. The Wicksells had taken off their jackets long ago. With the coat pockets bulging full of ammunition, Brad and Mitch placed theirs underneath the counter, far from any hostage's reach. Kent thunked his down on the table where he sat.

"Wait, hang on." Kent looked to Bailey. "*Why* you just sitting there?"

She licked her lips. "I'm done."

"How long ago?"

"I don't know." Her voice trembled. "A few minutes."

"Why didn't you *say* something?"

She swallowed. "You were busy."

He cursed under his breath. "Edwards, what's your email address?" He listened, then repeated it to Bailey. "Send the thing. *Now.*"

Mitch sniffed. "Better make sure she don't say nothin' else."

"I'll watch her." Brad pushed off the stool.

"Yeah, yeah, go ahead." Kent turned away, talked into the phone. "T.J.'s story is coming. We're finally getting somewhere."

Gripping his gun, Brad walked to Bailey and stood behind her, frowning at the monitor. "Send a blank email with the attachment. Put 'T.J.' in the subject line."

Bailey hit some keys. Brad looked to Kent. "It's done." He motioned to Bailey to slide her chair away from the computer. "Don't touch it again unless you're told."

She obeyed. Brad sauntered back to the counter. He smirked at Wilbur as he settled on the stool.

"The email's coming to ya," Kent told Vince.

Carla felt lightheaded. *Please, please.* They were so close . . .

Kent stalked back to his table. "Shut up—just get the TV! Don't call back till you do." He smacked a button to end the call.

Brad made a popping sound with his lips. "John's not bring-ing the TV?"

"No, somebody else." Kent waved a hand. "He'll be unarmed, and he ain't coming inside. And ain't none of us three going out there."

Brad worked his jaw. "You letting some cop come—"

"I'm *handling* it, Brad!" Kent shoved to his feet. "Now let it be!" He eyed his son, fuming. "What matters is, not long from now, everybody'll hear T.J.'s story. Once those reporters read the document, others will pick it up. It'll be across the nation in an hour."

Brad smirked. "That's a start. How about getting T.J. out of prison? Look how long we've been here."

Kent's face turned to stone. "You'd better find yourself some patience, boy. Sometimes things take longer than expected."

He eyed Carla and the girls, his lip curling. "Looks like we'll be breaking up your little party."

Carla closed her eyes. *Thank You, God!*

"No, we're not," Brittany blurted.

Carla gawked at her daughter. They were teetering on a cliff here. One wrong move and the whole thing could give way. *"What?"*

Brittany shot her a look, then fixed defiant eyes on Kent. Her mouth trembled. But she pulled her shoulders back and raised her chin.

"I'm not leaving without my mother."

FORTY-ONE

Vince pressed back in his chair and puffed out a long breath.

Awareness of his body flicked on. The back of his shirt was damp. His muscles felt drained, and his left hand cramped from holding the phone. He flexed his fingers.

"Good job." Justin took off his earphones.

Vince nodded and rose to greet the CRT commander. "Jack. Glad you're here."

"You're going to need help with that exchange. Sounds like we got here just in time."

Jack's tone remained factual, but Vince saw the anxiety in his eyes. The CRT commander had four daughters at home, two of them teenagers. He was a tough guy on the job, but those girls had their daddy wrapped around their fingers.

"Yeah, you did." A to-do list rapid-fired in Vince's brain. "Right now I need to look at that email and send it on. In the meantime, can you get the ISP helicopter in the air?" He turned to Justin. "Call Al to locate a TV. Remind him I want this exchange kept from the media until it's over."

"Right." Justin reached for the station phone. Jack headed for the lobby, tac radio in hand.

Vince sat down in front of the computer. Clicked over to his inbox. There sat the email with attachment. *Subject: T.J.*

He opened the document and printed it. The hard copy would soon be tacked near the situation board. As the printer whirred, the words from Wicksell's letter filtered through Vince's mind. *"There is evidence that should have come out in court..."*

Vince leaned forward. *Evidence? Okay, Wicksell. Show me.*

Arms folded, he began to read.

FORTY-TWO

My Story

My name's T.J. Wicksell. I didn't kill Marya Whitbey. I couldn't do that to anybody.

I'd never put this down on paper if I didn't have to, because some of it's embarrassing. But it ain't half as bad as what they're saying I did. So I just want to set the record straight for when my trial comes up.

I still can't believe I have to go to trial! I can't believe this is happening. Sometimes I wake up at night and think it's all a nightmare. Any minute now I'll wake up for REAL.

I met Marya at Mr. Kranck's store sometime last summer. Every now and then I'd see her, and we'd talk. She was sweet and pretty. Treated her little girl, Keisha, real good. I got to liking Marya. I wanted to ask her out but figured she might say no until she got to know me a little better. I could tell Marya wasn't the kind to just go out with anybody. I was going to have to earn her trust.

Every time I went into the store I hoped she was there.

That day in October I drove to the store to pick up some pasta and tomato sauce for my mom — she was making lasagna that night. Marya was there. I teased with Keisha, got her to giggling. It was cold outside, and Marya had a heavy bag to carry. I offered to take her home. She said okay.

I told myself while we drove I was going to ask her to go out. Maybe a movie or something. But she only lived about three blocks away, and we got there in no time. I did a U-turn and pulled up to the curb out front. Marya thanked me. I offered to take her bag inside for her, but she said no, she could manage. "What apartment's yours?" I said, and she pointed to the second one on the left from the building's front door.

I sat in my car and watched until I saw the light come on in that apartment.

My mom needed her groceries to make supper, and I knew she'd be mad if I hung around any longer. I drove away about a block, but then I got so ticked at myself for not asking Marya for a date. And how long would it be before I ran into her in the store again? I hadn't even gotten her phone number.

I turned around to go back to her apartment. As I got to the building I noticed a driveway going around back. I turned left onto it. It led to a parking area. There were some cars there, but still a lot of empty spaces. I parked and went in the building through a back door.

On the right was a staircase. I went straight ahead and hit the front hallway. Then turned right.

Way down the end of the hall, I saw something really quick. Like someone's foot as they disappeared around the corner. Then I heard fast footsteps, like somebody running up a staircase. I figured there must be another set of stairs down there, but didn't think any more about it.

I headed toward the second apartment on my left. And then I started to get nervous, which isn't natural for me. But I got to thinking what if Marya got mad at me for coming back? What if she told me never to come around her again? Then even if I saw her in the store, I wouldn't be able to talk to her.

My head was thinking all these things while I stood about five feet away from the door. And suddenly I realized it didn't look all the way closed. I walked over a little and looked at it. Yup. Open about an inch.

I heard Keisha crying.

I stood there, waiting to hear Marya's voice, soothing Keisha like I'd heard her do in the store. But the little girl just kept on crying.

What should I do? I looked up and down the hall. Didn't see anybody.

So I walked forward until I could touch the door. Keisha was still crying.

I knocked on the door. No answer.

Right then I got really scared, like something . . . I don't know, I just knew something. I almost turned and ran. But I was worried about Marya. So I knocked again and called her name. Still no answer.

Next thing I knew I had the door pushed open. I stuck my head inside. "Marya?"

Nothing but Keisha crying.

I saw the living room and the kitchen past it. The bag of groceries sat on the counter. To my right was a little hallway and a room—probably the bedroom. Keisha's crying was coming from there.

Something felt real bad. Inside I knew something had happened. My heart started beating hard, but I couldn't just leave. I went down the hall and looked around the corner into the bedroom.

There was Keisha. She had red on her all over. Wet red.

Marya was on the floor on her side. Not moving. She was bleeding. I saw cuts all over her body.

She looked dead.

I remembered that foot I saw in the hallway, and somebody running up the staircase.

I went crazy scared. I know I should have called the police. And should have gotten Keisha out of there. It's easy to think that now, but I'm telling you when something that scary happens, your brain *forgets* to think. You just *act.* I started to turn and run, but then I saw the knife on the floor. My brain cleared for just a second, and I thought—what if Keisha cuts herself with it?

I jumped into the room, picked up the knife by the handle, and threw it on the bed, where Keisha couldn't reach it. Then I tore out of the apartment and headed for the nearest door of the building. I ran out the front, my legs just pumping, still not thinking straight. Then I realized my car was in the back. I ran around the building. I must have wiped my hand on my shirt around then, but I don't remember. I jumped in my car and drove out of there as fast as I could. I didn't stop until I got home.

When I drove up to our house I noticed the blood on my shirt. I ripped it off so Mom wouldn't see the blood. I balled it up and took it inside the house. I stuck it under my bed and threw on another shirt. Mom was already calling me from the kitchen, mad that I'd taken so long. I told her I was sorry and that I'd had to go to a second store because Mr. Kranck didn't have the sauce she wanted.

I couldn't eat the lasagna that night.

Two days later the paper came out with a drawn picture of somebody seen running to a car in the parking lot of Marya's building. The picture looked like me. The cops came the next day. They wanted to talk to me. That *really* scared me because I realized how stupid it was not to call them in the first place. Now I'd look guilty just because I'd kept quiet. I told them I didn't know who killed Marya. Which was true. They came back with a search warrant. They found my shirt under the bed. It had Marya's blood on it.

I told them this story after they arrested me, but nobody listened. I told my lawyer too. I hope they'll listen in my trial.

FORTY-THREE

Mother. The word felt weird to Brittany. First time she'd ever called Carla that, even though it was true. It was hard, after sixteen years of thinking of one woman as Mom to suddenly call someone else *Mother.*

Brittany's legs shook. Her breathing sounded more like panting, and that made her mad. She didn't *want* to look weak in front of hateful, *disgusting* Kent.

He pushed to his feet and headed for her like some stalking lion.

"Kid, you better watch yourself," Brad said.

Brittany clamped her jaw, pressed her feet to the floor—and somehow managed to look Kent in the eye.

He'd left his gun on the table where he'd been sitting, near the front of the café. Purposely, for sure. Just to remind them all how out of reach it was for them. Meanwhile, Mitch and Brad pointed their weapons at the group. Cowards.

Sweat shone on Kent's ugly face. And she could smell him. All ratty and thick like a horse barn.

He stopped three feet away. His face twisted. "What is this 'I won't leave without my mother'?" His eyes drove daggers at her. "You'll leave when I tell you to leave."

"She will," Carla blurted. "She *will.*"

"No, I won't." Brittany stared at Kent. "Not without *her.*"

175

"Hey, girl." Mitch shifted his weapon in Brittany's direction. "Better get out while the gettin's good."

Kent swung his head around to give Mitch a black look—*I'll handle this.* He sniffed and turned back to Brittany. "I don't have time for your games. You'll do what I say, case closed. Now I'm going down to the bathroom—do you *mind*?"

Mitch sniggered.

Off Kent stomped, cursing under his breath like the cultured man he was.

Down the hall, the bathroom door opened and closed.

Ali gawked at Brittany like she'd gone crazy.

Come on, Ali, what would you *do if* your *mother was in here?*

"I got an idea." Brad's voice sounded singsong. Taunting. Brittany couldn't see his face without looking halfway over her shoulder—and she wouldn't give him the satisfaction. She focused on the table.

Footsteps. He'd gotten off the stool. Brad sauntered over to where his father had stood. Brittany could feel his evil.

Carla tensed.

Suddenly all of Brittany's courage melted away. Just like that. She pulled in her shoulders—but her gaze drifted up to Brad's face before she could stop it.

He gave her a smile that chilled her soul. "Maybe we *will* let your mom go with you. On one condition. First you and me take a little trip down the hall."

FORTY-FOUR

Vince looked up from the monitor to find himself alone in the office. He could hear Roger and Jack talking in the lobby. Justin must have taken a bathroom break. Vince had been concentrating so hard on T.J.'s story, he hadn't noticed him leave.

His gaze returned to the screen. *New evidence, Wicksell? Where's the proof?* There was nothing in that document but T.J.'s version of events. Anyone with half a brain could have made up that alibi while cooling his heels in a jail cell.

But something nagged at Vince ...

Wait, hold those thoughts. He needed to forward the email to the reporters.

Frowning, he typed in their addresses and shot them the document. Watched the *send* icon until it stopped moving.

He sat back, staring across the room at Kent Wicksell's photo.

As far as he knew, the jury had never heard T.J.'s story. Shouldn't Lester Tranning have presented it in court?

Not if there was nothing to back it up. And evidently there wasn't. No witness had ever come forward regarding another person running from the scene.

Still, Lester didn't have much of a defense. T.J.'s prints were on the knife. Marya's blood was on his shirt. He was the last person to see her alive. With such a strong case for the prosecution, why didn't Lester put T.J. on the stand and let him tell his story?

But then T.J. would have had to endure Mick Wiley's heavy cross-examination. *Let me get this straight, Mr. Wicksell. You lied to the police. You lied to your mother. Why should we believe you now?* Mick would have torn T.J. apart. And knowing how Tranning didn't trust the prosecutor to begin with ...

Vince had to wonder. If the old feud between Tranning and Wiley didn't exist, would Tranning have handled the case differently?

He pushed the thoughts away and stood. Time was ticking, and he needed to brief Jack Little.

Soon he and Jack stood before the situation board, figuring details of the TV exchange, what each of Jack's men would do. They would all be needed at various posts. Someone else would have to take the TV to the café's door. Jack was fired up, missing no details, his words in staccato. Vince knew when all of this was over, each of Jack's daughters would get an extra hug.

"Looks like those building plans for Java Joint are your copy." Vince pointed to the set Jack had laid on the floor by the board.

"Yeah. Let's just hope we don't need them."

"Agreed." If negotiations failed and they had to go tactical, those plans would provide critical information for the CRT. "You have a monitor you can bring in here for me? I'm going to want the helicopter to film the exchange."

"We have one. I'll have a tech set it up. You want connection to one of our frontal cameras afterwards?"

"Absolutely." Vince glanced at his watch. He needed to wrap this up so Jack could get back to his post. "Anything else?"

"Think we're set. I'll get down and brief my men."

"Good. Let's get those girls *out* of there." Vince held out his hand, and Jack gripped it hard.

FORTY-FIVE

John Truitt swallowed his last midday pill and stared at the kitchen sink. The faint scent of vegetable soup rose from his empty bowl. Somehow he'd managed to eat in order to take the medication. Now the smell threatened to turn his stomach.

He rinsed the bowl and spoon and put them in the dishwasher.

Not knowing what to do next, he leaned both hands on the tile and fixed his gaze out the window.

Everywhere he looked in the backyard, he saw Bailey's touch. In the multicolored flowers along the white fence, planted and tended by her hands. In the perfect arrangement of outdoor furniture on the patio. Even the grass reminded him of her. On summer evenings she loved to walk through it barefoot. She'd toss back her hair and smile at the sky, reveling in the joy of just *living* . . .

John's throat squeezed.

I can't stay here anymore.

The thought surged within him like a rogue wave. He swung away from the sink, one hand thrust in his hair. With food in his stomach he felt better. Now he needed to *do something*. At least while Vince had talked to Kent Wicksell on the blog, John knew what was going on. Now he'd been cut off. Abandoned. Couldn't even deliver the TV to Java Joint's door—and maybe catch a glimpse of his wife's face.

TV.

News.

He strode from the kitchen into the living room. Turned on the television and flipped to a local channel. A golf tournament. He changed to Channel 2.

A sagging front porch and run-down house filled the screen. The picture had the feel of live coverage. A reporter stood in the scruffy front yard.

"This is Tony Brewer at the house owned by Kent Wicksell, who, along with his sons Brad and Mitch, has taken a dozen people hostage in the Java Joint Coffee Shop in Kanner Lake. Lenora Wicksell, Kent's wife, and the mother of the two sons, is at home. We have knocked on her door repeatedly, but she refuses to answer."

Fisting his hands, John stared at the scene. Through a window—a shadow of movement. Lenora Wicksell was home all right.

John swiveled back to the kitchen. Pulled open the drawer that held the phone book and yanked it out. *Wicksell ... Wicksell ...* There it was! Listed under Kent and Lenora. Address included.

Lenora Wicksell. John tried to imagine her face. What was she thinking right now? Had she known what her husband and sons were going to do?

Could she talk them *out* of Java Joint?

Gripping the phone book, he practically ran for the office.

On the computer, he searched Yahoo! Maps for the address. It was a little road off Highway 95, north of Hayden. John pictured the drive from Kanner Lake. Over to Highway 41 and south. East on Hayden Avenue over to Highway 95.

He could be there in twenty-five minutes.

Energized with new purpose, he printed out the map.

FORTY-SIX

Brittany sat frozen, eyes fixed on a small dent in the table. Carla clung to her arm like she'd never let go.

"What d'ya say, Brittany?" Brad hovered nearby, his gun barrel feet from her head.

"She says no," Carla hissed.

Mitch had moved toward the other end of the café, where Bailey sat. He laughed in his throat. "I'll take second round."

"Leave her alone." Wilbur's shoulders reared back. "You two are a couple a big men, ain't ya. Twice her size, with guns—"

"Nobody asked you, old man." Brad's tone could have melted steel. He swung his weapon at Wilbur. "You know what's good for you, you'll shut up right *now*."

No, no. Brittany's eyes burned. This was her fault. She never should have said anything.

Okay, just get me and Ali out of here!

She pictured running out the door. The feel of freedom. The fresh air. Just on the other side of that door was *life*.

But what about Carla? What if they *killed* her? What if they dumped her out in the street like Frank? Brittany would never forgive herself.

Down the hall, the bathroom door opened. Kent's heavy footsteps approached. He stopped somewhere behind Brittany, near the first table. "Hey. What's going on?"

Brad drew a long breath. "Just having a little conversation with the girl."

"He's threatening her." Pastor Hank's voice sounded thick with disgust.

Brad swore. "I'm not threatening anybody."

"Yes, you are," Wilbur retorted.

Brad lurched toward him. "I told you, old man—"

Ali screamed. Pastor Hank and Wilbur shouted, and Carla half rose from her chair.

"Shut up, shut *up*, everybody!" Kent stalked to Brad and shoved him back. "Get over to that stool and *stay* there." He pointed at Carla. "*You*, sit down!" He stomped across the room toward his gun. "Can't I leave you two in charge for *one minute*?"

"Don't yell at *me*, I was just standing here!" Mitch's skinny face reddened.

"Don't yell at me either!" Brad hurled. "You couldn't have *done* this without me today."

Kent snatched his weapon from the table and marched over to Brad, getting in his face. "Then why we got everybody shouting, huh? Things was *just fine* when I left the room."

"Just fine, really? You had a *girl* telling you what to do!"

Kent's face went purple. He pushed Brad backward, his words low and shaking. "I said get over and sit down! Or you can leave *right now*."

Brad's mouth twisted. He shot Brittany a look to kill and stormed over to the counter.

"And you!" Kent glared at Mitch. "Get over here in the middle where you belong."

Mitch's eyes narrowed, but he moved.

Kent whirled on the hostages. Brought up his gun. "Any one of you says *one word*, you die. Got it?"

Nobody moved.

He strode over to Brittany. The smell of his sweat filled her nose. "Happy now?" He spat. "This is all your fault."

She tried to say something, but her throat swelled shut. Ali had both fists pressed to her mouth.

Kent breathed out like some mad bull. Suddenly he grabbed Ali's shoulder with one huge hand and yanked her out of her seat. She screamed. Carla and half the people in the room screamed. Kent stuck his nose in Ali's white face. "You want to leave this place, or you want to *die*?"

Ali's chin trembled. She opened her mouth but no sound came out.

Brittany's muscles turned to lead.

Kent shook Ali. "*Answer* me!"

"I—I want . . . to go."

He shoved her back down. She landed hard and burst into tears. Carla grabbed her arm.

"Then do yourself a favor." Kent lashed a finger at Ali's chest. "Tell your friend to keep her mouth shut."

Ali just cried.

"You want to live, girl?" Kent grabbed a wad of her hair and pulled. "*Say* it."

Oh, Ali, I'm so sorry. God, please . . .

Ali raised her eyes to Brittany. Her lips trembled so much she could hardly talk. "K-keep your m-mouth shut."

Kent grunted and pushed her head away.

Ali bent over the table, sobbing.

Hatred for the Wicksells flamed up and branded Brittany's soul. *I hope you all rot in jail.*

FORTY-SEVEN

Vince took a call from Al at the media site. Stan Seybert had volunteered his TV.

"His friend Bud Halloway drove him home to get it," Al said. "They'll be ready to deliver it to CRT in about ten minutes."

"Great." Adrenaline shivered Vince's bones. He'd rest a whole lot easier when those two girls were safe.

Roger hustled into the office, followed by Larry, who headed to the situation board. "I got through to Judge Hadkin, and he's on his way." Roger held out a piece of paper to Vince. "Here's his cell number. Larry's putting it up."

"Good. Tell Jim to have Lester and Mick wait until the judge arrives, then escort them all in together."

"Okay." Roger eyed him. "Can I talk to you for a minute?" He gestured with his head toward the other office.

"Sure." Vince followed him out.

In the second office, Roger shut the door. "We still need an officer to take the TV to Java Joint's door?"

"Yeah. I was just going to talk to Jim about that. He'll have to find someone from ISP."

"Let me do it."

"Why? I need you here."

Roger ran his tongue beneath his upper lip. "I got friends in there, Vince."

"We all got friends in there."

He dipped his head sideways—*Yeah, I hear you.* "Let me do it. I'm a skinny guy—don't look like a threat. I'll get those girls away from there."

Vince studied him. "This about your stepdaughter?"

Roger scratched his jaw. "She is that age."

"She hang around with Ali?"

Resignation flickered across Roger's face, as if he knew how Vince would respond to his answer. "Yeah. Good friends."

Vince's voice softened. "That makes you a little too close to the situation, doesn't it?"

"No closer than you. And you're negotiating."

Vince leaned against the doorway. He surveyed the worn brown rug, his gaze landing on a spot. Spilled coffee, maybe.

Roger didn't talk much about his private life, but Vince had gleaned bits and pieces of information. The man's crusty nature hid a loyal family man's heart. Forging a relationship with his stepdaughter, Tracey, hadn't been easy. The chasm between them had hurt Roger more than he'd let on. Rescuing Ali and Brittany just might elevate him in Tracey's mind.

Vince lifted his eyes to Roger. "Okay. You're in. I'll want the girls brought directly here. We need to debrief them before they go home."

"Thanks." Roger nodded. True to form, he wouldn't make a big deal out of being granted his request. "Before I leave—you want medical here for the girls?"

"Yeah. Find a female if you can. Coordinate with Jim about having the doc escorted in right away. I'm going to run down the hall, then I'll inform Tactical of our plan."

"Okay."

As Vince turned to head for the bathroom, Roger was already picking up the phone.

Back in his office, Vince could feel the rise in tension as the countdown for the exchange approached. His helpers scurried around, the phone was ringing off the hook, and he still had a dozen details to attend to.

First Vince updated Jack by radio and made sure he'd passed filming instructions to the ISP helicopter. "Also, is that monitor on its way to me?"

"Yeah. Coming up now."

"All right, thanks. Roger will be down there soon. He'll need to be informed about details of the exchange."

"Will do."

Next Vince took a call from an irritated-sounding Al. "Chief, afraid to tell you I noticed a reporter following Stan and Bud as they left. They know to keep their mouths shut, but it's going to look pretty obvious something is up. Don't be surprised if word of this exchange gets out."

Oh, great. Vince buffed his forehead. Al had been releasing information supplied by Roger. The media had already been told the HTs' identities and their demands, along with names of the hostages. But reporters were insatiable in their quest to get the jump on a story.

"Okay. Thanks for the warning."

As Vince hung up, Larry informed him a Dr. Liz Hughes was on her way from outside Spirit Lake, driven by an officer with lights running. Estimated arrival: fifteen minutes. "And the two reporters got their emails. They're filming and standing by until we tell them it's okay to air."

"Good. They—"

The rear door opened. Vince hurried out to the hall to see a couple of CRT techs carrying in the monitor. Vince had Justin dig a folding table out of a closet and set it at the end of the desk. With the monitor set up there, he and Justin could both see the screen.

As the techs set up the system, Vince pictured the exchange they would soon witness. The café door opening, Ali and Brittany running out ...

Everything should go smoothly. It was a good plan.

The techs finished and clicked on the screen. It showed feed from the helicopter, now on its way to Kanner Lake.

They were good to go.

Time to call Wicksell.

Vince picked up his phone.

FORTY-EIGHT

Helen Communs lifted her head and opened her eyes. She'd been praying a long time. Her neck was tired from bending, and she had to blink four or five times before her vision cleared.

All around her she heard murmuring. Sounded like a lot more voices than the last time she checked.

Slowly she pushed to her feet from the front pew, knees catching before she could straighten. She hung there, bent over like an old maid—well, more like the old widow she was—until her legs felt strong enough to hold her upright and her spine agreed to uncurl. One arthritic hand finding her aching hip, she tottered a few steps to turn around.

She pulled in a breath. My goodness! The church was chockfull. Had to be two hundred people in the sanctuary—more than any Sunday morning. Pastor Hank would be so proud—

Pastor Hank.

Lord Jesus, get him and the others out of there.

Folks sat in groups of all sizes. Others bowed their heads alone. A few lingered against the walls, talking on cell phones. Some time ago Harold Brune, Pastor Hank's new assistant, had asked everyone to put their phones on vibrate. The ringing had been distracting people from their prayers. No one wanted the phones turned all the way off since tidbits of information were coming in from folks down on Lakeshore.

Weeping rose from Helen's far left. She searched out the sound. Linda Brymes. Leslie's mother. "God, have mercy." Helen saw Matthew, Linda's husband, beside her. He slipped an arm around her shoulders, drew her close.

The couple sat in a circle of chairs brought in from the kitchen. Helen spotted Mark and Gayle Frederick, Ali's mom and dad. Gayle's face glistened with tears of her own. Next to her sat David Clanton, Angie's close friend. Soon to be her husband—Helen would bet on that, if she was the betting kind.

Other faces in the group registered in Helen's mind—Frank Jr., Angie's son in his thirties. Trudy, Wilbur's wife.

Helen made her way toward them. They all needed hugs. They all needed another shoulder. Hers might be bony and weak, but her faith was strong. And right now, faith was what mattered most.

By the time she reached them, Trudy, her good friend, had bent over, hands gripping her knees, tears dropping to the carpet. Helen laid a hand on her arm, and she pulled up to look. Her face crumpled. She leaned over, burying her face in Helen's chest, and cried. Others in the group looked up, shook their heads in weary despair.

No, not despair. We got God on our side.

Helen stroked Trudy's gray hair until the poor woman cried herself out.

"It's all right." Helen patted her veined hand. "The Lord puts our tears in a bottle, that's what the psalm says."

Trudy managed a nod.

Frank Jr. straightened suddenly, slid a hand into his jacket pocket. He must have come right out of work in Spokane as soon as he heard. He pulled out his cell phone, got up, and wandered over to face the wall, where his conversation wouldn't bother anybody.

Helen got a feeling about that call. She fixed her gaze on his back, trying to figure his body language. She saw his head draw back, his left elbow up and hanging in the air. He listened a moment longer, then snapped the phone shut. Turned around, eyes roaming the sanctuary. Helen followed his gaze to Harold Brune. Frank strode over to him, spoke words Helen couldn't hear. Harold's eyebrows rose, and he leaned back to aim a penetrating stare at Frank Jr. Angie's son nodded.

Harold squeezed his arm, then the two of them walked over to the Fredericks in the family circle. The men pulled them aside, their voices low, but Helen caught the words. Gayle gasped, a half cry of victory, half wail. She and Mark hugged each other like they didn't want to let go.

Oh, God—yes! Fear fluttered at her heart, but Helen renounced it in Jesus' name. *Keep them safe, Lord; keep them safe.*

Harold and Frank turned to the rest of the circle and told them the news. More gasps. Trudy's hand flew to her mouth, her eyes round. Hope freshened her face.

Harold faced the crowd in the sanctuary. "Can I have everyone's attention, please!" Heads looked up, worn faces hopeful for good news. All voices fell to a hush.

"We've heard word that something is happening down on Main Street," Harold said, "but we can't verify it. Somebody heard a reporter phoning his news station and saying he'd heard a television is being taken into Java Joint. Seems the men holding our loved ones hostage want to watch the news." Clothes rustled, murmurs of disgust rippling over the pews. "In return, *if this news is true*, Ali and Brittany will be released."

Gasps filtered toward the ceiling. Heads turned toward the Fredericks. Gayle and Mark gripped each other, faces pulled taut.

Harold held up a hand. "We need to pray—hard. We got to pray that this is true, that everything goes all right—and those girls get to safety." He glanced toward the Fredericks.

Helen saw in his expression more fear than he would put into words. So many things could go wrong. They'd all heard about the guns those men had—and they'd already shot one person. What if this was only a trick to shoot somebody else? Maybe even those precious girls?

Helen's heart folded in on itself. *Oh, Lord Jesus, get them out!*

Harold squeezed Gayle's shoulder. "Gayle and Mark will be driving down to Lakeshore now to see if they can find out anything more. Let's all get to praying they're united with their daughter soon."

Applause broke out in the sanctuary, amid a few shouts of "hallelujah" and "thank you, Lord!"

As the Fredericks hurried off, Helen sank into the chair Mark had occupied. Frank Jr. slid the remaining empty chair away from the circle, and everyone closed in. Helen bent over her knees. Soon the sounds of fervent prayers rose to the rafters of New Community Church.

FORTY-NINE

"Yeah."

Kent's voice snapped over the phone line. Apprehension flushed through Vince. He was up walking his office, too pumped to sit down. Justin sat at his desk, ready to take notes. Larry stood by the situation board, tapping the black marker against his palm.

Vince jangled keys in his pocket. "Kent, you okay? You sound upset."

"I'm fine. Nothing I can't handle."

Didn't sound fine. The man sounded like he was ready to chew somebody's head off.

Vince lifted his hand palm up at Justin—*Should I pursue this or move on?* Justin rolled his forefinger in the air.

"Okay. Glad to hear it. Want you to know your TV's being delivered. Everything will be ready to go soon."

"That guy who's bringing it ..."

"His name's Roger Waitman. He'll be unarmed, like we agreed."

"How I know you're not lying to me?"

"Kent, what would you expect one man to do when you've got multiple automatic weapons pointed at ten remaining hostages? I'm not going to risk anything going wrong."

Kent grunted. "Let's just get this done with. I want those girls *outta* here."

Justin raised his eyebrows — *That's a switch.*

"Me too. Now remember, we'll have someone waiting around that corner to take the girls away. But they don't need to concern you because they're not coming anywhere near Java Joint. They're only there to get the girls out of the area."

"Yeah." Kent sounded almost raspy. "Okay."

Vince gazed at the monitor at the side of his desk. The helicopter was now a few miles northeast of downtown. He watched the slow pan of rooftops and residential streets. He could make out dozens of people on the sidewalks, standing in clusters. Looking up.

Within a minute the copter would be in place, hovering. Vince would be able to see Lakeshore, Second Street, and Main.

"Kent, you'll hear the helicopter soon. It won't get close. It's only there to film what's happening so I can tell you exactly when the TV starts rolling and when you can expect a knock on the door. No surprises."

"Better make *sure* it's not close. That thing gets in my face, this whole deal's off."

"No need for it to. I want this to go as smoothly as you do."

Wicksell breathed heavily over the line. "How long once we get the TV before we see those reporters on the news?"

"Shouldn't be long, but I'll keep you informed. They're waiting for the signal from me that all's ready."

"They'd better make it good."

"They'll make it good."

His breathing whooshed in Vince's ear. Too heavy. Angry. Vince didn't like the sound of it.

A noise outside Vince's office. Larry hurried out to see who had arrived. He reappeared with an ISP officer and a woman. She looked about forty, with short blonde hair and a compassionate face. Large gray eyes. She carried a black bag.

"Hold on a minute, Kent."

Vince covered the phone's mouthpiece and motioned them in. The woman nodded to Vince. "Dr. Liz Hughes."

He nodded back. Pointed at a chair for her to sit.

"Need anything else?" the officer asked.

"No. Appreciate it."

As the officer left, the station phone rang. Larry swiveled to answer it in the second office.

Vince looked to Dr. Hughes. "Thanks for coming on such short notice."

"Sure." She looked grim. Determined.

He pointed to the phone. She raised a hand—*Go ahead.*

Vince turned back to check the monitor. The copter was in place over the target. Its camera shot covered the CRT team on Lakeshore, the ghostlike second and third blocks of Main. He stared at the top of the Java Joint building, picturing the hostages inside, the men and their guns. If ever he'd wanted X-ray vision . . .

Justin jotted a note and held it up for Vince to see. *Keep him talking.*

Vince nodded. "Kent, you all getting hungry in there?"

"Nah. Ain't had time to think about food. Besides, don't she have sandwiches and stuff here? Menu sign says so."

"Yes, she does."

"It ain't food we need. It's just so dang hot in here."

A certain amount of discomfort could be positive. Enough of it, and the captors' resolve might weaken. But heat was a bad one. Heat led to short tempers.

"I hear you. That's a lot of people breathing in a closed-off space. Everybody drinking plenty of water? You don't want people fainting on you."

Kent sniffed. "Yeah, suppose so." The phone muffled. "Bailey. You got bottled water? Go get everybody one." More rustled movement. "Okay, we're giving out water."

"That's good."

Vince watched the monitor. A pickup truck was heading up Lakeshore. A TV and table sat in its bed.

"Kent, looks like the TV is being delivered to its drop-off point."

"About *time*."

"I know this seems like it's taking forever. But everybody's moving as fast as they can."

Wicksell snorted.

The line fell silent. Vince's mind thrashed for something to say. "This is a good thing you're doing."

"Oh yeah. I'm a great guy."

The sarcasm bit. Vince flexed his jaw. "All right, give us a minute or two — "

"I'm tired of hanging on to this phone," Wicksell snapped. "You get everything in place, you call me back."

"No, wait, Kent, let's stay on the — "

"I'm *tired* of yakkin' to you, hear? And when this thing's over, I'm gonna expect things to go much faster. I'll be thinking on that, understand? Some kind of time frame for T.J. to get out of prison — like *real quick* — or I quit talking altogether."

The line clicked off.

Vince lowered the receiver and stared at it, wondering at Wicksell's unpredictability. A chill crept through his veins.

He punched the *off* button.

Vince exchanged a tense look with Justin, then checked the monitor. Down on Lakeshore, Roger had the TV on its stand. Two CRT members were running up Second.

They were getting into position. It wouldn't be long.

A sound behind him reminded Vince of the doctor's presence. He looked over his shoulder, gave her a stiff nod. She nodded back, her eyes round, fingers curled around the underside of her chair. Vince felt a pang of understanding. Doctors were summoned *after* the trauma. They weren't used to watching it unfold while all too aware of what might go wrong—and helpless to stop it.

He looked back to the phone in his hand. His fingers itched to redial Java Joint, but in Wicksell's fragile state of mind, calling before everything was set would probably just tick the man off more.

Vince set the receiver on his desk.

Don't let anything go wrong, God. Please don't let anything go wrong.

FIFTY

Ali tipped up the plastic bottle and drank until half the water was gone.

She plunked it down, breathing hard. Every passing second seemed like an eternity. She just wanted *out* of here. And the closer the chance came, the more scared she got that something would happen and they wouldn't be able to go.

She looked across the table. Brittany stared back. They didn't dare talk. But they sent friend messages with their eyes.

Ali, I'm so scared.

Me too.

I'm sorry I opened my mouth.

It wasn't your fault. I'd want my mom out of here too.

Ali's throat tightened. She couldn't imagine being in Brittany's shoes, having to leave her mother behind in this horrible place.

Ali despised Kent Wicksell. And Brad and Mitch. Just *wait* till she got out of here. She'd tell the *world* how awful they were.

"All right." Kent was still at his front table, where he'd been talking on the phone. Ali couldn't see him without turning around in her seat. "Time to get in place. Brad, you come two steps from the counter and angle in. But I don't want your back to the door. And, Mitch—over there even with the computer, angled the same way."

Mitch strode out of Ali's sight, over toward Bailey. Ali watched Brad push to his feet, aiming black looks at Kent, like he hated being told what to do. He planted his feet apart and turned his gun straight at Ali's head. Just for spite.

Her heart thumped.

Ali heard Kent walk to the center of the room. She kept her eyes on her water bottle, glad she couldn't see his face.

"Listen up, people." His voice sounded hard. "We're going to do this exchange soon, and *everyone's going to do exactly what I say.*"

Heavy footsteps, coming toward their table. Ali tensed.

Kent grabbed Ali's arm. She gasped. "Get up."

She half slid, half fell out of her chair. Her legs trembled. Kent jerked her upright. "Walk to three feet in front of the door and stop."

Ali glanced back at Carla. Her face looked like bleached cotton. She mouthed, "Go." Ali stumbled to the door.

She heard sounds behind her and turned. Kent had pulled Brittany from her chair. "Get over there behind your friend." Kent gestured with his head.

Brittany's shoulders hunched, her chin lowering. She started to cry.

"Move!" Kent shoved her. She heaved two sideways steps and nearly fell.

"*Stop* it — she'll go!" Carla half rose, her hands balled into fists.

Carla, no!

Kent leaned over the table, grabbed her forearm, and twisted.

"Aahh!" She doubled over.

Brittany swiveled back toward Kent. "Leave her *alone!*"

Brad leapt forward and seized her by the hair. Yanked her away from Kent. Her face twisted in fear and pain.

"*I don't need you telling me what to do understand?*" Kent thrust his face in Carla's. He pushed her back, and she fell into her chair.

Kent swung around toward Brittany and Brad. "Get her to the door."

Brad pulled her over to Ali. Brittany sobbed. *"Please* let my mom go with me!"

"Shut. *Up."* Brad shoved her behind Ali. "Now just *stand* there."

Brad stalked back to his place and stood, legs apart, his blue eyes like steel. He moved the barrel of his gun to aim at the second table. "Brittany. I got this gun aimed at your mom. You want her to live to see another day, you'll stop crying *right now."*

Brittany's head came up, her eyes wide. She stuttered in air, trying to stop the tears.

Carla hunched in her seat, holding her arm, pain creasing her face. She nodded at Brittany and tried to smile. It came out all warped.

Kent strode over to Ali and Brittany, dark-faced and anxious. He turned to point his gun at the hostages.

"Nobody moves, hear? Any minute now I'm going to get a phone call that they're coming. After that things will happen fast. We'll hear a knock. When we do"—he glared at Ali—"I'll open the door and check outside first. When I give you the word, you two run out. Got that?"

She and Brittany nodded.

Seconds passed. Nobody said anything.

Ali's throat got so tight she couldn't breathe. She held on to Brittany, drinking in the sight of the people they were leaving behind. Everyone's face was stretched and bleak. Angie and Carla were crying. Pastor Hank looked tense. Ted and Leslie gripped hands. Leslie caught Ali's eye and tried not to look scared. Leslie raised her chin. *You'll be okay.*

Ali tried to nod but couldn't. She clung to Brittany.

Kent stood one foot away, holding his gun so hard his knuckles went white. His anxiety made Ali feel all the more terrified.

Brad swore. "This better work. Some cop coming here, no telling what'll happen."

Kent's face turned dark. "It'll work."

"Let's hope."

"I didn't ask for your opinion, Brad, so shut up."

"If you'd just—"

"Shut *up*!"

Ali looked at Mitch. His face was hard, jaw set. The end of his gun barrel was four feet from Bailey's head.

More time passed. Ali started to shake. Brittany and Carla were staring at each other like they'd never be together again. Ali's heart cracked, seeing that.

"You two, turn around!" Kent spat.

Ali jumped. She shuffled around until she could see nothing but the door. Brittany stood right behind, clinging to her shirt.

The room fell silent except for hard breathing and gulped tears. And the faint sound of the ticking clock.

Kent paced over to his table. "Come *on*, Edwards, come *on*."

They waited.

FIFTY-ONE

In civilian clothes concealing his Kevlar vest, Roger stood on Lakeshore behind the building that cornered Second. The distant *whap-whap* of the ISP helicopter sounded from above. Stan Seybert and his friend Bud Halloway were unloading the television and table from the back of Bud's truck. They'd been escorted into the inner circle by an ISP officer, who stood by to escort them out as soon as their task was done. Milling about in the street were the seven men from CRT, each in gear, all forty-five pounds apiece of it. Fairchild's APC hulked in the middle of the street, a fortified monster ready to protect everyone involved from possible fire. Behind it sat the CRT van. CRT's mobile command post was parked at the curb, leaving room for the other two vehicles to maneuver.

Adrenaline already pumped through Roger. His brain beat the steady drum of his mission: *Get the girls to safety*. The face of his own stepdaughter hovered in the background. What if it was Tracey in that café? The *desperation* he and his wife would feel. Camille would be wild with terror.

Get the girls to safety.

Stan and Bud set the TV on the table. Roger checked the TV's stability. Stan secured its cord to the table with masking tape.

"All set?"

Stan stepped back. Sweat dripped down his temple. "Ready."

Roger laid a hand on his shoulder. "You've done a lot today. We appreciate it."

Surprise tinged Stan's expression. Roger understood. The gesture was out of character for him. Something Chief would have done.

"Thanks." Stan wiped his face. "Be safe, man."

Roger straightened his back. "No worries." He looked to Bud, and they exchanged nods. Roger gestured toward the ISP officer. "He'll take you two back."

Bud's eyes roamed over the Tactical team, their vehicles, before landing on Roger. "Go get 'em."

It hit Roger then—the task he was about to undertake. Walk up to a café guarded by men loaded with firepower. *Unarmed.* Yes, he had a vest on under his shirt, but all Wicksell had to do was stick a gun barrel out that door, aim at his head, and pull the trigger. Some Tactical member might pick Wicksell off, but not before he pumped out plenty of bullets. He'd already shot one officer today. Why not a second?

The CRT members gathered around. The temperature was around 85°, and they were sweating already in their heavy gear. They wore thick Kevlar vests, boots, and helmets, carrying M4s with backup .45 Glocks strapped to their thighs. Their faces were calm, but their jaws were set. Missions were what they lived and trained for. But the stakes weren't usually this high, Roger knew. Often they went out on search warrants for drugs, faced down gun-wielding perps holed up in some building. Two teenage girls' lives on the line—that was enough to blanket the team with grim determination. Most of these guys had kids of their own.

Bud and Stan returned to Bud's truck and drove away, following the ISP vehicle.

Roger cleared his throat. "Okay, Jack. Ready on our end."

He stood back, out of the men's way. They were a well-oiled team, that he could see. He'd picked up on some of their nicknames. Apparently every man except Jack had one.

"All right." Jack trailed a hand across his wide forehead. "Dust-up, get the APC going. Swank and Frenchie, proceed to the rear door of the building. Harley, in the van. But let's get the APC set before you move. Lightning and Goose, wait till I'm in the command post to move out with Roger."

Guns in hand, Swank and Frenchie ran with amazing agility for all the weight they carried. Roger watched them disappear around the corner and up Second. From there they would veer left into the alley that ran in back of Java Joint. Dust-up climbed in the bulky APC, drove forward on Lakeshore past the intersection, then reversed around the corner and up Second. On the curb to Roger's right up near Main sat the Wicksells' parked pickup truck—a barrier they'd had to plan around. The APC stopped about four feet from the left curb and just below the truck.

Jack signaled for Harley to go. He reversed the van up Second along the right curb and stopped within inches of the Wicksell truck's rear bumper. The APC now provided cover for occupants of the van should anyone run out of Java Joint and fire diagonally down Second.

With the two vehicles in place, Jack headed for the mobile command post. From inside he would watch all points of action on multiple monitors, communicating with his men via radio. The three snipers remained in their rooftop positions.

Jack disappeared into the mobile unit, then radioed. "Everybody set?"

Lightning radioed back. "Goose and Lightning ready."

"Swank and Frenchie ready."

"Dust-up ready."

"Harley ready."

"Okay," Jack answered. "Chief Edwards, we're set."

"Got your vehicles on Second in sight." Vince's voice filtered back. "I'll tell Wicksell you're coming."

Roger looked to the two men who would follow him, providing cover. Lightning's helmeted head wagged back and forth, black-gloved hands cradling his M4. Goose—surely called that because of his beaklike nose and beady eyes, pointed up Lakeshore. "Heave ho."

Roger placed his hands on the TV table and began to push.

FIFTY-TWO

Lenora Wicksell peeked through the dusty blinds she'd yanked down over the kitchen windows. The reporter was still there—in her *backyard*. How dare he trespass on her property! But what could she do—call the police? As if they'd care.

No need to look through the shades on the front windows—she already knew two other reporters had set up camp practically on her porch. Another man and a woman. They'd called her name, rung her doorbell who knew how many times. And phoned her. Over and over. Every time she'd answered, then banged down the receiver.

She couldn't afford not to answer. What if it was Kent calling?

Her pail of dirty water, brush, and cloths stood where she'd left them by the baseboards. No desire to touch them now. Even with the blinds closed, she imagined the TV camera somehow filming right through the slats, catching her on both knees, scrubbing. She could hear the lead-in to the story now: *Wife cleans kitchen while her husband holds a dozen people hostage.*

They would never understand.

As if sensing her presence, the backyard reporter turned, caught her eye. "Mrs. Wicksell, Mrs. Wicksell!" He lurched toward the window, thrusting out his microphone. She jerked back and dropped the blind.

Lenora stood before the dirty dishes in her sink, palms together, fingers pressed to her mouth. Nowhere to go. No one to turn to. A prisoner in her own home.

The sound of a car out front. Her shoulders slumped. Another reporter come to torment her.

She heard the voices of the two reporters who'd already staked out their territory. And a new man: "Is Lenora Wicksell in there?"

"Yes." The male reporter. "But she's not talking to us. Who are you?"

"A friend? Relative?" The woman.

"What can you tell us about Lenora Wicksell?"

"Sorry, I can't talk to you now," the new arrival said. "I'm here to see Lenora."

Who *was* this? One of Kent's friends? She didn't recognize the voice.

Lenora slipped into the den and muted the TV, then sidled toward the front door. Cocked her head, listening. Rapid footsteps climbed the porch steps. Stopped.

Loud banging on the door. She jumped.

"Lenora Wicksell! Please let me in!" The voice sounded desperate, driven. "Please. I'm not a reporter. I need to talk to you about your husband."

He knew something about Kent?

Was this a trick? What if she opened the door and the reporters barreled inside?

"Lenora, *please*." The voice muffled, as if he cupped his hands around the door to keep the reporters from hearing. "I was there this morning. I saw Kent and your sons. Please let me in."

Before she knew it, Lenora found herself at the door. She threw back the bolt, stood aside, hidden from any outside cameras, and opened the door a few feet. The man hurried through.

On the porch the reporters clamored. Lenora slammed the door and rebolted it.

She and the man faced each other, breathing hard, in the dingy entryway.

FIFTY-THREE

Vince focused on the monitor as he connected to Wicksell. The helicopter camera fixed downward on a waiting Main Street and the CRT members on Second and Lakeshore. The view seemed surreal, as if Vince were playing some video game.

If only.

Tension bunched his shoulders, hardened the muscles in his neck. Five minutes, that was all. Five minutes, and those two girls could be right there in the station, safe.

Justin leaned forward in his chair across the desk, headphones on, pen and notebook ready. His gaze, like Vince's, was glued to the aerial shot. He looked as nervous as Vince felt. Larry stood four feet away, arms crossed, chewing on his lip.

The tac radio sat nearby on the desk, ready to grab if needed. Its volume was turned low so Wicksell couldn't hear any CRT communications through the phone.

Wicksell answered on the first ring. "Yeah." His voice sounded tight. Anxious.

"We're set. TV's just started on its way. You'll hear the knock in about two minutes."

"'Bout *time*."

"I'll stay on the phone with you."

"Whatever."

"Everything okay in there?"

"Yeah, now it is. We just got a lot goin' on."

"Want to talk about it?"

"No. Just get your man here."

"Understood."

Vince watched Roger pushing the TV as the camera panned in on him a third of the way up Second Street. Two CRT members escorted him, one in front, one in back.

"It won't be long until the reporters read T.J.'s story, right? That's what you said." Wicksell's tone had hardened.

"Right. As soon as you're ready and we give them the go-ahead."

Wicksell heaved a sigh.

"You all right, Kent?"

"I'm fine — stop bugging me. Just want this to be done with."

"That makes two of us."

"You'd better come through on this, Edwards. You'd better come through, or things are gonna get real bad around here."

"I'll come through, Kent. I don't want anyone in there getting hurt."

Roger passed the alley, midway up Second, then pushed on, the APC and waiting van on his right.

Wicksell made a sound in his throat. "Cops ain't exactly been our friends, know what I mean? They're the ones arrested T.J. Cops, lawyers — we ain't been able to trust any one of them."

Vince had the impression Wicksell was talking just to fill dead air. "You wrote your letter to me, Kent. You reached out to me. You must have thought I could be trusted."

"Who else would I talk to? You're the head of this town. I seen what you done for it in the last two years. Figured you could make things happen for my son."

"And that's what I'm trying to do right now."

The CRT member in front of Roger reached the corner of Second and Main. He checked around the building, then signaled to

Roger an all clear. Roger turned left—alone. The CRT members hung back, just beyond the corner of the building. Vince could see the two frontal snipers on rooftops, covering Roger.

Wicksell exhaled. "Just know I got my gun in my hand. I see anything through that door I shouldn't see, we're gonna have trouble."

"You'll see a television, Kent. That's it. Right now—"

"Where *is* that guy?"

Vince kept his voice calm. "He's almost to your door. Any second now."

"If he don't—" Wicksell cut off abruptly. "He just knocked." The phone muffled. Wicksell's command was hurled at someone in the café. "Don't move! I'll open the door."

The clack of plastic against wood. Wicksell had put down his receiver.

Vince reached for his radio and turned up the volume.

FIFTY-FOUR

Ali stood near the door, Brittany clinging to her from behind. She could feel Brittany shaking. Ali brushed a hand across her face. Her muscles were tight enough to break. And her heart was fluttering.

She thought of her parents. Did they know she was coming out? Were they okay? How soon would she see them? She wanted to fly straight into their arms. Just picturing their faces made her legs weak.

Her eyes were going crossed from staring at the door. As if the harder she stared, the quicker the man with the TV would come. She closed her eyes, took a long, slow breath. Kent was talking on the phone to Chief Edwards. What was taking so long? Every second seemed like forever. If this fell through now, if she and Brittany had to go back to their seats at that table, Ali would come totally unglued. Now that they were this close . . .

Please, God, get us out *of here.*

Specks of dust mixed with the stifling air and swirled into Ali's nose. She hiccupped, then sneezed.

She needed water. Why didn't she drink the rest of her bottle when she had the chance? Her body felt so hot. She needed to *breathe.*

Two hard knocks banged on the door. Ali nearly jumped a foot.

"Don't move!" Kent commanded. "I'll open the door."

He tossed down the phone, picked up his gun, and strode over. Ali and Brittany shrank from him. He stank from sweat, and the evil around him felt like a live beast ready to pounce.

"Move!" Kent pushed her shoulder.

She and Brittany shuffled back farther.

Kent undid the locks with his left hand, gripped the handle. Cautiously, he opened the door, the muscles in his arms and neck tense. His head disappeared as he stuck it in the opening. Ali saw the movement of his body as he turned his head right and left, surveying the street.

All of a sudden somebody outside spoke. A man's voice. "Okay, Kent, there's your TV. Where are the girls?"

"Yeah, yeah, just checkin' things out first."

Kent pulled his head back inside, grabbed Ali's arm, and yanked her forward. "Go! And you behind her." He turned hard eyes on Brittany, then stood with feet apart and aimed his gun at them.

Ali didn't look back. Heart beating in her throat, she squeezed through the foot-wide opening.

Air and bright light hit her like two fists. Her eyes squinted shut. The fresh, clean, *breathable* air. It swarmed into her nostrils, down to her lungs, almost too much to take. Was this what good air felt like? The café had been a dungeon.

She fumbled a blind step, then forced her eyes open. Directly in front of her, on the sidewalk near the curb, sat a TV on a table.

The air made her feel all dizzy. Her brain lifted right out of her head. Waves of joy at being rescued surged through her, so strong she was going to drown.

Maybe this wasn't really happening. Maybe she was back in the café, dreaming.

The happiness melted away.

Ali wobbled. Her muscles turned soft.

Brittany ran into the back of her.

To her right—a man. He was reaching for her, saying something, but she couldn't hear for all the blood pounding in her ears. Her thoughts gummed up. What now? Where should she go?

The man gripped her arm. "This way, hurry. Hang on to each other."

A fog covered Ali's brain. Her thoughts got lost in it.

Go, girl. Breathe. Run.

She tried. Hard. Were those her legs? *Somebody's* legs were running beneath her. She felt Brittany's hand in hers, heard the stomps of their feet and her own heartbeat. The man half pulled them up the sidewalk. They were almost to the curb ...

Sudden panic clawed at her.

Where was Kent surely he was following he would grab them both and force them back inside he wasn't really going to let them go, he would never let them ...

Ali's vision clouded.

Those legs under her. She couldn't feel them anymore.

Brittany's hand fell out of hers. The running man turned and caught hold of Brittany. Ali stumbled. Swayed to her left. She felt the horrible sensation of one heel on the sidewalk, her toes in empty air ...

The curb.

Ali fell.

She hit the pavement hard on her left hip. Her hand scraped. Burning pain shot through her palm and one ankle.

"Go, I've got her!"

Who was that some other man's voice—

Somebody gripped her hard. Pulled her up. *No, no, it's Kent!*

"Come on, get around the corner!"

Her bleary eyes saw this *thing* a person all clad in black with a big gun helmet on his head pulling her up the curb down the sidewalk. He gripped her *hard*.

She ran blindly.

"Hey!"

Kent's voice. That *was* Kent, behind her, coming to get her ...

Running down the street, bricks on her right—the side of a building.

Radt-dadt-dadt-dadt-dadt-dadt...

Her mind exploded. Somebody was shooting. Kent was *shooting.*

Help me, God, he's coming after me.

The man beside her yanked her onto the street. A big gray vehicle loomed in front of them. They ran around it. Ali saw Brittany and the first man, and there was a van, and he was pushing Brittany inside, and the man with Ali pulled her toward it, and then he was forcing her head down, pushing her inside the second row of seats too, and the man shut the door then climbed in front, and some other man behind the wheel smacked the car in gear and squealed down the street and careened left around the corner.

The force sent Ali slumping toward the door. Brittany fell into her. Ali twisted around and grabbed on to her, and then Brittany was crying and Ali was crying and the men were saying, "It's okay, it's okay, you're safe now."

Ali couldn't thank them. She couldn't even talk. She just clung to Brittany and bawled.

FIFTY-FIVE

Vince clenched his teeth when he saw Ali fall, and Larry groaned. A CRT member jumped to the curb and helped her up. Pulled her away. At that instant Kent ran out onto the sidewalk, weapon aimed up the street.

Vince froze. Justin gasped.

"He's got a gun!" a voice surged over the radio.

Wicksell started shooting.

Vince's eyes jumped back to Ali and the CRT guy. They'd just passed the corner of the building. *Just.* A second earlier, Ali would have been hit.

"Hold fire!" Commander Jack Little's voice.

Vince clutched the phone in his left hand, radio in his right. *No, Wicksell, don't pursue—*

Kent darted back into Java Joint and slammed the door.

"Gunman is back in the building," Jack clipped.

Still, Vince held his breath. He focused on the running girls, one CRT member pulling them to the van, the other darting backward, gun aimed toward Main should Wicksell reappear.

Go, Brittany and Ali. Go!

The Java Joint door remained closed. Wicksell's TV sat on the table by the curb.

The girls and CRT members ran around the APC. Reached the waiting van. Clambered into the side door. A CRT member slammed their door and jumped into the front passenger seat.

215

"Targets in vehicle." The breathless report came from the radio.

The van took off.

A long exhale seeped from Vince.

"Whoa." Larry dragged a hand down his face.

"All clear." Relief coated Jack's voice. "Whoo, that was close. Good work, men."

It took a few seconds for Vince's heart to start beating again. He found his fingers cramped from squeezing the phone. Unwinding them, he put the receiver down and spoke into the radio. "Jack, Vince here." He envisioned Jack at the monitors in his command post, eyes darting from Wicksell to Brittany and Ali. The split-second decision he'd had to make. "Good call, holding fire. Although for a second there you had me worried."

Jack knew what Vince did. The only thing worse than Wicksell back in Java Joint all riled up was a dead Wicksell on the street, leaving Mitch and Brad with a whole new vengeance to take out on the hostages.

"Only because he stayed where he was, and I saw our people were out of range. If he'd have taken two steps up that street, he'd be a dead man."

Vince rubbed a hand across his forehead. On the monitor he could see the CRT van heading toward the station. "I see your vehicle's on its way. Thanks for your work."

"What we're here for."

Vince started to set down the radio and took a deep breath. Looked to Justin with a questioning expression—*Heard anything on the phone?* Justin shook his head.

If he had the time, Vince would lean over his knees and fill his lungs with oxygen. Send up a prayer of thanks for the girls' safety. Instead, he turned down the radio volume and picked up the phone. "Kent? Can you hear me?"

No answer. Just background noise. Kent yelling.

"Kent. Talk to me."

Vince counted two seconds.

"Kent!"

No answer.

Vince imagined the man, furious, gun in his twitchy fingers, stalking the café.

"Kent, can you come to the phone?"

A noise behind his back, startling him. Vince jerked around.

Dr. Hughes stood before her chair by the wall, chalk-faced, a hand to her heart. She'd obviously watched the whole thing on the video from across the room. Vince had been so focused, he'd forgotten she was there.

She dropped her hand to her side. "Sorry. I just ..."

Vince muffled the receiver against his chest. "You all right?"

She swallowed and nodded. "You sound so calm. How do you do it?"

Calm?

Sounds filtered from the rear of the station. The door opening, footsteps, voices. Larry darted out to investigate.

"They're here." Relief flushed through Vince. "Go on and get started. I'll be there when I can."

Dr. Hughes leaned over to pick up her bag. For a moment Vince saw the mirror image of himself as the worry lines on her face disappeared, replaced with the placid confidence of a professional. She hurried toward the office door.

Vince raised the phone. "Kent? Kent."

No answer.

He heard the girls' crying, the doctor's voice greeting them. Roger's voice. Vince stood up, torn. Should he stay on the line and try to reach Kent, or start the girls' debriefing so they could get to their anxious parents as soon as possible?

He set down the phone, threw a look at Justin. "Keep listening and call me if he comes back on. I need to go talk to the girls."

Vince swiveled and hurried from the office.

FIFTY-SIX

The cries rose the second Kent Wicksell started shooting.

Terror sliced through Bailey at the sound of the gunshots. She and every other woman in Java Joint screamed. Bailey's hands flew to her mouth, tears leaping to her eyes. *Ali and Brittany! Did he shoot the girls?*

Carla shoved to her feet. "Brittaneeee!"

Brad jumped forward, thrust his gun in her face. "Get *down*!"

Carla swayed, both arms waving, her face bleached white. "No, Brit—"

"Sit down or I'll cut you in half!" Brad shoved the barrel against her chest.

Carla stumbled backward. Her head hit the wall. She bounced forward, her mouth open and keening, grabbed the back of her chair for support, and slumped into it.

Mitch aimed his gun straight at Bailey. "Everybody *stay* where you are, or this one gets it."

Bailey shrank back in her chair, looking down the gun barrel. Every limb in her body shook.

Hate skewed Brad's face as he leered at Carla, his jaw locked and eyes spitting fire. "*You* don't want to lose a daughter? *We* already lost a brother. Now you know—"

The door crashed open and Kent Wicksell stumbled inside, clutching his weapon. His expression was blacker than Brad's, spittle on his mouth, his barrel chest heaving.

"They had a SWAT guy out there!" He slammed the door shut, locked and bolted it with one hand. "Right up the street, a guy in full uniform!" He swung left, then right, blindly propelled by rage.

Brad backed up two steps and half turned his head, eyes still on Carla. "Did you get him?"

"I got *nobody*—they were all already around the building." Kent stormed across the floor like a mad man. "I wasn't about to run after 'em. Coulda had a dozen men around that corner."

Around the corner. The girls were safe. Nauseating relief swept through Bailey. She looked at Carla, her throat so tight it ached. Carla's chin dropped. She huddled in her chair, arms drawn across her chest, and cried.

Kent jerked toward her. "Shut *up!*" He stomped toward the hostages. "Shut up, all of you! I don't want to see *anybody* crying. Your precious girls got away, all right? Don't worry about the fact that your cop *lied* to me, and I almost got myself *killed*."

"He shoot back?" Mitch shuffled backward, away from Bailey, and aimed his weapon toward the table where Paige, Ted, and Leslie sat.

"No, or I'd be dead. He grabbed the girls and ran." Kent paced to the counter and slammed his fist against it. Turned around and stomped the other direction.

"And *you!*" He swung suddenly toward Jared. In a second he'd closed the space between them. His hand lashed out, grabbed Jared by the shirt, and pulled him to his feet. Kent pushed his purpled face into the older man's.

Leslie gasped and clapped a hand to her mouth.

"This whole thing came from *your* bright idea," Kent spat at Jared. "Let me tell you something. Those reporters don't do exactly what they're supposed to do, or your cop out there lies to me again?" Kent ground his teeth. "I. Will. Kill. You."

Jared hung before him, head pulled back, frightened eyes fixed upon Kent.

"You *hear* me?"

Jared managed a slight nod. Kent growled and shoved him down. The chair surged sideways a few inches, its legs stuttering across the linoleum.

Kent swung around and strode to his table near the front window. He snatched up the phone.

"Edwards!"

He burst into a stream of curses.

FIFTY-SEVEN

Vince stepped into the hall and spotted the girls. Roger led them, both stumbling and wild-eyed, into the second office. Larry flattened himself against the wall, letting them pass. "Stay with Justin," Vince told Larry. He entered the office in time to see Brittany collapse into the desk chair and Ali fall into a second one Roger had pulled from the wall. Brittany leaned over, crying into her hands. Ali's body shook, all color gone from her cheeks. Half dazed, she stared at her left palm, scraped and seeping blood.

Dr. Hughes headed for Ali first. She placed her bag on the desk, stooped down to look the girl in the face. "Hi." She took Ali's uninjured hand in her own. "I'm Dr. Hughes. I'm here to make sure you're all right. Will you let me look at your palm?"

Ali nodded numbly.

Vince walked over and put a hand on her head. Gave her a small smile. "Ali. We're so glad to see you and Brittany safe. Very glad."

She looked up at him, chin trembling. "Where's my mom and dad?"

Out of nowhere, thoughts of his own son pierced Vince. How Tim had died half a world away, without his mom or dad. *Tim, how could I not have been there with you?*

Vince steadied his voice. "You'll see them soon, Ali, I promise. They're near one of our officers and have been notified that you're safe. We just have to make sure you're okay first and talk to you for a few minutes."

Ali's gaze lowered, as if she was too tired to argue. She fixed her eyes on Dr. Hughes. Her scraped palm must have hurt, but she appeared not to feel it.

When the shock wore off, she would.

Vince patted her shoulder, then focused on Roger. "Good work."

Roger gave him a wan smile.

The phone rang. Roger turned to answer it.

Vince went over to Brittany. He squatted beside her, placing his hand on her arm. "Brittany. My name's Chief Edwards. I don't think we've met before, but I've heard a lot about you from Carla. She's very proud of you."

The girl raised a tear-streaked face, her mouth trembling. "You have to get her *out* of there!"

Her grief wrapped around his heart. "We're doing everything we can to get *everyone* out of there."

She held his gaze, as if deciding whether she could believe him.

He offered her a tiny smile. "Promise."

Her eyes dropped. She swallowed hard.

Vince took his hand away. "When Dr. Hughes is finished with Ali, she'll examine you and make sure you're okay. Can you just sit here a minute?"

She nodded.

"Good. In the meantime, it would be a big help if you can tell me about the men in Java Joint. Anything you can remember may be very important. The more we know about what's going on in there, the better I know how to deal with them."

Brittany wiped her eyes with sudden impatience, her jaw jutting forward. The expression reminded Vince of Carla when she was ticked off. "I can tell you *plenty*. They're mean and nasty, and they *smell*. Kent's the one in charge. The other two stand around pointing their guns at everybody. They've got this duffel bag that

I think has extra guns in it. And bullets. They've each got a jacket with pockets stuffed with ammunition too. The youngest one, Brad, is a—" Her lips pressed. She didn't need to say what she was thinking.

Vince's legs were tiring in the squat position, but he didn't want to stop Brittany's flow of words. He reached for the arm of her chair to steady himself. "Do the other two men have the same kind of gun as Kent Wicksell?"

"Oh yeah. They're *big*." Brittany held her hands apart in measurement.

Three MP5s. Maybe more in the bag.

"The windows are all blacked out, right?"

"With sheets."

"Any spot left open where someone could see through them?"

"No. There's tape around every sheet, all sides. And they've turned off all the lights."

The tape made sense. Wicksell hadn't given any clues that he could see a thing through those windows as the TV was being delivered. As for the lights ... Maybe they were worried about throwing shadows against the sheets.

"What about the back door?"

Brittany shook her head. "It's locked. And there's a desk turned on its side and pushed in front of it."

Vince absorbed that piece of information. "Are the three men up front all the time?"

"Yeah. Except to go to the bathroom."

"What about the hostages—where are they?"

Pain flicked across Brittany's face. "They're all sitting at tables along the back wall."

"How many tables?"

"There's ..." Her gaze wandered to the ceiling as she thought. "Four. No, five, counting the computer table where Bailey's sitting by herself."

"So the rest are maybe three to a table?"

Brittany bit the inside of her bottom lip. "Three at the first table nearest the counter and the hallway. Then Mom." Her eyes teared up. "She's alone there now." Vince waited while she wiped her face. "The next table has two—Wilbur and Pastor Hank. The fourth one has three people. That's where Leslie is. And S-Man and Paige. Then Bailey at the computer table."

"Wow." Vince spoke gently. "I'm impressed at your memory."

She tightened her mouth. "Pretty hard to forget."

"I'll bet." He paused. "I'd like you to draw a diagram of those tables for me before you leave, okay?"

"Okay."

"Where in the room are the three Wicksell men?"

Her face twisted. "Brad's sitting on a stool at the counter most of the time. Making a big deal of it 'cause it's Wilbur's stool—that's how *childish* he is. Mitch is mostly right in front of everybody, like in the middle of the room. Kent moves around, but when he's talking on the phone, he's at a table near the front window."

"Which window?"

"The one farthest to the right. If you're inside looking toward the street."

"So—in that corner of the room."

She tilted her head. "Not really in the corner. But not far from it."

"All right. Put that in your diagram too, okay?"

She nodded.

Vince could stoop no longer. He pushed to his feet, feeling tingles in both legs. "Thanks, Brittany. Everything you've told me is very helpful. I'll need to ask you some more questions, but for now just sit tight, and the doctor will be with you in a minute."

"Okay." She looked up at him, her expression morphing into forlorn exhaustion. "Can I use a phone to call my parents? I lost my cell phone 'cause they took everybody's away and threw them in a bag."

"Absolutely, you can call your parents. We just need to get you a free line." He looked to Roger, who was still on the phone—the second call he'd answered since arriving. "Officer Waitman will help you with that. Can you wait a sec?"

She leaned back in her chair and nodded.

Vince reached for Brittany's hand and squeezed. "I can't tell you how glad we all are that you and Ali are safe."

"Thanks."

A simple response, but Vince could hear the blend of emotions behind it. Relief for herself, hatred of the men, fear for those left behind. Especially her mom.

Roger waved a hand to get Vince's attention, the phone pressed against his chest. Vince gave Brittany a little smile and stepped away, raising his eyebrows at Roger.

"Jim has heard the judge and both attorneys have now arrived at their given location. Someone can bring them in whenever you're ready."

"Let's do it."

"What about media?"

With parents being notified of the girls' release, word would spread quickly. Better to keep reporters properly informed. "Call Al and give him the basics of the exchange to tell media." Vince lowered his voice. "Let's not go into shots being fired—"

"Vince." Larry stood in the doorway. "Justin says Kent's on the line."

"Okay, coming." He looked back to Roger. "Gotta go."

As Vince hurried into the hallway, Larry whispered, "Justin says the man's in a *rage*."

Vince strode toward his office, the back of his neck prickling.

FIFTY-EIGHT

John stared at Lenora, his brain scrambling for words. The woman was tall and thin. Straggly brown hair, a worn, weary face. She eyed him with a mixture of expectation and dread. But now that he'd gotten in the door—a miracle in itself—what could he say? *Your husband is holding my wife hostage* ... The strangeness of their connection tied his tongue.

She folded her arms. "Who are you?"

"John Truitt. My wife, Bailey, owns Java Joint. She's in there with your husband."

Lenora's eyes widened, then a veil fell over her face. Her jaw hardened. "What do you want?"

Anger welled within him. What did he *want*?

He opened his mouth. Shut it. No, no, he couldn't lose his temper with this woman. He had to *reach* her.

Dear God, show me how.

Motion caught John's eye. He focused over Lenora's shoulder into a cluttered den. The TV was on but muted. Its screen showed a reporter standing on Lakeshore.

Briefly, Lenora's gaze followed his to the television.

"You want your innocent son freed," John blurted. "T.J."

Lenora's expression flickered. "Yes."

"I want my innocent wife freed."

She pulled in her shoulders. "I can't help you."

"Are you ... talking to your husband?"

226

"No."

"Do you have a computer? Did you see the comments on the blog?"

She frowned and shook her head.

Some of the tension slid from John's muscles. Suddenly he pictured the world through Lenora Wicksell's eyes—a desperate world of perceived injustice. A husband and two sons putting their lives on the line for the youngest in the family. And she, left alone.

"I read the first communications between your husband and Vince Edwards, Kanner Lake Chief of Police. I can tell you what I know."

She studied him with suspicion, then motioned him into the den. They perched on opposite ends of a saggy blue couch.

John told her about the blog comments, the plans to air T.J.'s document. Hope stirred across Lenora's face as she drank in his words. She looked to the silent-mouthing female reporter on the TV. "Maybe she's reading T.J.'s story now."

Story. Apropos choice of words.

She reached for the remote and turned up the volume. "... repeat, we are trying to substantiate reports that Brittany Hanley and Ali Frederick, the two youngest hostages, are being freed ..."

Lenora sucked in a breath. John leaned forward.

Time seemed to stop as they listened. The reporter spoke of an exchange—a TV set for two hostages. Showed film of Stan Seybert and another man from Kanner Lake, Bud Halloway, loading a TV onto a truck. Skimming below his concentration, John considered the irony of his and Lenora's entwined anxiety in this room. He on one side of the battle, she on the other.

He pulled his cell phone from his pocket. "Want me to find out if it's true?"

She nodded. The creases in her forehead belied her need to know something, *anything.* Knowledge connected her to her husband.

John knew the feeling.

He dialed the Kanner Lake Police Station. An unknown voice answered. That small surprise threw him. What if they told him nothing? He could lose what ground he'd gained with Lenora. "Hi. It's John Truitt."

"Yes, I saw your ID come up. This is Larry Emmet. I'm helping answer phones."

"Oh. Is it true—about the girls?"

A pause. "I'm not supposed to say anything."

"Then put Roger on the phone."

"He's really busy right now."

"Listen to me, Larry, my *wife* is in there. Now tell me what's going on."

Larry cleared his throat. "You'll be hearing on the news soon anyway. Yes, it's true. The girls are here. Safe." He related details.

Emotion swept through John. Relief for the girls and their families, hope for Bailey and all who remained. He exhaled, tilted his head back. "Thank you." He closed the cell phone.

Lenora watched him, hands tightly clasped beneath her chin. He told her all he'd heard.

She soaked in the news, then blinked her gaze away to stare at the floor. John saw something steal over her body. Her mouth tightened, eyes narrowing. She straightened her back.

"Get out."

"But—"

"Now." She stood up.

John pushed to his feet. "Look. You can help. The world is going to hear your son's story now—isn't that what you wanted? Maybe you can talk to your husband, ask him to let everyone—"

"Do you see T.J. home and safe yet, huh?" She slashed a finger toward the floor. "Do you have *any idea* what we've gone through? Kent let those girls go to get something he wanted, but my son's still in *prison*. Nobody else is coming out of there until he's free!"

"Please."

"Leave this house *right now.*"

She stepped forward, pushed hard against his chest. Then drew up, back arched and fingers curved like claws. "Go this minute, or I will run outside and scream to those reporters you tried to hurt me."

John stared at her openmouthed.

"Get *out!*"

He turned on his heel and headed blindly for the door. Lenora scurried in front of him, unbolted the lock, and threw it open. He forced himself through.

"And *don't* come near me again!" she yelled. The door slammed behind him.

He stood staring at the paint-peeling wood. Dear God, what should he do now? Where to go? He had blown this so badly.

To the church. To pray.

John's vision blurred with tears. He turned and stumbled down the Wicksell porch steps—and only then noticed that two cameras were rolling.

FIFTY-NINE

"Hello, Kent, I'm here." Vince leaned one hand on his desk, willing his voice steady.

No response.

"Kent? You there?"

Silence.

Vince aimed a questioning look at Justin.

"He was on just a minute ago. Cussing a blue streak."

Vince worked his jaw. "Kent?"

Noises filtered over the line. "Edwards!" The word was spit from Wicksell's mouth.

"I'm here." Vince sat down on the edge of his chair. "I understand you're upset at the way the exchange went. I want to assure you that you're safe."

Wicksell spewed curses. "What do you call *safe*? We had a deal! You told me nobody would be armed! You said *not armed*!"

"I told you the man delivering the TV would not be armed, and he wasn't. The man you saw was only there to get the girls to safety. Apparently one of the girls fell, and he helped her get up. That was it. No one shot at you—even though you fired multiple times."

Wicksell breathed over the line like a fuming dragon. "So much for trust." His voice was hard, cold. "I should have known I can't trust *any* cop."

Fear trickled through Vince's gut. He thought of all the negotiating scenarios he'd practiced. The vocal nuances he'd learned, that thin line between balancing at the edge of a cliff and falling over it. Wicksell was at that edge. If Vince couldn't turn this around, things could get nasty very quickly.

"You *can* trust me. We got you the TV—"

"You had a *SWAT* member here. On *my* street! He could have gunned me down!"

"He was not there for that purpose, Kent. He was only there to take the girls to safety, and that's what he did."

"He'd have shot me if he could."

"He wasn't there to shoot you. Remember, *you're* the one who fired shots. No one returned fire."

"How do I know you didn't have ten more men like him around?"

"No one is anywhere near you on the street. We sent people in to take the girls away, and they are all gone now."

Wicksell's breathing rattled.

Larry entered the office and headed for the hostage photos tacked to the wall. He wrote "RELEASED" across the pictures of Brittany and Ali.

Justin jotted a note for Vince and held it up: *Change subject. TV.*

Vince nodded. "Kent, did you get the TV inside?"

"What, you think *I'm* gonna bring it in while you got armed men on the street? No, it's not inside!"

"Nobody is out there. You said you were going to send someone else out to get it. Go ahead and do that. It's safe."

"I'll *bet* it is."

Vince wrapped his fingers around the arm of his chair. He wanted to bring Wicksell's temper under control. On the other hand, if the man needed to vent, best let him do it. Maybe the anger would play itself out.

"Okay, Kent, the television isn't going anywhere. When you're ready to bring it in, we can proceed."

For another five minutes Wicksell argued and cussed. Vince maintained a calm tone, but Wicksell ranted on. Twice Vince reminded him they couldn't move forward until someone pulled the television into Java Joint. The reporters were standing by. T.J.'s story would air—but not until Wicksell gave the word that he was ready to watch the coverage, because that's what the two of them had agreed upon, and Vince was holding up his side of the bargain.

"All *right*," Wicksell finally seethed, "just get *off* me!"

A *crack* shot through Vince's ear. Wicksell had slammed the phone down.

SIXTY

"You!" Kent spun on his heel and pointed. "Get up!"

S-Man felt Leslie's hand tighten on his. He eased his fingers from her grasp. *It's okay*, he told her with his eyes. To his left, Paige fixed him with a wide stare, her forehead crinkled. Her face said it all—*Ted, don't let them kill you too!*

S-Man pushed back from the table and stood up.

Surprising, under the circumstances, how good it felt to stretch his legs.

He was used to sitting for hours at a time to write, but that was different. Ensconced in his Saurian world, he wouldn't register that his rear end was tired or his back muscles tight—until the lapse of concentration that tumbled him back into the real world. It was like a switch being thrown. *Bam*, all the aches and pains shouted at him.

S-Man stole a glance at his contracts lying on the edge of the counter. The papers that promised his new life as a novelist. It seemed like days ago he'd been signing them.

Kent plucked his gun off the table where the telephone lay. Pointed it at S-Man. "You're gonna go outside and bring the TV in." He threw a look at Mitch, who stood guard near Bailey. "Get hold of her." He pointed to Leslie. His calculating eyes cut back to S-Man.

Mitch stepped to Leslie and clenched scrawny fingers around her arm. Dragged her to her feet. She cried out and stumbled backward. He wrapped one arm around her neck.

White-hot rage shot through S-Man. His muscles jerked, every nerve within him straining to let his fist fly at Mitch. In a split second he willed himself to hold back. Whatever he did would only be taken out on Leslie.

"Good choice, Space Cowboy," Kent sneered. "Yeah, I saw the look on your face." He jerked his head toward the door. "Nice and slow now. I'll be watching from inside the door. Get the TV and bring it in here. No fast moves, no running for it—and your little blonde reporter will get to sit back down beside you, all nice and quiet."

S-Man's eyes briefly met Leslie's as he moved around the table. He limped across the café, unbolted the door. Opened it—to strong sun and fresh air. He blinked at the light, the heady sweetness of the air caressing his face. He breathed in hungrily.

The barrel of Kent's gun poked into his back.

"Go."

Squinting, S-Man stepped over the threshold and onto the sidewalk. Warm sun poured down over him, reflecting against white pavement. His narrowed eyes took in the eerie, empty street, the shot-out buildings on the other side. The Simple Pleasures storefront lay in ruins, windows shattered. Glass everywhere.

Not a person in sight. Like some abandoned war zone in Sauria.

Before him at the curb sat the TV.

S-Man walked toward it, taking in all he could through his peripheral vision. No SWAT man peeked around a corner, no sniper visible on the Simple Pleasures rooftop. For the first time since the gunmen had appeared, S-Man felt overwhelmed by the sheer *aloneness* of it all. Had the entire town abandoned all of the hostages to their fate?

He crossed to the curb, hearing his own hollow footsteps and nothing more.

Like walking into The Outer Limits.

He reached the table, saw it was on wheels. Pulled it toward him, then got behind it. His back to the Main Street he once knew, S-Man pushed the table to Java Joint's door and over the threshold. Its wooden wheels bumped across the metal strip.

Brad and Kent were arguing again about things not moving fast enough. Kent threw cuss words over his shoulder as he kept a steely eye on S-Man. Mitch tossed in his own opinion. Kent shouted him and Brad down.

"Get out of the way!" Kent screamed at S-Man.

He moved aside, and Kent slammed and bolted the door.

Java Joint's claustrophobic, sweat-laden air clawed at S-Man. His eyes opened wide in the dimness.

Lingering sensations from his seconds of freedom fled from his mind.

He looked to Leslie. Mitch had her even tighter by the throat, anger at his father goading his moves. Her wide eyes spelled terror, but her clamped jaw screamed indignation. His independent, fighter Leslie.

"You don't have to choke her, Mitch," Kent spat.

Mitch eased off.

Kent swung back to S-Man, his face dark. "Don't just *stand* there—roll it to the counter."

S-Man did as he was told. He wanted Mitch's hands *off* Leslie—the woman he loved with all his heart.

The woman who was leaving him in a couple of weeks.

If they survived.

In that inopportune moment—with the wood of the table under his hands and a crass comment from Brad hitting his ears—a giant movie screen of his and Leslie's future unfurled in S-Man's brain. The picture was so vivid, so *right*, he marveled that he'd not seen it before. Why wait while Leslie went off on her own, hoping she'd come back to him? Why not go with her? He'd convince her to marry him. Together they'd go wherever the reporting jobs took her. He was seeing his dreams come true; so was she. Why should they have to choose between those dreams and each other?

A novelist could write anywhere.

"Stop! Leave it there." Kent's voice drilled into his thoughts. "Go sit down."

S-Man turned around, feeling almost light, a tiny smile on his lips. Kent gave him a suspicious look. "Move it."

When S-Man reached the table, Mitch unwrapped his arm from Leslie's throat and pushed her. She fell into her chair as S-Man lowered into his. He took her hand, squeezed it hard. Gave her a reassuring nod.

Leslie's eyes misted, but she hefted her chin and blinked the tears away. Throwing a glance to kill at Kent, she muttered one word under her breath.

"Pig."

SIXTY-ONE

Vince hunched at his desk, dragging a hand back and forth across his chin as he strained to hear the muted noises from within the café. When Kent slammed down his receiver, he'd left the line connected. Vince couldn't make out what was happening.

With every passing minute, his tension ratcheted higher.

Larry had left the office, but not before pointing to the word he'd written across the girls' pictures. Vince reminded himself of that victory.

He heaved back in his chair, exchanged a frustrated look with Justin. Got up. Walked around. Sat down again.

Still no Wicksell.

Suddenly—a voice in his ear.

"Edwards!" Wicksell sounded no calmer. "I had Mr. Science Fiction Writer bring the TV in. And the door's locked and bolted again, so don't go getting any ideas."

Ted Dawson—S-Man.

"Good." Vince spoke easily, as if the last five minutes hadn't made his gut churn. "As soon as you get it turned on, let me know. I'll proceed with the reporters."

"You're gonna screw us on that too, ain't ya?"

"No. They're going to read the document on air. Just like I got you the TV."

"Oh yeah, they'll read it. But there'll be something in the background goin' on. Something I don't know."

237

"There's no hidden agenda. But we agreed not to move on this until you're ready."

"Brad!" Wicksell yelled. "Get the TV turned on!"

Vince tried to picture the hostages in Java Joint. Were they still at tables as Brittany had told him? What condition were they in? All this shouting, the gunshots—they had to be terrified. Did they even know the girls hadn't been hurt?

"Let me tell you something, Edwards—*nobody's* comin' near this place again. Hear me? Not for *anything*."

"All right, if that's the way you want it."

Wicksell growled in his throat. "It's not all right. Nothing's all right. I come to your town, ready to deal, and all you can do is *lie to me*."

"No, I asked you at the very beginning if you wanted me to lie or tell the truth. You picked the truth. That's what you're getting."

"Yeah, yeah."

"Kent, I need you to trust me—"

"I already told you I *don't* trust you."

"As long—"

"You want me to shoot someone else, huh?"

"You know I don't."

"I think you do! Or maybe it's what you *need* to show you I mean business."

"Kent, listen to me." Vince spoke slowly. "You and I can't move forward as long as you're threatening hostages. I'd rather focus on what you want me to do for you."

"I want you to *shut up*, that's what."

Vince focused on his desk. Maybe the arrival of the judge and attorneys would help. When Wicksell heard all three men were meeting to discuss T.J.'s case, maybe he'd calm down. *Something* had to work.

"Edwards!"

"I'm here."

"Just letting you know the TV's on."

Good. Something else for Wicksell to think about. Watching the airing of T.J.'s story would give him time to settle down.

"All right. I'll contact the reporters, tell them to go ahead."

"They'd better make it good, Edwards. I mean *real* good. They don't do my son's words justice, a few of your friends are going to be sorry."

The threats chewed Vince's ears. He wouldn't hesitate to go tactical if he had to, but the thought twisted his stomach. If he sent CRT storming in there, people would die. Maybe some of the hostages.

"I'll contact them, but I need to see that you're going to calm down first."

"Don't *tell* me what to do!"

"Kent, I cannot proceed as long as you're threatening anyone in there with you."

Wicksell snorted. "Like *you're* making the rules."

"You and I agreed to work this out. I'm carrying out my part. I have the reporters standing by. You need to do your part. Can you do that?"

"I *am* doing it."

"Doing your part includes making no more threats."

"Yeah, yeah, fine. Just get the reporters on TV."

Vince and Justin exchanged a glance. "All right, Kent. Don't hang up. I'll have someone here make the phone calls, and as soon as that's done, I'll let you know."

"Make it fast."

"I'll work as quickly as possible. I'm going to put the phone down just a minute."

Vince set the receiver on the desk and hurried out of the office. As he strode down the hall, he erased all tension from his face. No need for the girls to be any more frightened.

He stuck his head in the second office's door, motioning to Roger. Larry sat at a desk, writing in the log. Dr. Hughes was examining Ali's left ankle. Brittany waited with shoulders pulled in, clasped hands at her mouth. She glanced at Vince.

"You all right?"

She nodded.

He threw her a quick smile, then looked to Roger. "I need you to call those reporters, tell them we're ready. Find out how long it'll be, then let me know. We'll need to stagger the times so Wicksell can watch both channels."

"Will do."

When he returned to his office, Justin shook his head. "More yelling going on in there."

Vince snatched up his receiver. "Kent?" Wicksell was shouting obscenities, not directly into the phone. "Kent."

The cursing broke off. "Yeah!" Kent's tone seethed. "What d'ya want?"

"Just want to let you know we're calling the reporters. I'll have an update for you in a minute. Who are you yelling at?"

"Anybody. Everybody. What's it to ya?"

Kent was pacing. Vince could tell by the way he breathed, the sound of hard footsteps.

"Is everyone all right in there?"

"*No one's* all right in here; who do you want to hear about first?" Kent's words pulsed. "My son, Brad, who *wasn't even supposed to be here*, keeps trying to tell me what to do. He has his way, there'll be a body out on the street in the next minute. Then there's Mitch, suddenly all paranoid about somebody outside the windows ready to bust in. Making me downright nervous."

Paranoia — a symptom of meth. Not a good attitude with a gun in your hand ...

"I got all these people to keep under control, and it's so stuffy in here you'd think we was in a closet."

"It must seem like a long time you've been in there."

"*Way* too long. This thing is taking *way too long.*"

"Sounds like it's really getting to you."

Wicksell snorted, then chewed out a few more curses. "You think we came this far to give up now, you got another thing coming. You and me got a lot left to work out yet."

"We're working with you as fast as we can, Kent. Next thing is to get T.J.'s story aired, and that'll be soon. Past that I have an idea—" Vince cut off as Roger appeared in the doorway. "Hang on a minute. I may have word about the reporters."

Roger gave him a thumbs-up. Vince placed his hand over the receiver's mouthpiece. "How long?"

"They're ready to go. By the way, we got a TV being delivered here along with the judge and attorneys so we can watch what's going on. In about two minutes."

"Thanks." Vince checked the clock. Just after twelve. "Tell Channel 2 to air at 12:15 and Channel 4 to go at 12:30."

"Right." Roger swiveled on his heel and left.

Vince turned back to the phone. "Kent? All systems are go." He gave the air times for each channel.

Wicksell grunted. "About time." The phone line muffled, and he yelled at someone in the café. Vince couldn't make out the words.

"Edwards?" Wicksell bit off the name. "Call you back after we're done watching the news."

"Wait, Kent, let's stay on the—"

"*No.* I'm *tired* of talking to you."

"Kent—"

The line went dead.

Justin let out a breath. He pushed back in his chair and slipped off the headphones.

Vince stared at the receiver, then slowly replaced it. Prickles danced around the back of his neck. Lack of contact was not good, especially with Wicksell's present state of mind. As long as the man stayed on the phone, he was less likely to hurt anyone.

Of course, there were always the two sons ...

The station's back door opened. Men's voices. Footfalls.

The attorneys and judge had arrived.

SIXTY-TWO

Jared Moore clasped his bony hands, feeling the heavy drum of his heart. It had refused to slow since Kent Wicksell dragged him out of his chair. Jared did not doubt Kent was capable of carrying out his threat. Tension in the café vibrated like a live wire. These men were out for blood. Frank's life had not been enough. They'd kill again without blinking an eye.

The television was turned on to Channel 2. Its picture wasn't cable-sharp, but not bad. The hostages sat woodenly, watching a car commercial.

"They'd better make it good." Kent's words to Chief Edwards. *Why* had Jared ever opened his mouth? Why should he have believed these men were able to act logically?

At the time he'd suggested the emails to reporters, it had seemed like a smart idea. Give them a sought-after story, and they'd come through with the professionalism expected of their field. Now, thanks to Kent's rage, Jared's faith lay deflated, a pricked balloon on the dusty floor. No matter how professional the reporters, Kent would find something wrong with their performance.

On the TV, the commercial flipped to pictures of local houses for sale. *Paid programming.*

What a strange parody, all of them listening to a narrator sing the praises of a house in Coeur d'Alene with four bedrooms and large walk-in closets.

243

Jared shook his head, wishing he could clear it. His mind was a slough of thoughts. Fear, dread, shock, slushed with phrases of the article he would write were he merely reporter rather than participant. He couldn't help the flow of words in his head. They were as natural to him as breathing. Now they kept him sane.

He blinked at the screen. A new property—a five-bedroom ranch house on three acres in Spirit Lake. Jared pictured couples in their homes right now, safe, watching the program. Seeking just the right house for their family of five and two dogs ...

Amazing, how the world out there just ... rolled on.

Java Joint hung thick with stale sweat. Some of that sourness surely was his own. Fear had a way of oozing out one's pores. Without fresh air, the place seemed worse by the minute. The air-conditioning in this old building wasn't keeping up. And Jared's rear end had gone numb from sitting on the hard chair for so long. Being shoved around hadn't helped.

Kent Wicksell perched on the first counter stool, rapping a knuckle against his weapon. A Freudian gesture? *This works or I kill somebody.*

Brad scoffed at the TV. "Who watches this stuff?"

"People with nothing better to do." Mitch rocked from one foot to the other.

"Yeah, like us."

"Won't be long now." Kent's knuckle kept rapping, like a woodpecker against Jared's temple.

Brad shook his head. "Like you can trust what that cop says."

"I can trust this." Kent slid a black look at his son. "Because he knows what'll happen in here if he don't come through."

Brad's eyelids flickered, but he said nothing.

Behind Jared, Wilbur coughed. Jared hoped he was holding himself together. Not an easy situation for a man who'd had triple bypass surgery two years ago.

Yet another house on TV. Then the screen flashed and reporter Jeremy Cole appeared. "Kanner Lake Breaking News" ran in red letters across the bottom of the picture.

"All *right*." Kent leaned forward. Brad hissed through his teeth.

Cole stood at the edge of town on Lakeshore, the camera zooming out to show milling reporters and townspeople, news trucks, police cars, and flashing lights.

Bev and Angie gasped.

What a strange feeling to know those people were a mere five, six blocks away. They may as well have been a planet apart.

Chairs creaked as every hostage leaned forward, straining to make out the face of a friend, a loved one. Jared scanned the TV screen, wanting, *needing* to see his wife, Tricia, but the camera was too far away to make out faces.

Still, he knew she was there, somewhere in that crowd. He could feel her.

"We interrupt normal programming once again with more breaking news from Kanner Lake." Jeremy Cole's face appeared solemn. "On Main Street this very minute, three desperate men are holding a remaining ten people hostage in the nationally known café Java Joint. Kent Wicksell and his two sons, Mitch and Brad ..."

Scenes of his years with his wife trailed through Jared's mind. Tricia, with a nervous smile and little white flowers in her hair, walking down the aisle toward him on the arm of her father. Tricia, after labor, exhausted and sweaty, but so anxious to hold their newborn son. Tricia in the backyard, fretting over rosebushes that wouldn't grow. The way she hummed while stirring soup at the stove. Her tsking comments as they watched the news — "Jared, you'd have written that story so much better." She'd gone from brown-haired to gray in their forty years of marriage, and somewhere along the way wrinkles had set in. But her walk was still quick-stepped, her hand in his still firm.

Tricia, I'll get out of this, you'll see. Our life together isn't over yet.

"… in his own words, emailed by his father, Kent Wicksell," the reporter continued. "The document is about three pages long. I will now read it in its entirety."

Angie drew a loud breath. Jared could see the desperate curiosity in her face. He felt it too. Among the hostages, only Bailey knew what T.J. had written.

Let's hope it's enough to get us out of here.

Kent's back went rigid, his shoulders hunched as he focused on the TV, as if daring the reporter to do him wrong.

SIXTY-THREE

As the "Breaking News" shot of Jeremy Cole filled the TV screen, everyone in the lobby of the Kanner Lake Police Station fell silent.

Here it comes. Vince stood with arms crossed, feet apart. Adrenaline tingled through him, setting his stomach at a low tremble. On his right, defense attorney Lester Tranning towered over Vince, lanky arms on his narrow hips. Tranning was dressed in khakis and a blue knit shirt. He'd been pulled off the golf course to come to the station. On Vince's left, prosecutor Mick Wiley had drawn up a chair. He perched forward, legs spread, one fat hand stroking his chin. To Mick's left stood Judge Marcus Hadkin, a wiry, dry-witted man in his sixties who'd seen it all and had the hard face to show it. Hadkin had shown up in paint-splattered jeans and an old T-shirt.

"Your man Roger caught me shopping for paint in Spokane," he'd told Vince with a shake of his gray head. "I got my family room half done. Promised my wife I'd finish today. When I told her why I had to come here, she thought I was making up the wildest excuse she ever heard."

The two attorneys hadn't been so talkative. Vince sensed the ancient feud between them, animosity an undercurrent in their voices and eyes.

Roger stood on the other side of Tranning, rocking on his heels, watching the TV out of the corner of his eye. Vince knew he was keeping one ear attuned to the doctor as she spoke to the girls in the second office. Justin and Larry stood beyond Roger.

Jeremy Cole's lead-in to the story was fine. The basic facts. Nothing Vince saw that should upset Wicksell.

So far, so good.

The reporter raised the pages of the document and began.

Tranning made a knowing sound in his throat, then shrugged as if to say, *"Heard this before."*

Then why didn't you use it in court?

Wiley sat like a stone through the entire reading. He would soak everything in, Vince knew, filtering it through his steel-trap mind before responding.

Cole finished reading and looked into the camera. "Kanner Lake Police Chief Vince Edwards continues to negotiate for the release of the remaining hostages. Kent Wicksell has not moved from his initial demand that T.J. be freed from prison. We will continue our coverage soon with further footage and information. For now, this is Jeremy Cole, Channel 2 News."

The TV screen flicked back to the infomercial on local real estate.

Judge Hadkin sucked air through his nose. He lifted both hands. "That's no new evidence—that's a *story*. A poor one at that."

Wiley grunted his assent.

"No. T.J. saw someone running away—a key piece of information that the police ignored." Tranning's voice sounded even more nasally when he was complaining. "They zeroed in on my client and never looked back."

"Maybe because there was no other place to look." Wiley shook his head. "I didn't see *you* coming up with anything to support that claim."

Vince stepped to the TV. "We should listen to the one on Channel 4 too."

He flipped the station. Soon Teresa Wright appeared and read the document. Her statements before and after were similar to Cole's. Nothing, Vince thought, that should set Wicksell off.

Please, Lord.

Vince snapped off the TV. "Okay. Would you three sit down and start discussing what we can do? I need to give Wicksell something. Right now he doesn't even know you're here. Just telling him that ought to placate him a little. But I'm hoping you can come up with something that'll help me talk him out of there." He looked from Wiley to Tranning with a silent message: *Put your differences aside.*

Vince focused on the judge. "Marcus, I'd appreciate it if you lead the discussion and take notes. I'll get back to you all as soon as I can."

"Just like the courtroom. *Somebody's* got to keep these two in line." Judge Hadkin sparked with energy. "Go on and talk to that lunatic, Vince. I'll take care of this. Too bad I didn't bring a gavel." He scratched his nose and surveyed the area for chairs. "All right, gentlemen, let's pull those over and get to it."

Vince flashed him a tight smile.

"Roger, would you continue debriefing the girls?" he asked. "I've got to get back to Wicksell. Have Larry take notes. I want to know the dynamics between the three men, and between them and the hostages. And make sure Brittany draws the diagram of where everyone is in the room."

"Okay."

As Vince headed for his office, his private line rang. He hurried to his desk and picked up the phone. "Kent. You hear the newscasts?"

Justin stepped through the door, and Vince motioned for him to close it. No need to be distracted by the drone of voices from the lobby.

"Yeah, I heard 'em." Wicksell sounded mad as a wet hen.

Whoa. Vince lowered into his chair. "You sound upset. What's wrong?"

"We got trouble, that's what."

SIXTY-FOUR

Angie Brendt felt the first strange flutter in her heart as the despicable Kent Wicksell switched the TV to Channel 4. They'd already heard the reading of T.J. Wicksell's story once; now they were going to hear it again. Wonderful.

Her heart fluttered a second time. Worse.

She stiffened. What *was* that?

Bev leaned toward her with a questioning expression. Angie shook her head—*It's nothing*—even as she felt her cheeks go hot. Bev eyed her askance, clearly not believing her. Well, too bad. Bev had been through enough today. That *monster* had stuck a *gun* at her head. Far be it from her best friend Angie to make her worry any more.

Angie's heart fluttered a third time.

Then—pain. Deep under her rib cage, radiating out to her left arm.

Angie held her breath. Forced herself to count to ten. *I don't feel it, I don't feel it.*

She felt it, all right.

Help me, Lord. Was this what she thought it was? These horrible killers with their guns and meanness and vile language, and seeing Frank shot, and now worrying about Jared. Had this nightmare of a day worked her right into her first heart attack?

Angie clamped her fingers around her upper left arm and massaged. It didn't help. Oh, it *hurt*.

251

She tried to focus on the TV to distract her mind. Kent Wicksell cursed half under his breath as the second reporter started reading that silly story written by his son. As if anyone would believe it. Angie had watched the news about that trial every night. That boy was *guilty*. Stabbing a mother in front of her own baby girl and leaving the child to walk through her blood.

Even if Angie hadn't believed in T.J.'s guilt before, she would now—after seeing his family in action.

The pain pulsed. Under her ribs and down her arm. She *was* having a heart attack.

No, Lord, not here, not now! These men will kill me!

Her breathing came in shallow gulps. Moans escaped her lips, though she tried to stop them. Bev looked at her, eyes round, her gaze taking in the massaging fingers, the quick rising of Angie's chest. Alarm creased her face.

"What are you feeling?"

Bev spurted the question—loudly. Not caring about the gunmen. But that was Bev. She was brave. Unlike Angie.

Brad's head snapped toward her. "Stop talking!"

"But she's—"

"Shut *up*!" Kent swatted the air in Bev's direction. His gaze never left the TV.

Shut up—his favorite phrase. That and the cusswords. Had he grown up in a barn? These weren't men; they were animals.

Oh, her arm hurt. Angie rubbed it hard, but it didn't help. She groaned.

Jared Moore reached over and held on to her shoulder. "Are you okay?"

Angie shook her head. That was all she could do. Just shake her head while random wild thoughts started rattling around inside it. Thoughts about the Wicksell men, and what would happen now, and the *pain*—and David Clanton. David, her longtime friend, who had finally become her boyfriend over a year ago. He, a widower, she, having lost her dear husband years before. They'd started dating slowly, taking it easy, making sure. They'd both loved their spouses so deeply . . .

As she clutched her arm, afraid she might pass out and terrified her life would end with a bullet in her brain, Angie wondered what on earth she and David had been waiting for. Why hadn't they married when they had the chance? She loved him, didn't she? Well, *didn't* she? Now their chance would never come.

And Frank Jr., her son. In his thirties and still not married, despite all her tries at matchmaking. If she died in this café today, she'd never live to see him with a family.

The pain chewed at her. *God, please help me!*

Angie closed her eyes and groaned louder.

"She's having a heart attack!" Bev cried.

Angie heard jumbles of sound — Jared's voice, Brad's curse, her other friends' calls for help on her behalf, the *brrr* of chair legs against linoleum. *No, be quiet, I'm all right. They'll shoot me.* She struggled to say the words, but only moans rose from her throat.

She slumped to her right — and felt Jared catch her.

Blood whooshed in her ears. Through the pounding she heard Kent Wicksell cursing.

"You two — put her on the floor! The rest, stay back!"

Bev and Jared whispered soothing words as they edged her out of the chair, lowered her down. Angie couldn't open her eyes. They nudged her on her back, told her to lie still. She had no energy to resist.

"You've got to call for help," a man said.

Angie's thoughts swirled around the pain. *That was Wilbur's voice. He should know. He's had a heart attack. Triple bypass . . .*

"She needs an ambulance!" *That's Leslie.*

Then Brad and Kent and Mitch were all shouting, telling every-body, "Shut up, or I'll shoot and put her out of her misery!" and "Throw her outside and let her die!" and "I can't hear the TV!"

The pain roiled. The floor felt so hard and uncomfortable. Angie's head rolled back and forth, her legs drawing up.

She was going to die.

David, I'm so sorry.

"Everybody, move over there. Now!"

The café exploded with noise. Footfalls around her. Yelling. Crying. Chairs scraping. What was *happening*?

Suddenly it all fell silent, except for the TV reporter's voice.

"Hey!" A gun barrel poked in her ribs.

Angie forced her eyes open. She looked up to see Kent Wick-sell towering over her, his expression cold as ice. She could see no one else.

Sounds from her right. Angie rolled her head and saw her friends clustered near the computer table where Bailey sat, Mitch and Brad guarding with guns. They all watched her with alarm and righteous anger. Bev glared at Brad like she was about to blow a gasket.

Angie's bleary gaze wandered back to Kent.

He sneered down at her. "See all the trouble you caused? And don't pretend you can't hear me. You'd better pull yourself together, 'cause I ain't callin' no ambulance for you. That cop ain't sendin' *nobody* near this place again. *Got* it?"

Angie's eyes slipped shut.

He dug a foot into her ribs. "If you're pretending just so you can get out of here, it ain't gonna work."

"I'm ... I'm not ..."

Angie tried to push out the words, but they wouldn't come. She could only lie there and hope to God he wouldn't shoot her.

SIXTY-FIVE

Paige saw Angie groaning on the hard floor—and something snapped within her soul.

She could almost hear the *crack*, like an ice-encased branch giving way. Until then, from the moment Frank had slumped, shot, at her feet, Paige had felt only the cold. Numbing, deadening cold. And she'd welcomed it. Sitting at her table hour after hour, Paige couldn't have borne the knowledge that Frank was dead if she'd allowed herself to feel.

Paige knew fear. She knew helplessness. She'd grown up with both. Numbing out had been her defense against an abusive mother and her equally abusive "stepdads" since Paige was a little girl. It was better that way. When you felt the pain too much, you'd go under. You'd think you were going to die. You'd *want* to die.

"Get over there and don't move!" Mitch yanked Paige to her feet and shoved her toward the wall. He pulled Leslie up next. Out the corner of her eye, Paige saw Ted reaching for Leslie, trying to push her behind him. Brad, Mitch, and Kent started shouting at once.

Paige hit the wall and whipped around, shrinking back against it. The pandemonium died away, her friends pressed together like panicked sheep, looking down the barrels of Mitch's and Brad's guns. They craned their necks to see Angie amid the tables and overturned chairs. Paige could see her face.

White, twisted in pain. Her eyes rolled as if she was only half-conscious.

Paige clenched her hands. "You have to *do* something!"

"Shut up!" Brad's blue eyes hardened into lasers.

Her friends yelled back. Wilbur, Ted, Bev, how many others Paige didn't know. Their voices mixed and rose, taking strength from each other. Brad and Mitch shouted louder, waving their weapons.

Kent ran toward them, gun raised. "Next person who says a word *dies*!"

The noise cut off. Paige found herself cowering before Brad, her face half hidden in Pastor Hank's shoulder.

She peeked up through strands of hair. Kent glared at them, a vein pulsing in his neck.

On the TV, the female reporter read T.J.'s story.

"Now." Kent's teeth gritted. "*Nobody* talks. Nobody *moves*."

He turned and stalked to Angie. Sneered down at her about the trouble she'd caused.

He's going to kill her.

Suddenly he straightened. Focused slitted eyes on Paige and the others around her. Started toward them, then veered as if hooked by an invisible hand to the phone on the front table. He threw down his gun, snatched up the receiver, and smacked it on.

Paige knew then. She'd seen enough of the signs as a child. The stone face, jaw moving from side to side, the stiff shoulders. Kent Wicksell's rage had burned down to pulsing red coals, just waiting for one wrong word, one wrong action ...

When that happened, someone was going to die.

SIXTY-SIX

"Kent, what's going on?" Vince asked. Across from him, Justin started taking notes.

Wicksell growled in his throat. "I got a woman on the floor, claiming she's having a heart attack. I don't need this. She don't get up, I just might get a *little riled*, get what I'm saying?"

"Who is it?"

"I don't know, some—" The sound of a palm rubbing against the mouthpiece. "Who is she?" Wicksell's voice was directed away from the phone. Vince heard numerous voices reply but couldn't make out their answer.

"Angie," Wicksell told him.

Angie Brendt. Vince's eyes shifted to her photo on the wall. Angie was full of life and fun. Known for her laughter, her positive attitude. "What are her symptoms?"

"She's lying on the floor, massaging her left arm and groaning." Wicksell's voice remained hard. "I told her no use faking it, I ain't letting her out of here."

"I don't think she's faking. She's in her midsixties, and she *has* seen some stress today. You need to let her go right away so she can get to the hospital."

"I *told* you I ain't letting anybody else near this place!"

"If she's—"

"If she's sick, too bad! I'll put her out of her misery!"

Vince's options flashed through his head. If Angie was having a heart attack, every minute counted. But Wicksell's attitude screamed he was nowhere close to letting her go.

"I don't believe you really want to do that. And you've got enough to deal with in there. Do you want to worry about a woman who needs medical care?"

"I'm telling you, I'll do it! I'm *tired* of these people. They went crazy on me two minutes ago. If I wasn't such a patient man, they'd all be *dead*."

Vince kept his voice level. "Kent, I understand this is upsetting for everyone. The others are certainly worried about Angie. It will be helpful to calm *everyone* down by assuring that Angie gets the medical atten—"

"And listen, don't tell me 'I did this and that for you,' hear? I don't care if those reporters read T.J.'s story, it's not enough! I want to get my son *out of prison. Now.* You're not doing *anything* to help me. We came in here at eight o'clock, now it's after one. Five hours. *Five!*"

Dread rolled through Vince's stomach like a ball of wax. The newscasts had been so important to Wicksell. They should have placated him for a while at least.

"Kent, I have been working on it. Right now the prosecutor, defense attorney, *and* Judge Hadkin are here, discussing T.J.'s case. They'll figure out what to do legally to help—"

"So they're talking. So what? They talked plenty in the courtroom—and look what happened."

"Kent, a jury convicted T.J. Not the attorneys, not the judge. Hadkin has plenty of jurisdiction to reopen a case if he thinks it should be done. Of all people, he's the one who matters most. And he's *here*."

"He won't do nothin'."

Wicksell had *demanded* that these men hear what he had to say. Now he didn't even care that they were here? What did Vince have left?

"I don't think that's true, Kent. I think he'll help."

"Then get him on the phone with *me*, saying T.J.'s being freed *right now*. No, wait, I know. There's cell phones in here. When I can call *home* and hear T.J. and his mom *together*—*then* we'll come outta here."

Vince needed to talk to Lenora Wicksell himself—one phone call he hadn't yet had time to make. Now with Kent in such a state, perhaps a taped message from her could help calm him down.

"Tell you what, Kent, I'll—"

"You'll tell me nothing, Edwards! Just go get T.J. out of prison! Until the judge can tell me that's happened, you and I ain't talkin' *no more*."

The line clicked in Vince's ear.

SIXTY-SEVEN

Bailey pressed against the wall, both hands to her mouth. Praying for Angie, praying that Kent would calm down and let an ambulance come. Mitch and Brad stayed close, guns up, expressions dark. Not caring in the least about Angie's groans.

Kent broke off his call with Vince and smashed down the phone.

No one dared move. On TV, a series of ads flipped back to the female reporter who had read T.J.'s document. "We now have further news about the hostage situation in Kanner Lake ..."

Bailey's gaze pulled from Kent's purple face to the television. The picture switched to a new scene. *John!* Her eyes widened. John was on the screen.

Beside her, Bev drew a sharp breath and nudged Bailey.

Brad turned to see what they were looking at. His chin came up. "Hey—our house!"

Our house?

Kent swiveled around.

"... A little over an hour ago," the reporter continued, "this man visited the house of Kent Wicksell, wanting to talk to Kent's wife, Lenora. We have since learned the identity of the man—John Truitt, husband of Bailey Truitt, owner of Java Joint and one of the hostages ..."

Kent and Mitch threw furious glances at Bailey. Her veins iced over.

The footage showed John walking up a broken sidewalk toward a dingy white house with peeling paint. He mounted the steps onto the porch. Knocked on the door. It eventually opened, and he went inside.

The picture cut to John hurrying out of the house, a woman behind him. "And *don't* come near me again!" she yelled. The door slammed.

Shocked silence stretched out in the café. They watched John head to his car and drive away.

The Wicksells went wild. Mitch whirled on Bailey. "What'd he do to my mother, huh, what'd he *do*?" Brad stormed toward her. Kent shouted a stream of curses and yanked his gun from the table.

Radt-a-tadt-a-tadt-a-tadt-a-tadt. The TV screen exploded.

The hostages screamed.

Mitch and Brad whipped toward their father. Kent hunched like an enraged grizzly, his feet planted wide and teeth bared. *Radt-a-tadt-a-tadt.* Bullets punched the counter and stools, shattered pastry cabinet glass, riddled the cash register and espresso machine and purses and S-Man's contracts. Bailey's ears sizzled. The gunfire and screams blasted and screeched and burst and shrilled until the whole world would surely cave in. Bailey bent low, cringing, hands over her head. The next bullet would be hers.

The shooting stopped.

Shrieks filled the café. Bailey pulled her arms from her head.

"Shut up, all of you, *shut up!*" Kent swung his gun around.

Screams dissolved into gasps and crying. Bev lay crumpled across Bailey's feet, her legs drawn up and face covered. Was she hit? Bailey bent down, shook her shoulder. Bev pushed to her knees and looked up. No blood to be seen. Bailey reached for her hand.

Mitch and Brad cussed and threatened. Kent stomped across the café floor with his gun, cursing John and every person in Kanner Lake.

The phone rang.

Bailey pulled Bev to her feet, cast wild looks right and left. Was everyone else safe? Hank and Ted had hold of Leslie. Carla hung on to Wilbur, her face streaked with tears. Jared shielded Paige with his body.

Bailey cut her eyes toward Angie, who still lay across the room on the floor, not far from the counter. If anyone had been hit from a ricocheting bullet, it would be her. The phone kept ringing. Kent ignored it.

Angie's legs were moving. Bailey couldn't see her face but heard her choked prayer: "Jesus, Jesus, Jesus ..."

"What are you trying to do, kill us *all*?" Brad strode to his father and hit his shoulder.

Mitch stormed after Brad. "Leave him alone!"

Kent shoved Brad away. "That man went after *your mother*!"

"So kill his wife and throw her outside! Kill every last one of them, for all I care! But now you've busted the TV. And what if you'd shot out the front windows? The cops would pour right in here!"

"You see any windows shot?" Mitch jumped in front of him.

"Maybe we won't be so *lucky* next time." Brad's teeth gritted.

Kent shook his gun at them. "Don't tell me what to do! Either of you!"

The three men faced off, chests heaving.

Angie's weeping rose from the floor.

"Shut *up*!" Kent spun around, a thick vein bulged in his forehead. He surged toward Angie, kicking abandoned chairs from his path. "I've had *enough* a you!"

Bailey grabbed Bev's wrist. Terrified groans spilled from the hostages.

Brad and Mitch aimed their guns at the group. "Don't move!"

Kent grabbed Angie's arm with his right hand. "Get up." He yanked hard. Her body bent from the waist like a pulled puppet. "Get *up*!" He wrenched again, and she staggered to her feet, hair disheveled and face without color. Kent sneered. "Shooting's too *quick* for you. Get out and die in the sun!" He flung a vile name in her face, dragged her forward. "Unlock the door!"

Mitch sprinted over, undid the bolt.

"Open it." Kent's teeth clenched as he jerked Angie across the café. Mitch pulled the door back. Instant light and fresh air wafted into the room. Bailey squinted. Kent leapt behind Angie and thrust his hand hard against her back. "Go *die*!"

"Uh!" Her head whiplashed. She staggered, then stumbled over the threshold onto the sidewalk. Sunshine lit up her pink outfit.

Angie collapsed on the pavement.

Mitch slammed the door and bolted it.

"There." Kent slumped against it in triumph. *"There.* Hope it's slow and painful."

Mitch and Brad exchanged vindictive glances and made their way back to stand guard over the hostages.

The phone rang again. Kent made a face at it, stomped over to click it on, then off. He slammed the receiver on the table.

Nobody moved. The air hung still and choking. Bailey's wide eyes traveled from Kent to the ruin of her café. *Dear God, help Angie.* Bailey's ankles trembled, and numbness crept over her body.

"Now." Kent stalked toward the hostages, gun cradled in both hands, his barrel chest rising and falling.

The phone rang. He stopped in his tracks and swore.

It rang again.

He heaved a sigh. "Okay, Edwards. You wanna keep bugging me? You're about to be sorry."

He swung back to the table and picked up the phone.

SIXTY-EIGHT

"Shots fired!" A voice cut through the tac radio.

Vince's head jerked. He leaned toward the monitor, eyes fixed on Java Joint's door, looking for signs of bullets. Justin pushed to his feet.

"Still shooting."

An eternity passed. Vince's heart beat in his throat.

Dear Lord, please save them.

No movement on the screen.

"Gunfire ceased."

Vince grabbed his phone and punched on the line. Pressed it to his ear, listening to the rings. Once, twice. A third time, a fourth.

Come on, Kent . . .

On the monitor the Java Joint door flung open. A woman clad in pink staggered out to the sidewalk and collapsed.

The door closed.

Vince's veins chilled. He hunched forward, eyes narrowed, desperate to make an identification.

Pink clothing. Short, grayish-brown hair. *Angie Brendt.*

Had she been shot?

The phone line connected, then went dead.

Vince punched *talk* again.

Angie lay on her stomach, one arm flung out. Vince could see no bloodstain on her back, her head.

The Java Joint phone kept ringing. Vince kept the receiver to his ear as he picked up the tac radio. "Frontal position, one of you called in gunfire?"

"Yes."

"Second frontal—I heard it too."

Vince watched the screen. "Can either of you get a visual for any wounds on the woman who just came out?"

A pause. "No wounds, far as I can tell."

"Ditto for me."

Vince felt sick. This was it. His negotiations had failed.

But one thing at a time. First, he had to get Angie out of there, whatever her condition. Second, assess the situation inside Java Joint. *If Kent would just pick up the phone!*

"Jack." Vince spoke into the radio. "Can you get some men up there to retrieve the victim? I have reason to believe she may be suffering from a heart attack, so we need to get her out quickly."

"Understood. Two men are on their way."

Onscreen, Angie's stretched-out arm began curling inward.

"She's moving," Jack said.

They fell silent, watching. The phone rang in Vince's ear.

Angie rolled to her side. She struggled to her knees, then managed to push to her feet. She stood, swaying, facing up the sidewalk.

Come on, come on, get her out of there. At least she was conscious and on her feet. The men wouldn't have to bodily carry her away. Even so, the café door could open any minute. Angie would be cut down in seconds.

The phone line connected.

"Edwards!" Kent seethed. "You *better* be calling to tell me T.J.'s free."

"I'm calling because I heard reports of gunfire. Everybody all right?"

"Sure, we're great."

"No one hurt?"

Kent laughed low in his throat. "The place has seen better days."

"You mean the café?"

"What you *think* I'm talking about — the Chamber of Commerce?"

"So — no one was shot?"

"Not yet. But soon."

Vince closed his eyes. "What about Angie?"

"I kicked her out."

"You kicked her out?"

"Yeah. Got tired of her whining."

Vince looked back to the monitor. Angie was dragging herself up the sidewalk.

"Listen, Edwards. You pushed me too far with that man going to my house. *My house*!"

"What are you talking about?"

Kent swore. "*Don't* act like you don't know!"

"I—"

"Shut up!" Kent's breathing fumed.

Angie listed to one side. She stepped sideways and slumped against a building.

Come on, Angie, you can make it.

"Now hear me, Big Chief. I'm *tired* of waiting around. And after what you done — I swear, if Lenora's hurt, I'll come after you personally and kill you with my bare hands. It's just past one thirty now. You got *one hour* to get T.J. out of prison and on his way home. If two thirty comes and that ain't happened, I shoot a hostage. Every half hour after that, I shoot another one."

Vince kept his voice even. "Less than an hour doesn't give me much time."

"Better hurry then."

"Kent, I don't have the authority to open the prison cell for T.J. I can put in the request, but I can't—"

"You got *one hour*. You and I *ain't* talking until then. And by the way—just to keep myself entertained, I've decided to play a little game with the folks in the meantime. *They* get to decide who goes first."

The line went dead.

PART THREE

Ultimatum

SIXTY-NINE

The two men nearly scared Angie to death. They came out of nowhere, covered in dark gear like those policemen on TV shows. Carrying guns.

"Oh!" Her hands flew up, and she almost fell over against the building.

Was she hallucinating? All the pain, and her wobbly legs, and the sun was so *very bright* . . .

"Police." One of the men ran toward her. "We're getting you out of here." He grabbed her around the waist and pulled her away. He was *strong*. Her feet hardly touched the pavement.

Next thing she knew, they'd stumbled around the corner building and turned down Second Street. A van idled in the middle of the road, pointed toward Lakeshore. The man steered Angie toward it. She heard hard steps behind them. *Kent?* She threw a wild look backward.

No. The second policeman, running backward, his gun aimed toward Main.

They reached the van. The first man pushed her into the backseat and crawled in after her. The door slammed. The second man jumped in front.

"Go!"

A third man behind the wheel sped the van down the street.

Angie fell back against the seat, her eyes closing. Oh, she *hurt*. "Where are we going? I want to see David."

"We're going to get you to an ambulance. You still in pain?"

"Yes. Which hospital? What about my friends? I want to see David."

She prattled on. Angie knew she sounded like a fool, but she couldn't stop herself. She gripped her left arm, massaging. Wanting the pain to *go away*. Wishing she could just fall asleep, wake up on another day.

"Where are we—which—?"

"Just stay calm now." Angie felt a hand on her shoulder.

The van stopped. Doors opened. Angie kept her eyes closed. The pain was too much, and all the *commotion*. Her brain couldn't handle it.

Other voices. Footfalls. A hard metal *snap*.

Gurney?

"Ma'am, come on, let me help you get out."

Then she was sliding over ... on her feet for two seconds ... hands helping her down. The sun was bright, turning the insides of her eyelids mottled red. She was lifted, slid into the ambulance. She felt someone climb in behind her. Doors closed.

The ambulance moved.

"Which hospital are we going to?"

"Kootenai Medical Center." A woman's voice. "Just be still now."

A blood pressure cuff around her arm. Tightening. "Please. You have to tell David."

"Is David your husband?"

The *pain*. Angie's breath came in puffs. "No. But. Soon. Maybe. Tomorrow."

"Tomorrow, huh?" A smile in the woman's tone. "Well then, we better get you fixed up quick."

SEVENTY

Angie had gotten to safety.

Vince lowered the phone, relieved for her. But the feeling was short-lived.

Justin put down his pen and sat back.

One hour.

Briefly, Vince focused on the pictures of the hostages, envisioning their positions within the café.

Tactical wouldn't need an hour. While he'd been negotiating, Vince knew Jack and his men had been doing their homework. Thanks to the building plans, they knew every inch of Java Joint's layout by now. What kind of front door it had, the lock system. They'd studied the photos of the hostages and HTs. Each CRT member would know his exact job. Who would go in first. Who would be last. Who carried the shields, who wielded the gun with frangible ammunition to breach the door.

In the meantime, Vince would try to keep Kent Wicksell on the phone, despite his unwillingness to talk. Vince would call until he answered. Distracting him was important. One, he was the one most likely to storm out the door or harm someone inside. Two, according to Brittany's information, he tended to sit at a certain spot when he was on the phone. The more Tactical knew about the HTs' positions upon entry, the better.

Vince needed to get Brittany's diagram down to Jack immediately.

He picked up the radio, prepared to speak the words he'd so hoped to avoid. The CRT commander would be expecting this. With the gunfire, the HTs had left Vince with no other choice.

"Jack, this is Vince."

"Yeah, Vince."

"I'm giving you the green light to go tactical."

SEVENTY-ONE

"*They* get to decide who goes first."

Pastor Hank watched, nearly numb with shock, as Kent punched off the call and smirked at the phone.

Leslie gasped. She eased away from Hank into Ted's arms. Bev and Bailey clung to each other, shivering. Wilbur cussed under his breath.

Hank thought of Janet. *Dear Lord, thank you that she's not here.*

If God had ever used sickness for good, it was now. Janet would be in Java Joint right now if their youngest daughter wasn't fighting mono.

But she and all three daughters must have heard the news by now. Hank's heart squeezed, thinking of their terror.

Lord, help them be strong. And surround us in here. Protect us with your angels . . .

Hank knew his church members were praying at this very minute. The prayers of everyone combined were what had kept them all alive until now.

Except Frank.

Hank looked to Paige. Her face was white, her blue-green eyes lifeless. She held on to Jared.

Kent laid the phone on the table with a firm *clack*. He turned evil eyes on the group. "Everybody, go sit down where you were."

Brad and Mitch backed up, their weapons following the hostages' movements. No one spoke, the only sounds their footsteps and chair legs scraping into place.

All hope had fled the room.

Hank sat down at his table across from Wilbur. The older man looked ready to bite somebody's head off.

Two tables over, Jared dragged his chair into place, facing Bev. Angie's seat between them screamed its emptiness. Anger and fear welled in Hank, and he curled his fingers, fighting the emotion. Did anyone out there even know Angie was on the sidewalk? Surely she'd been rescued. The thought of her lying on the hot pavement in the sun, in such pain ...

Lord, please. No.

The phone rang. Hank started at the sound.

Kent swore and threw a black look at the receiver. He grabbed it, punched it on, then off.

The clock ticked.

Sweat ran down Mitch's temple. He jerked his shoulder up and wiped it away.

Kent glowered at the hostages, his large nostrils flaring. "What're you all so quiet for? *You* don't decide who I shoot first, I'll do it for ya." He pointed to Bailey. "And it'll be *her.*"

SEVENTY-TWO

Vince perched in his chair, phone pressed to his ear. Wicksell kept disconnecting the line. *What's going on in there?* Vince's focus glued to the monitor, even though he hadn't yet heard from CRT. The screen froze on the empty second block of Main, Java Joint in the center. The scene looked like a movie set, waiting for action to begin.

If only this were a movie.

The line jangled in his ear. Vince's nerves thrummed.

Larry, Justin, Roger, Wiley, Tranning, and Judge Hadkin all crowded around the desk, their attention fixed on the screen. Roger rubbed the side of his face, back and forth, back and forth. A nervous, helpless gesture after running on all four cylinders only to be brought to a screeching halt. Wiley stood with fat legs apart and arms crossed. Hadkin pushed his lower lip up against the top one, plucking at loose skin on his Adam's apple. Larry gripped the black marker from the situation board. He'd marked "RELEASED" across Angie Brendt's photo. No need now, but it gave him something to do.

Another ring.

They spoke little. Nothing left to say. All the activity—the negotiating and information gathering; logbook and situation board maintenance; the discussion between attorneys and judge, once so important—cut to the ground like a sword through the knees. All for nothing.

If Vince had learned one thing in his training, it was that incidents like this were unpredictable. And fluid, never static. One idea might work—like the TV/hostage exchange. The next could fail.

The station line jangled. Roger answered it and walked across the room, facing the situation board. He spoke in low tones. Vince couldn't hear the words.

In his ear, the Java Joint phone rang again.

The line connected, then cut off.

Vince exhaled in frustration. He lowered the receiver.

"What's the use?" Tranning held up his hands. "They won't answer."

Vince ignored him, punched the *talk* button again.

Roger turned around, relief on his face. "Great news from Al. Channel 2's reporting Frank's out of surgery. He's still in critical condition, but everything went well. Unless some complications come up, looks like he'll make it."

"Yeah." Justin raised a fist.

Vince's shoulders sagged with relief. "Thank You, Lord."

Now, save the hostages . . .

"One more thing," Roger said. "Al's asking if you know anything about John Truitt going to Kent Wicksell's house to talk to his wife. A Channel 4 reporter was there, and they got it all on film. She let him in the house but then threw him out, yelling at him to not come back."

John. Vince blinked at Roger, the implications sinking in. That's why Kent was in such a rage. "They air that footage?"

"Apparently so. Not too long ago."

"Oh man." Wiley ran a hand across his forehead. "Kent saw it on TV."

Tranning nodded. "Yeah. Bet so."

No wonder he wasn't answering the phone.

Too late to fix it now. Too late.

Vince checked the monitor. Still no movement. Suddenly he registered that the Java Joint phone hadn't rung for some time. Kent had disconnected again.

Stubbornness rose in Vince. He clicked off the dead line and pushed *talk* once more.

SEVENTY-THREE

"Okay, let's go over the lineup one more time." Jack Little wiped sweat off his brow as he grouped with his six men on Lakeshore. The three snipers remained at their posts. Adrenaline knocked through Jack's veins. It was always that way at gear-up, no matter how many times he and his team were called out. And *this* time—it wasn't every day they did a frontal assault facing three hostiles holding nine hostages. "Harley's breaching the door. Dust-up's rolling in the flash-bang, followed by tear gas. Then we go in stacked. Swank's point, followed by Dust-up, me, Goose, Frenchie, and Lightning. Harley's covering rear. Questions?"

The men shook their heads. Dust-up scratched the underside of his chin—his gesture of impatience. Harley's deep-set blue eyes squinted in the sun, his lips in a thin line.

"Let's do it." Frenchie tapped his mask against his leg.

Swank's face was set in that calm-and-cool expression of his that made the girls swoon, his square chin jutting forward, eyes narrowed. "Good to go."

Full gear for their dynamic entry called for masks to protect them from the tear gas, and eye and ear protection against the M84 stun grenade, or flash-bang. The gas masks were a necessity in this situation, even though they carried the downside of diminished visibility. Not a good thing with three hostiles spread out in the room, but each CRT member had his area to cover. And after the flash-bang went off—with a blinding light of one million candela and deafening 180-decibel blast—every person in that building would be stunned and most likely on the floor. The bright light in a flash-bang rendered blindness for about five seconds. In those seconds the eyes would continue sending the same message to the brain, causing each person to see a freeze-frame effect until normal sight returned. It revved Jack's blood, thinking the frozen picture the hostiles would see was their locked and bolted door blowing open. Meanwhile, the loud blast would disturb inner ear fluid, sending each person reeling.

Unfortunately, the hostages would be stunned too, but the effects would soon wear off.

"All right." Jack nodded once. "Mask up."

SEVENTY-FOUR

Wilbur stuck his tongue under his top lip and drilled Kent Wicksell with a look to kill.

If only he was a soldier again.

He tried to guess Kent's age. The man was probably young enough to have squeaked out of the Vietnam draft. Just as well. His kind would have run to Canada for sure with the rest of the cowards.

Kent and his sons. What a lowly bunch of humanity. God was supposed to love everybody. Looking at these pieces of scum, Wilbur found that hard to believe.

He looked at Bailey. Poor thing, sitting over there all by herself. Best little woman in the world after his Trudy. Now her café was shot up, and they'd told her *she* was to blame for them even coming here.

Rage burned through Wilbur's limbs.

The phone started ringing again. Kent smacked it on and off.

Wilbur pictured the carnage behind him. He'd seen enough when he was over against the wall. Just as well he wasn't looking at it now. The counter was a wreck. The top of his own stool was blown away. Only good thing about that was now Brad couldn't sit on it. The punk now parked himself on the second stool. Only one left in one piece.

Mitch jitter-paced in the middle of the café. That boy had some big kinda humdinger drug running through his veins. *Won't get it in jail, now, will ya?*

"Here, Mitch." Kent shoved a chair toward him. "Might as well take a load off." The chair slid to a stop two feet from Mitch. He pulled it over and sat down. His gun pointed straight ahead—which put it at Carla Radling's chest.

Oh yeah. These men were real brave.

Kent pushed to his feet, knocked his knuckles against his gun. "Everybody's so *quiet* in here. What's the matter, cat got your tongues?"

Wilbur's mouth opened before he knew it. "It ain't got mine." His voice rattled with phlegm like some old man's, which made him madder. He cleared his throat and jutted up his chin. Looked lowlife Kent Wicksell in the eye.

Kent snorted. "You always got somethin' to say, don'tcha?"

Mitch cut a curious look at Wilbur.

Wilbur's heart beat hard. Good for it. Triple bypass two years ago—and listen to the thing. He would have lived to be a hundred—if he'd had the chance.

"Yeah, I got somethin' to say, you lily-livered thumbsucker."

Brad sniggered.

"You want somebody to die first, it ain't gonna be Bailey. It's gonna be me."

SEVENTY-FIVE

Jack keyed his radio. "Edwards. We're moving in."

"Roger."

Jack put on his mask.

As usual, Lightning was the first one ready to go. He jigged his right leg, left hand on his hip as if to say, *Come on, why you guys so slow?* Jack ignored him—as Lightning expected. Jack tugged his mask in place, hearing the sudden closed-in sound of his own breathing, and picked up his M4. As point—first man in—Swank got the added privilege of carrying a sixteen-pound ballistic shield. It was already in his hand.

Jack looked each man over. All ready.

They fell into line and set out. Within forty seconds they would reach the corner of Second and Main. Ten more seconds, and they'd stop short of the first Java Joint window. The fact that the HTs had so cleverly blacked out the glass only served to help the good guys. Using hand signals, they would run past those first two windows without being spotted—and breach the door within seconds.

Jack and his team had one mission upon entering the building: shoot to kill the three HTs. No time for mercy, no "go for the leg to wound" like in some movie. They'd pored over photos of the hostages and HTs, committing the faces to memory. The diagram from the released teenagers, delivered to their mobile command post within minutes of the command to go tactical, provided further critical information. The team had studied the arrangement of the Java Joint tables, the most likely placement of the three HTs. No guarantee the men would still be in those positions, but their guns and faces would give them away.

Five seconds of stun time was all CRT needed.

Heart pumping, the familiar bulk of gear weighting his body, Jack ran up Second Street with his men, gloved hands firm on his weapon.

SEVENTY-SIX

Wilbur glared at Kent.

"No, Wilbur, don't!" Bailey cried. Other voices said, "*No!*" Paige swiveled in her chair, and shot him a wide-eyed gaze. Those pretty blue-green eyes. Wilbur had carried a soft spot for Paige since the day they met. She shook her head hard.

Well. Who'd-a known he had so many friends?

Kent surveyed Wilbur like he was a cootie under a rug. "Whatd'ya know. We got ourselves a hero."

"His stool's all shot up—he ain't got nothin' to live for," Brad crowed.

"Ha-ha-ha-ha!" Mitch laughed like some machine gun.

Wilbur cranked his stiff torso around to look Brad in his ugly mug. "Tell you somethin'. I wouldn't *want* to live if you was my son."

Brad's face contorted. He jerked his gun toward Wilbur. "You—"

"Shut up, Brad, ain't worth it," Kent said. Wilbur eased back to face him. Kent's mouth dragged down at the corners as they sized each other up. His eyes slitted. "You ready to meet your Maker, old man?"

The phone jangled. Anger pinched Kent's expression. He punched the button to connect and slammed the receiver on his table. "*There.* Now it ain't gonna ring anymore."

Paige kept shaking her head at Wilbur. Her cheeks looked pale and hollow.

Wilbur took a slow breath. "First of all, nobody calls me 'old man' but Preacher here." He gestured toward his buddy Pastor Hank. "After his years of puttin' up with my spotty attendance at church, he's earned the right."

Kent shrugged.

"Second, yeah, I'm ready. I done told God I'm sorry for everything I did wrong, and if He wants my soul today, He can have it. Don't mean I want to go yet. But I'm the oldest one here, so I'm your man."

Drat that Jake Tremaine—gone off on a trip this weekend. He was near as old as Wilbur. If he was in here, he coulda been the brave guy.

Except Jake was never brave a day in his life.

A sound seeped from Bailey. Wilbur looked over to see her eyes tear up. The sight nearly ripped his heart in two.

Kent sniffed. "You got a wife?"

Wilbur moved his jaw from side to side. "Yup. Best woman a man could ever find. Name's Gertrude. Called Trudy."

"Trudy, huh? What's she gonna say when she hears what you done?"

Wilbur made a sound in his throat. "She'll want to take the fryin' pan to my skull—if I wasn't already dead."

Mitch laughed. "I'd like to see that." He stood up, looked back at Kent. "I'm going to the bathroom." He headed for the hall, toting his gun. The bathroom door closed.

Kent stretched out his legs. "Maybe you'll live to see another day, old man. Long as your chief comes through."

"I ain't countin' on it. He ain't gonna let no killer outta jail."

Brad spewed curses.

Hank shook his head in warning at Wilbur.

Kent's eyes hooded like a snake's. He ran his fingers along his gun barrel. "You're not careful, you just might get yourself shot early."

Paige was still turned around in her chair, watching him. "Wilbur," she whispered, "don't—"

"Shut up!" Kent shot her a black look. "I ain't talkin' to *you*."

"Don't you talk to her like that!" Wilbur half rose.

"No, *stop!*" Paige gripped her forearms until they turned white. Her beautiful face looked hard and cold as stone. She shot Wilbur a look of pain and defeat, then turned her eyes on Kent. He stared at her, heavy eyebrows raised.

"Don't take him. Take *me*."

Bailey gasped. Wilbur grabbed on to the table. "Paige, sit *down!*"

If Bailey's tears had started the crack in Wilbur's heart, Paige finished it off. *Frank.* These evil men took her man from her. Grief welled up in Wilbur's chest so strong his legs went weak.

"Paige." Leslie reached across their table toward her, but she drew away.

Paige stared at Kent with cold defiance. Then her face crimped, and she pushed to her feet. "I hate you." Her mouth mushed and tears plopped out of her eyes. She took a step toward Kent. "I *hate* you, and I hope T.J. *rots* in jail."

Rage pulled Kent's back up straight as a stick. He yanked his gun off the table and swung the barrel toward her head.

SEVENTY-SEVEN

The police station line rang, and Roger jumped. He and the other men in the room had been intent on the monitor now that CRT was on their way. He could picture the men in their gear, running up Second—the same route he'd taken.

It rang again. Everyone else ignored it. Vince was still on his private phone until the bitter end. Wicksell had connected the line but wasn't responding. Roger almost let the station line keep ringing, until his sense of duty pulled his arm toward the phone. His eyes stayed on the screen.

"Kanner Lake Police Station, Officer Waitman." He spoke in low tones, not hiding his distraction. He backed up two steps from the transfixed group of men, peering at the monitor between the heads of Wiley and Justin.

"Hello." A female voice. Sounded fairly young. Nervous. "I, um ... I used to live in the building where Marya Whitbey lived. Died."

Wiley shifted on his feet, blocking the monitor. Roger moved a little to the right.

"Yes?"

"I saw the thing on the news a little while ago. That reporter reading the statement from T.J. Wicksell?"

"Kent?" Vince said into his receiver. "Come on, talk to me."

Nothing yet onscreen. *Under sixty seconds,* Roger thought. "Yes, I'm listening."

The young woman started to cry. "I'm s-sorry."

"It's all right. Take your time."

Judge Hadkin hit his palm with a fist. "They're going to come around the corner any minute."

The woman sniffed. "I'm just kind of scared. Maybe it's nothing, but ... With all those people being held in that coffee shop, I thought you should know. Maybe it would help somehow."

"We're happy to hear anything that might help."

"And the way he *looked* when he said it." Her voice trembled. "Totally cold and sort of smirking. Like he was proud of pulling off something big."

The words triggered Roger's instincts, pulling his attention away from the screen. "Who?"

Justin threw a curious glance over his shoulder at Roger.

"This friend of mine. We were watching the news. And when the reporter read about that T.J. guy seeing somebody running away down the hall? He said, 'That was me.'"

Roger's eyes cut to Lester Tranning's back. The defense attorney stood with head tilted to one side, fingers drumming against his thigh.

"Did he tell you why he was there?"

"I didn't ask, but it was like ... I was supposed to understand what he was saying. He freaked me out. I just shrugged and acted like I didn't get it."

"There they are!" Larry pointed.

On the monitor a CRT member's gas-masked head appeared as he checked around the corner building toward Java Joint.

"Kent?" Vince's voice remained calm. No giveaway from him of what was about to happen.

The CRT man swiped a hand forward in an all clear.

Roger's heart skipped a beat. One side of him whispered this phone call meant nothing. A wrong hunch on the woman's part—too little, too late. Or merely a sick joke by her friend. "Tell me what you think he was saying."

The CRT's lead man stepped around the corner, followed by a second . . . a third. Within two seconds the team was moving in a swift line down Main.

SEVENTY-EIGHT

At the edge of Java Joint's first window, Jack and his men halted. Jack's hands tightened around his weapon.

In front, Dust-up checked over his shoulder. Swank nodded. And Harley.

The three of them would run first—Swank, toting his shield, to the right of the entrance, Dust-up to the left. Harley gripped his twelve-gauge shotgun fit with an XM26—the lightweight modular accessory system attached beneath the M4's barrel, capable of firing frangible bullets to breach the door. Harley would shoot out the lock at a forty-five degree angle. The frangible ammo could blow down a door in seconds, turning to dust upon striking its target, so that no fragments could fly back at the shooter. Once the door was breached, Harley's weapon would transition to firing lethal bullets as he provided rear cover for the men going in.

Dust-up pointed to the door. He, Swank, and Harley bent low and ran into position. Jack and the other three men followed to stack behind Dust-up.

Jack's mind shifted into overdrive, picturing in the final second the sequence of actions.

Harley aims his shotgun at the proper angle and fires.

Java Joint's door locks blow apart.

Harley kicks in the door.

Dust-up rolls in the flash-bang followed by tear gas.

All seven men swivel their heads away, eyes closed.
The flash-bang explodes.
They storm inside, Swank in the lead ...
Harley lifted his weapon and aimed it at the door lock.
Now.

SEVENTY-NINE

Paige's body felt stone-cold numb. Death didn't matter. She welcomed it.

In the second that she saw Kent Wicksell reach for his gun, memories flashed through her mind. The day she arrived in Kanner Lake, lonely and terrified, fleeing her secret past. The first time—in this very café and with these very people—when she allowed herself to begin accepting the friendship they offered. The kindness on Bailey's face that day, in S-Man's voice. And Wilbur, most of all. He'd raised his shirt and proudly shown her the scar from his surgery. The others had moaned. But the look in Wilbur's eyes said so much more. He wasn't just showing off his battle wounds. He was saying, *See what I've been through? And I made it. Don't hide your own scars, Paige. Friends help friends heal.*

Kent swung his gun barrel at her and sprang to his feet. Rage rippled across his big face. "You gone and said the wrong thing, girl."

Time slowed. Paige looked at the barrel of the gun and felt nothing. Saw only Frank's face, remembered the sound of his voice ... their first date.... first kiss.

All gone.

"Paige, sit *down*." Wilbur's voice gruffed.

Her feet took another step toward Kent. "Go ahead, shoot me."

Leslie heaved a sob. "Paige, *please stop*."

The sights and sounds all came at once then. Bailey and Ted and Jared shouted at her. Brad shouted back. Kent yelled, "Shut *up*!"

Paige moved toward Kent.

Wilbur hustled to reach her. Brad shoved to his feet. "Stop!"

Kent's gun jerked.

Gunshots split the air.

Paige froze. Funny she didn't feel the bul—

The door blew open.

A canister rolled in.

Brad and Kent swung their guns around.

The room flashed like a thousand lightning bolts.

Exploded.

Paige toppled backward, stunned. As she hit the floor, Java Joint's bright, yawning doorway froze in her brain.

EIGHTY

Vince watched CRT rush into Java Joint, a fist pressed to his mouth, telephone forgotten, his back muscles like iron. None of the men in the office uttered a word.

The seconds ticked by, an eternity.

Roger had answered a phone call and faded out the door. Vaguely, Vince registered him standing out in the hall, talking to someone.

A blur of movement inside Java Joint. No way to make out what was happening.

Faces flashed in his head. Bailey, Wilbur. Leslie, S-Man. Bev, Pastor Hank, and Jared. Carla and Paige.

Please, Lord, don't let us lose any of them.

EIGHTY-ONE

"On the ground, on the ground!" Jack and his men swarmed inside Java Joint, their shouts muffled in the gas masks.

Jack saw Dust-up veer left. Swank jumped to the right with his shield and rammed a gunman—*Brad*—already staggering. Brad fell, loosening his grip on an MP5.

In an instant Jack took in the scene—dazed people at tables, a young woman and elderly man on the floor.

He aimed at Brad and fired.

Gunfire to the left. Jack swiveled around, saw Dust-up had taken down a second HT.

Kent.

The gunfire silenced.

The third, where was the third?

Swank and Goose ran for the hall.

Jack swung right, left, finger on the trigger.

One, two hostiles.

The *third*?

The stunned hostages started to move.

Tear gas expanded, seeking every square inch of space in the building. They needed to get the hostages outside.

Gunfire erupted down the hall. Jack sprinted toward Goose and Swank, Dust-up on his heels. *Radt-a-dat-a-dat.* Shots from inside the second room, closed door. *Bathroom.* The door splintered. Goose reeled back, hand flying to his leg.

Jack poured bullets through the bathroom door. Shots fired back. The lock gave way. Swank moved in with his shield, kicked in the door. Jumped back. The third hostile in the room—*Mitch*—fired at Swank. Bullets pinged against the shield. Jack ducked around Swank and let his own bullets fly.

The man jerked around like a wild marionette. His gun clattered against the wall. He collapsed across the toilet, then slid to the floor.

Sudden, stark silence. Jack could hear his own breathing.

He kicked aside the hostile's gun. Checked to make sure he was dead.

In the hallway Swank was helping Goose get up. Jack jabbed his finger toward the front—*Out, out, out!* Goose half limped, half ran up the hall, aided by Swank, Dust-up behind them. Jack followed and headed for the hostages.

Lightning and Harley were helping people up, looking for wounds. Tear gas clouded the air. Jack ran for the elderly man and young woman on the floor near Kent. The woman lay crumpled on her side.

Paige.

Dust-up set his gun on the floor and squatted down to aid the older man. *Wilbur.*

Jack helped Paige sit up. Her eyes were squeezed shut and watering. No sign of a bullet wound. Wilbur hacked and moaned. Older people, especially those suffering from emphysema or other lung problems, could be more affected by the gas. The man needed fresh air immediately. Dust-up pulled him to a sitting position, trying to get him on his feet.

Sudden sound behind Jack. Cursing, the scrape of a hard substance across the floor. Jack swiveled—and stared down the barrel of a gun.

EIGHTY-TWO

In the police station hallway, Roger listened to the woman on the phone.

His brain turned numb.

Tense whispers filtered from Vince's office. "Where *are* they?" "What's happening?" Roger barely noticed. He knew only that it was too late. If this caller was on the level—and she sounded like she was—it was too late to help the Wicksell men.

He turned toward the second office. "Thank you for calling." His voice sounded wooden. "Just hang on a minute, I'll need to take down your contact information."

"But I don't want . . ."

Roger reached the desk, picked up a pen. "I understand your concern. But you did the right thing. It's important that we check this out."

"I don't want him to know I called!" Fear pulsed in her tone.

"He doesn't need to know."

"But he *will*. I'm the one he said it to."

"If he bragged to you, he'll probably brag to others. We'll keep your name out of it." Roger poised the pen over the paper. "Please now. There are lives on the line."

But it's too late.

A long silence.

"Okay."

Roger wrote down her information.

EIGHTY-THREE

I'm dead.

Jack froze.

An eternal second spun out. Kent raise up on one shaky elbow, aiming Dust-Up's weapon. His neck muscles were rigid, face red with anger, eyes watering.

All those bullet holes in his chest. *How* was he still moving?

Regrets flooded Jack's brain. His wife, his daughters. He wouldn't live to see his girls go off to college, get married—

Paige screamed.

Dust-up jerked around.

Jack heaved to the right.

Kent pulled the trigger.

Dust-up yelled through his gas mask. He leapt up, kicked the gun from the hostile's hand. Kent's elbow gave way. He slammed back to the floor, writhing.

Lightning sprinted over, aimed point-blank between Kent's eyes and fired.

Kent's body twitched, then stilled.

Jack's heart nearly beat out of his ribs.

Dust-up cursed, snatched up his gun. Stuck the barrel in Kent's chest and pumped out more bullets.

Jack pushed to his feet, shouting in his mask. "Dust-up, stop! He's dead."

Dust-up paid no heed, terror and shock and rage burning in his eyes. Jack's death would have been *his* fault.

The CRT commander gripped him hard by the shoulders. "Stop! We've got to get the hostages out!"

Dust-up's eyes cleared. He blinked, shrugged out of Jack's grasp. Kicked Kent's body hard, looked around for any other unsecured weapons, then turned back to Wilbur.

Jack took a deep breath. His pulse still ran double time.

Later in debriefing, he and his men would assess what went wrong. Now they still had work to do.

He checked around for his other team members. Signaled them a thumbs-up.

Swank had put down his shield to help the hostages. Jack recognized a blur of white, shell-shocked faces from their photos. Hank ... Leslie ... Ted ... They all helped one another up, holding on to each other. In their own addled states, most didn't seem to realize Jack had nearly lost his life. One woman (*Bailey*) grabbed onto his arm and spewed thank-yous, even through her coughs and tears.

Where was Goose? They had to get him to a hospital.

It's over. We did it.

You're alive.

As the knowledge sank in, Jack felt the familiar energy drop of a mission completed. But no time for emotion now. He had to get out of there, peel off his mask, and radio an all-clear to Vince. Minutes later, cars and ambulances would come swooping down. He'd need to help.

Images of his daughters' faces crowded Jack's head as he hurried to help the battle-weary hostages out of Java Joint.

EIGHTY-FOUR

Vince skidded his vehicle to a stop on Main and ran down the pavement toward the ragtag, hacking hostages.

Bailey had collapsed on the curb, shoulders sagging and legs askew in the street. Carla slumped beside her. Vince stooped down in front of them.

"Bailey, Carla. You all right?"

They blinked at him, eyes watering and noses running. "M-my throat burns." Carla still looked half in shock.

He nodded. "That's normal. It'll pass. Medical teams are on their way to check you over." He heard the sirens. "There they are now."

Bailey grabbed his arm. "John! Is he okay?"

John. Vince gave her a wan smile. "Haven't talked to him in a while, but I'm sure he's fine. You'll see him real soon."

"The girls?" Carla swallowed hard.

"They're fine. With Ali's parents."

Carla's eyes closed. She hitched in a breath. "What about Angie?"

"They took her to the hospital to check out her heart."

Vince heard crying farther down the sidewalk. He pushed to his feet and spotted Leslie, Paige, and S-Man. In the street, one of the CRT men was attending to Wilbur, Pastor Hank looking on. Jared held a shivering Bev.

Sirens shrieked, then died away. Vince turned to see two ambulances at the intersection at Second. A third pulled in behind. EMTs jumped out.

"Over here!" Jack yelled at a medical team. He stood by one of his men who lay on the sidewalk, one leg bloodied. Vince trotted over. "He going to be all right?"

"Yeah. A leg wound, bleeding pretty bad, but no main artery hit." Jack's face looked pinched. Vince understood. He knew what it felt like to have a man down.

The EMTs drew near. Vince backed off and let them work on their patient.

He looked back to the sound of sobs. Leslie held Paige in both arms, Paige's head against her chest. They rocked back and forth. Paige's shoulders heaved.

Frank.

He hurried over to them. S-Man's face was drawn and haggard.

"Paige." Vince touched her head. She shrugged him away. Leslie turned helpless, bloodshot eyes upon him.

"Listen, Paige." He placed both hands on her shoulders. Nudged her away from Leslie. "Have you heard about Frank? He came through surgery. He's in critical care, but they feel real good about his recovery."

Leslie's eyes rounded, and Ted tilted his head up toward the heavens. Paige swiveled her head to Vince, her mouth hanging open, hair stuck against her cheek. "He's *alive*?" The words croaked.

"Yes. And I'm sure he can't wait to see you."

More sirens keened.

Paige fell still, as if the slightest movement might change his story. She stared at him. "But ... but he was ..."

"Shot three times. But they all missed his heart. He's alive because John pulled him to safety and we were able to get him to a hospital in time."

Paige wailed long and loud. Heads turned. Pastor Hank started toward her. Wilbur pushed an EMT away and wrestled up on his elbows. "Go help that girl before she does something stupid; I'm fine!"

"She just found out Frank's alive, Wilbur!" S-Man swiped his watering eyes with the back of his hand.

"Oh!" Bailey and Carla gasped. They pushed to their feet and stumbled toward Paige, Ted, and Leslie, arms out, breaking into sobs. Vince stepped out of their way. They needed this.

The five of them hugged each other, then moved down the curb into the road. The EMT helped Wilbur up, and he, Pastor Hank, Bev, and Jared met them in the middle of the street. All nine rescued hostages threw their arms around one another, some still coughing, but managing to laugh and cry at the same time.

Vince's eyes burned. Energy rushed out of him like air from a popped balloon. He sat heavily on the curb. For the first time since the phone call from dispatch that morning, he let his head drop into his hands and *breathed.*

PART FOUR

Rebuilding

EIGHTY-FIVE

T.J. Wicksell lowered his aching body carefully into the plastic chair behind the Plexiglas, trying not to wince. His right arm felt heavy in the cast. His cracked ribs had hurt most of all. Even after a month they were still sore.

The visiting area smelled of dust and sweat and hopelessness. Like always.

He peered at his mom on the other side and tried to smile.

She looked ten years older. Used to be so pretty. Now just looked worn out. She placed her palm against the glass, and he did the same. His hand was way bigger than hers.

They picked up their phones.

"Hi, Mom."

Suddenly nothing else would come; the words all gummed together way deep inside him.

"Hi. It's so good to see you." She started to cry.

No, don't.

T.J. pushed the emotions down. *Feel those, man, and you die.*

He waited until her breathing evened out. "Thanks for coming. I know it's a long drive."

She shrugged. "I made it in three and a half hours."

It would be a long day for her, driving all the way down, then back. To an empty house.

But at least she could leave. At least she was free. He had to go back to a prison cell.

Last time, his dad and Mitch and Brad had come with her to see him.

It was so hard, believing the three of them were gone. Day in, day out, his life hadn't changed. Even during this visit he could tell himself they were all just busy. Mitch was high, and Brad was out chasing women, and Dad was selling parts for somebody's old pickup. They'd come next time.

If he really thought about it, if he let himself picture his mother *all alone* day after day in their house—because of him—he'd curl up and die.

He fingered the plastic receiver in his hand. "I saw you on TV."

"Which time?"

"When you were talking about the guy who said he was the one running away from Marya's apartment. The guy whose girlfriend called the police."

His mother closed her eyes, a sick expression on her face. "I was so sure he was the one. *Finally*, I thought. After . . . it was the one bit of hope I could hold on to."

Guilt bubbled up in him. How'd the lid come off? He rattled around inside himself, trying to clamp it back on.

"It was so unfair." His mom drew in the sides of her mouth. "Why would somebody tease about something like that? Why would somebody just *make it up*?"

The lid still wasn't working too good. T.J. shifted in his chair. If only the running guy could be for real. He lifted a shoulder. "Doubt he expected his girlfriend to call the police."

His mom stared at her lap for a long time. Her shoulders looked so thin. T.J. found a black mark on the wall below the Plexiglas to stare at.

"Well, I'm still looking." Her voice took on an edge. She leaned forward until he raised his eyes. Her jaw flexed. "I'll look forever, T.J. The real killer's out there somewhere. Knowing he did what you're being punished for. I was on TV again—after the police questioned the man who teased his girlfriend about being there—and his alibi checked out. Did you see me that time? Had a whole hour session with a reporter. He got to ask me anything he wanted, long as I could tell everybody there *is* a *real* running man out there somewhere, and I'm going to find him." Her eyes teared. "It's all I got now, T.J.—proving your innocence."

Her chin quivered. She covered her eyes with one hand.

T.J. pulled himself in, like trying to fit in the little crawl space under their front porch when he was a kid. He tucked his shoulders and tightened his thighs. Pictured his insides drawing up like a cocoon around his heart. That's how you lived with yourself in prison. That's how you survived.

Especially when your lies cost three members of your family.

His throat felt raw. "I never meant to hurt you, Mom."

Even though Marya deserved it, saying no to me. Pushing me away.

His mother dropped her hand. "*You* never hurt me. The system did. The man who killed Marya did. It's not your fault, T.J. You're the one thing that keeps me going."

Guilt bubbled out of the pain again, and he scrambled to crash down the lid. Had to push on it—hard. He nailed it in place on four sides.

"You're the one thing that keeps me going." His mom needed that. He could never, ever take it away from her.

T.J. lifted his casted arm and spread his palm against the glass. "Don't worry, Mom, I'll always be here for you. I won't ever let you down."

His mom gave him a sad smile. She matched his handprint with her own and pressed until her fingers turned white.

EIGHTY-SIX

The morning sun shone on Bailey's face as she and John walked hand in hand toward the new and freshly painted red door of Java Joint. Before they'd left home, Bailey had the presence of mind to stuff her purse with tissues. She needed one already, just looking at her café.

"You know, I like this new door better." John smiled as he pulled out the key. "Nice bright color."

"Me too."

In the past four weeks, Bailey had wept again and again at the outpouring of love her friends and neighbors displayed. The owner of the building repaired the windows and door amazingly fast. Donations of money and volunteered time ensured that she and John wouldn't have to pay a penny of their business insurance deductible to replace their own property. In fact, she'd had enough extra money to outfit Java Joint with the latest in espresso machines and equipment, not to mention fancier stools.

The stores on the opposite side of Main were also being cleaned up in a hurry. Townsfolk simply couldn't bear to see the damage day after day. Simple Pleasures looked beautiful once more, inside and out. Even with her recovering left arm, Sarah had managed to create new displays, mostly giving orders while her husband and Paige and a few other friends did the work.

Bailey and John stepped into the café. She gazed at the round tables and chairs all in place, the new Formica countertop, this one a light blue. The room just sparkled, as if it couldn't wait to host the celebration they'd waited four weeks to complete.

Now it would be more of a celebration than ever.

Java Joint would not officially open for two more days. Bailey and John wanted this special party to be private, with a few extra invited guests. The rest of the Scenes and Beans gang had agreed.

After taking a vote, they'd also agreed to no longer post on the blog. After all that had happened, their hearts just weren't in it. Bailey deleted all of the interchange between Kent and Vince, then she wrote a final post, explaining the decision to their readers. For now Scenes and Beans would remain up, with all its previous posts. She didn't know just yet when she would take it down.

John shut the door and pocketed the key. He looked around, admiring all the handiwork. Nodding his head. Bailey squeezed his arm.

She checked the wall clock—one of her possessions that had survived the conflict without a scratch. Eight forty-five. In fifteen minutes everyone would be gathering.

Bailey walked around the counter to start her preparations. John followed, stooping down to check that the wrapped box still lay on its shelf. S-Man's new pen, recovered from Main Street, had managed to find its way back into John's hands. He'd saved it for this day.

John straightened. "Amazing that he'll get to sign those contracts with this after all."

"Can't wait to see him do it."

The publisher of *Starfire* had sent new copies of the contract after hearing the first batch had been scattered by bullets. S-Man could have signed them days ago but asked if the publisher wouldn't mind waiting until this morning. No problem, came the reply. Plans for Book One were forging ahead in the meantime. In fact, the publisher was even more excited. *Star-fire* had received national attention through news accounts of the attack on Java Joint. The publisher now believed it would sell more copies than ever. An "early buzz," they called it.

At nine o'clock the gang started arriving. By nine fifteen Java Joint flowed with voices, laughter, some tears—and coffee. All the Scenes and Beans bloggers were there except Angie, who was recuperating after surgery. Bailey knew David had hardly left her side since the triple bypass—in the hospital and once she got home. "He's a great nurse," Angie told her over the phone. "I've decided he'll make a great husband too."

Bailey had slapped a hand to her heart. She *knew* it!

Carla brought Scott Cambry to the party—Brittany's biological father, who was visiting from his home in Washington. Even as Bailey foamed their drinks—Carla's usual latte and a caramel mocha for Scott—she watched them from the corner of her eye. There was another couple she sensed was headed in the right direction.

After all these years, wouldn't that be something, God. The surprises you come up with.

Vince and Nancy Edwards had been invited, as well as Roger and Camille Waitman. Jim and Al were on duty. Frank was recovering from his bullet wounds and surgery. He was out of the hospital and now expected to heal completely, but it would be a long process. Like David with Angie, Paige had spent a lot of time at Frank's bedside.

"How are you, Vince?" Bailey asked as she poured him coffee in a biggie cup. Nancy was across the room, talking to Pastor Hank and Janet. Vince's regular drink was the same as Wilbur's—black, no sugar. Bailey looked deep into his eyes, signaling she wanted an honest answer.

Surprise flicked across Vince's face. "I'm okay."

"You sure? 'Cause you don't fool me. Calm as you look on the outside, I know these things weigh on you as much as anybody."

He drew a long breath. "Yeah. But that's okay. Keeps me praying."

"I understand that. Me too."

"And how are *you*?"

Bailey pulled her top lip between her teeth. "Better. The nightmares are gone. Like you say, prayer helps. In fact, prayer is *everything*." Her vision blurred. "We could have lost so many people this time, Vince. We came so close. But we didn't. Not a *one*."

His jaw moved back and forth. "I know." He picked up his drink. "Thank God."

She swallowed. "Thank God."

Bailey thought of John's part in the trauma but said nothing. It had all been said. John had apologized a dozen times for visiting the Wicksell house. He could have gotten someone in Java Joint killed. Nearly did. But he also saved Frank.

Leslie sidled up to Vince, nursing a biggie latte in her right hand and holding out her left, fingers pointed down. "Seen it yet?"

Vince smiled, and his face softened. "No. But I sure heard about it enough. Let me get a gander at this rock." He grasped her hand, pulling it close to examine the half-carat diamond. "Wow. Bet that's being paid for out of advance money."

She grinned. "Yeah, when he finally gets the check. Signing the contracts will *help*." She flicked a look at the ceiling. "Right now it's on credit."

After all the trauma, Leslie had postponed leaving for her new job in Seattle until next week—plenty of time for S-Man to find the right ring. No wedding date yet—but that would be decided soon.

Bev sidled up to the counter next to the third stool, occupied by Jake. "Have time to make my drink now, Bailey?"

That would be a biggie latte. "You bet."

"See how I beat you here, woman?" Wilbur leaned around Jake to mug at Bev. "Didn't trust you not to take my new stool."

Jake hitched his shoulders. "Don't blame ya." He'd heard about the stool-stealing escapade. He pulled his ever-present red baseball cap lower over his big ears.

"Oh, for heaven's sake, Wilbur." Bev hefted her chin in disapproval. "You act like some king sitting there. As if all our troubles haven't taught you there are more important things in life."

He raised his gray eyebrows with a regal stare. "Who says I *ain't* king?"

Jake chuckled.

She huffed. "Well, at least you won't be the only one in here with a scar on your chest. Once Angie feels good enough to come back, hers will be newer than yours."

Wilbur folded his arms. "You really think she's gonna go 'round *showing* it, woman?"

Bev's mouth opened, then closed. She made a point of turning away as her powdered cheeks flushed.

Wilbur shot Jake a victorious look and wagged his head.

Bailey poured Bev's drink and fitted it with a plastic lid. "Wilbur, all I can say is—it's a good thing Trudy didn't come after you with that frying pan. Things just wouldn't be the same around here."

He hunched over the counter. "Don't think she ain't tried a few times."

"That's whatcha get for wantin' to be a hero." Jake lifted his coffee cup. "You'd-a gone on a trip that weekend, your wife would be kissin' on you all day."

Wilbur's mouth twitched. "Don't think she ain't done that too."

Bailey looked across the café, checking to see who hadn't been served. Carla, Scott, and Paige were laughing with Sarah, who was brightly dressed as usual—today in bold yellow. It was so good to see Paige smile again. Sarah's left arm was out of the sling, but Bailey could tell it still gave her pain. All four of them held drinks.

Her gaze fell on Jared Moore. He was talking to Roger and John.

"Jared!"

He turned toward her. "Yes, ma'am."

"Ready for your drink?" She smiled. "You're the last one."

"You bet."

Bailey caught John's eye and motioned with her head. He excused himself from the trio and walked over, coffee cup in hand.

Wilbur and Jake leaned in, always ready to eavesdrop. "You two." She feigned a stern look in their direction.

As John reached the counter, she pulled the gift box from the shelf underneath. "I've got one more latte." She handed John the present.

He winked at her.

Two minutes later John's voice boomed through the café. "Okay, everybody, time to gather at the counter. I hear S-Man has some contracts to sign."

"Yahoo!" Leslie crowed.

Ted looked around. "Let's do it." He was trying to keep his poker face, but Bailey could see the smile brush his lips. He picked his black computer case off a table and pulled out the contracts. Held them high.

"Come on over here and have a seat." John plunked the present on the counter near the first stool. "You need to open this before you sign."

"All *right*." Ted started unwrapping the gift.

"Whatd'ya say, S-Man?" Jake grinned, knowing the answer.

He tossed the paper aside and opened the box. "I say *wuchak, rikoyoch*."

Thanks, friends, in Saurian.

He held up the pen. "Oh. Beautiful." He smiled at John. "Thank you. It's perfect."

Bailey started clapping as S-Man put pen to the first contract page. Leslie set down her drink and joined in. Everyone else did the same. Soon they were whooping and hollering as they applauded.

This is where we were four weeks ago, Lord. And here we are again. By Your grace, dear Jesus. By Your grace.

"Remember, it's going to take awhile." S-Man had to shout over the din. "I've got to initial every page and sign at the end—all three copies."

"Then we'll clap a *long* time," Paige cried. "Until you finish every one!"

And they did.

ACKNOWLEDGMENTS

My deep gratitude once again to Tony Lamanna for his help with all of the police work issues in this story. In law enforcement since 1969, Tony is the former chief of police of Spirit Lake, Idaho, and now diligently serves as school resource officer in his own town of Priest Lake. He is a nationally certified hostage negotiator. Tony patiently answered months of questions about the complexity of negotiations, command posts, and the way SWAT teams work. If you found an error or simplification in *Amber Morn*, it was entirely my doing. Sometimes the pace of a story demands that not every detail be presented.

Tony, I could not have written the Kanner Lake series without you.

Thanks once again also to Stuart Stockton, aspiring science fiction novelist who has allowed me to use his manuscript, *Starfire*, for S-Man. Stuart has also written all of the S-Man posts for the Scenes and Beans blog, which chronicle the creation of his Saurian world and his writing of the novel. I look forward to the day when *Starfire* is published.

To Marilyn and Terry Cooper, owners of the real Simple Pleasures in Coeur d'Alene, Idaho, thank you again for allowing me to use your beautiful store in this series. Uh, sorry for the damage in this book. But I fixed it for you.

Brink of Death

Brandilyn Collins

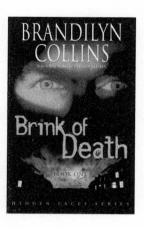

The noises, faint, fleeting, whispered into her consciousness like wraiths in the night.

Twelve-year-old Erin Willit opened her eyes to darkness lit only by the dim green night-light near her closet door and the faint glow of a street lamp through her front window. She felt her forehead wrinkle, the fingers of one hand curl as she tried to discern what had awakened her.

Something was not right . . .

Annie Kingston moves to Grove Landing for safety and quiet — and comes face-to-face with evil.

When neighbor Lisa Willet is killed by an intruder in her home, sheriff's detectives are left with little evidence. Lisa's daughter, Erin, saw the killer, but she's too traumatized to give a description. The detectives grow desperate.

Because of her background in art, Annie is asked to question Erin and draw a composite. But Annie knows little about forensic art or the sensitive interview process. A nonbeliever, she finds herself begging God for help. What if her lack of experience leads Erin astray? The detectives could end up searching for a face that doesn't exist.

Leaving the real killer free to stalk the neighborhood . . .

Softcover: 0-310-25103-6

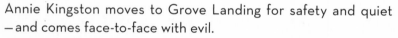

Pick up a copy today at your favorite bookstore!

ZONDERVAN®
.com

Stain of Guilt

Brandilyn Collins

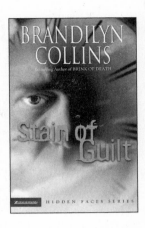

As I drew, the house felt eerie in its silence. . . . A strange sense stole over me, as though Bland and I were two actors on stage, our movements spotlighted, black emptiness between us. But that darkness grew smaller as the space between us shrank. I did not know if this sense was due to my immersion in Bland's face and mind and world, or to my fear of his threatening presence.

Or both . . .

The nerves between my shoulder blades began to tingle.

Help me, God. Please.

For twenty years, a killer has eluded capture for a brutal double murder. Now, forensic artist Annie Kingston has agreed to draw the updated face of Bill Bland for the popular television show *American Fugitive.*

To do so, Annie must immerse herself in Bland's traits and personality. A single habitual expression could alter the way his face has aged. But as she descends into his criminal mind and world, someone is determined to stop her. At any cost. Annie's one hope is to complete the drawing and pray it leads authorities to Bland — before Bland can get to her.

Softcover: 0-310-25104-4

Pick up a copy today at your favorite bookstore!

Dead of Night

Brandilyn Collins

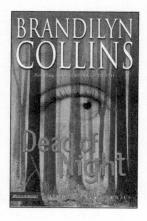

All words fell away. I pushed myself off the path, noticing for the first time the signs of earlier passage—the matted earth, broken twigs. And I knew. My mouth turned cottony.

I licked my lips, took three halting steps. My maddening, visual brain churned out pictures of colorless faces on a cold slab—Debbie Lille, victim number one; Wanda Deminger, number three . . . He'd been here. Dragged this one right where I now stumbled. I'd entered a crime scene, and I could not bear to see what lay at the end. . . .

This is a story about evil.
This is a story about God's power.

A string of murders terrorizes citizens in the Redding, California, area. The serial killer is cunning, stealthy. Masked by day, unmasked by night. Forensic artist Annie Kingston discovers the sixth body practically in her own backyard. Is the location a taunt aimed at her?

One by one, Annie must draw the unknown victims for identification. Dread mounts. Who will be taken next? Under a crushing oppression, Annie and other Christians are driven to pray for God's intervention as they've never prayed before.

With page-turning intensity, *Dead of Night* dares to pry open the mind of evil. Twisted actions can wreak havoc on earth, but the source of wickedness lies beyond this world. Annie learns where the real battle takes place—and that a Christian's authority through prayer is the ultimate, unyielding weapon.

Softcover: 0-310-25105-2

Pick up a copy today at your favorite bookstore!

Web of Lies

Brandilyn Collins

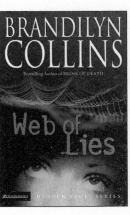

*She was washing dishes when her world
began to blur.*

*Chelsea Adams hitched in a breath,
her skin pebbling. She knew the dreaded
sign all too well. God was pushing a vision
into her consciousness.*

*Black dots crowded her sight. She
dropped a plate, heard it crack against the porcelain sink. Her
fingers fumbled for the faucet. The hiss of water ceased.*

God, I don't want this. Please!

After witnessing a shooting at a convenience store, forensic artist Annie Kingston must draw a composite of the suspect. But
before she can begin, she hears that Chelsea Adams wants to
meet with her — now. Chelsea Adams — the woman who made
national headlines with her visions of murder. And this vision is
by far the most chilling.

Chelsea and Annie soon find themselves snared in a terrifying
battle against time, greed, and a deadly opponent. If they tell the
police, will their story be believed? With the web of lies thicken-
ing, and lives ultimately at stake, who will know enough to stop
the evil?

Softcover: 0-310-25106-0

Pick up a copy today at your favorite bookstore!

Eyes of Elisha

Brandilyn Collins

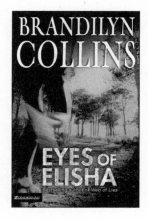

The murder was ugly.
The killer was sure no one saw him.
Someone did.

In a horrifying vision, Chelsea Adams has relived the victim's last moments. But who will believe her? Certainly not the police, who must rely on hard evidence. Nor her husband, who barely tolerates Chelsea's newfound Christian faith. Besides, he's about to hire the man who Chelsea is certain is the killer to be a vice president in his company.

Torn between what she knows and the burden of proof, Chelsea must follow God's leading and trust him for protection. Meanwhile, the murderer is at liberty. And he's not about to take Chelsea's involvement lying down.

Softcover: 0-310-23968-0

Pick up a copy today at your favorite bookstore!

Dread Champion

Brandilyn Collins

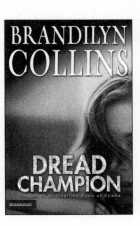

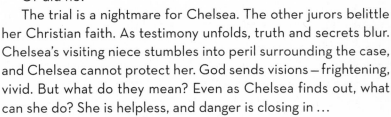

Chelsea Adams has visions. But they have no place in a courtroom.

As a juror for a murder trial, Chelsea must rely only on the evidence. And this circumstantial evidence is strong — Darren Welk killed his wife.

Or did he?

The trial is a nightmare for Chelsea. The other jurors belittle her Christian faith. As testimony unfolds, truth and secrets blur. Chelsea's visiting niece stumbles into peril surrounding the case, and Chelsea cannot protect her. God sends visions — frightening, vivid. But what do they mean? Even as Chelsea finds out, what can she do? She is helpless, and danger is closing in …

Masterfully crafted, *Dread Champion* is a novel in which appearances can deceive and the unknown can transform the meaning of known facts. One man's guilt or innocence is just a single link in a chain of hidden evil … and God uses the unlikeliest of people to accomplish His purposes.

Softcover: 0-310-23827-7

Cast a Road before Me

Brandilyn Collins

A course-changing event in one's life can happen in minutes. Or it can form slowly, a primitive webbing splaying into fingers of discontent, a minuscule trail hardening into the sinewed spine of resentment. So it was with the mill workers as the heat-soaked days of summer marched on.

City girl Jessie, orphaned at sixteen, struggles to adjust to life with her barely known aunt and uncle in the tiny town of Bradleyville, Kentucky. Eight years later (1968), she plans on leaving—to follow in her revered mother's footsteps of serving the homeless. But the peaceful town she's come to love is about to be tragically shattered. Threats of a labor strike rumble through the streets, and Jessie's new love and her uncle are swept into the maelstrom. Caught between the pacifist teachings of her mother and these two men, Jessie desperately tries to deny that Bradleyville is rolling toward violence and destruction.

Softcover: 0-310-25327-6

Pick up a copy today at your favorite bookstore!

Color the Sidewalk for Me

Brandilyn Collins

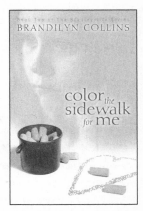

As a chalk-fingered child, I had worn my craving for Mama's love on my sleeve. But as I grew, that craving became cloaked in excuses and denial until slowly it sank beneath my skin to lie unheeded but vital, like the sinews of my framework. By the time I was a teenager, I thought the gap between Mama and me could not be wider.

And then Danny came along. . . .

A splendidly colored sidewalk. Six-year-old Celia presented the gift to her mother with pride—and received only anger in return. Why couldn't Mama love her? Years later, when once-in-a-lifetime love found Celia, her mother opposed it. The crushing losses that followed drove Celia, guilt-ridden and grieving, from her Bradleyville home.

Now thirty-five, she must return to nurse her father after a stroke. But the deepest need for healing lies in the rift between mother and daughter. God can perform such a miracle. But first Celia and Mama must let go of the past—before it destroys them both.

Softcover: 0-310-24242-8

Pick up a copy today at your favorite bookstore!

Capture the Wind for Me

Brandilyn Collins

One thing I have learned. The bonfires of change start with the merest spark. Sometimes we see that flicker. Sometimes we blink in surprise at the flame only after it has marched hot legs upward to fully ignite. Either way, flicker or flame, we'd better do some serious praying. When God's on the move in our lives, He tends to burn up things we'd just as soon keep.

After her mama's death, sixteen-year-old Jackie Delham is left to run the household for her daddy and two younger siblings. When Katherine King breezes into town and tries to steal her daddy's heart, Jackie knows she must put a stop to it. Katherine can't be trusted. Besides, one romance in the family is enough, and Jackie is about to fall headlong into her own.

As love whirls through both generations, the Delhams are buffeted by hope, elation, and loss. Jackie is devastated to learn of old secrets in her parents' relationship. Will those past mistakes cost Jackie her own love? And how will her family ever survive if Katherine jilts her daddy and leaves them in mourning once more?

Softcover: 0-310-24243-6

Pick up a copy today at your favorite bookstore!

ZONDERVAN®
.com

Be sure to read Brandilyn Collins' next exciting novel, *Vain Empires* — here's a sample

ONE

"Ever hear the dead knocking?"

Leland Hugh watches the forensic psychiatrist ease back, no reaction on the man's lined, learned face. His body lists to one side, left elbow supporting the fist under his sagging jowl. Legs spread apart, right fingers across his thigh. The picture of unshakable confidence.

"No, can't say I have."

Hugh nods once and gazes at the floor. "I do. At night, always at night."

"Why do they knock?"

His eyes raise to look straight into the doctor's. "They want my soul."

No response but for a mere inclining of the head. The intentional silence pulses, waiting for an explanation. Psychiatrists are good at that.

"I took theirs, you see. Put them in their graves early." Deep inside Hugh, the anger and fear begin to swirl. He swallows, voice tightening. "They're supposed to *stay* in the grave. Who'd ever think the dead would demand their revenge?"

From outside the door, at the windows, in the closet, in the walls — they used to knock. Now, in his jail cell the noises come from beneath the floor. Harassing, insistent, hate-filled and bitter sounds that pound his ears and drill his brain until sleep will not, *can not* come.

"Do you ever answer?"

Shock twists Hugh's lips. "*Answer?*"

The psychiatrist's face remains placid. The slight, knowing curve to his mouth makes Hugh want to slug him.

"You think they're not real, don't you? That in my room if I'd just pad-
ded over and opened the door, no one would have been there. I'd have
seen it's all in my imagination." He wags his head, steepling his fingers
together with mocking erudition. "Yes, esteemed colleagues." He affects
a serious, highbrow voice. "I have determined the subject suffers from
EGS—Extreme Guilt Syndrome, the roots of which run so deep as never
to be extirpated, with symptoms aggrandizing into myriad areas of the
subject's life and resulting in perceived paranormal phenomena."

He drops both hands in his lap, lowering his chin to look derisively at
the good doctor. The man remains unfazed.

Hugh sniffs. "Do you know, Doc, that psychosomatic pain hurts just as
much as pain caused by actual physical trauma?"

"Yes, I believe that's true."

"Then what difference does it make?" Hugh surges forward, palms
planted on his knees. His tone falls to one of cold steel. He is sick of the
psychiatrist's face, sick of these sessions in this nasty, dirty little room.
"If mere guilt makes the dead knock, I hear them just as clearly. I am still
reduced to a trembling idiot who can do nothing but pull the bed covers
over my head." Indignation pushes Hugh to his feet. "And they taunt me too.
Whispering of the symbolic clues I left behind, insisting the explicit actions
to which I was driven became my downfall." He throws his hands toward
the ceiling. "I *hate* them, every one. I wish I could *kill* them all over again!"

The gray-haired doctor inhales slowly. "Yet you do feel guilt for their
murders."

"No, I don't! Why should I? They *deserved* it."

He slumps back into his chair.

~~He slumps back into his chair.~~ He paces the room.

~~He slumps back into his chair. He paces the room.~~

~~The psychiatrist.~~

~~Hugh's hands fist,~~

~~He cannot~~

~~He can only~~

~~He~~

328

"Aaghh!" Novelist Darell Brooke smacked his keyboard and shoved away from the desk. All concentration drained from his mind like water from a leaky pan.

His characters froze.

Darell lowered his head, raking gnarled fingers into the front of his scalp. For a time there he'd almost had it—that ancient joy of thoughts flowing and fingers typing. In the last hour he'd managed to write three or four paragraphs. Now—nothing.

Absolutely nothing.

King of Suspense. He laughed, a low bitter sound that singed his throat. Ninety-nine novels written in forty-three years. Well over a hundred million copies sold. Twenty-one major motion pictures made from his books. Countless magazine articles about his career, fan letters, invitations to celebrity parties. Now look at him. Two years after the auto accident and still only half mobile. And wielding a mere fraction of the brain power he used to have.

What good is an author who can't hold a plot in his head?

Darell stared at the monitor, reading over his words, struggling once more to settle into the story. Pictured the psychiatrist, his killer ...

No use.

Face it, old man. You'll never write that hundredth book. You've been put out to pasture for good.

He wrenched his eyes from the screen, reached for his shiny black cane. With effort, he pushed himself out of his leather chair to unsteady feet. The broken bones in his leg and ankle had long since healed, but the ligament damage had not. Despite painful physical therapy his left foot never regained its full flexibility. Amazing—the constant flexing of a foot to maintain equilibrium. He hadn't realized the importance of those muscles and tendons until his were torn apart.

Daryl shuffled across the hardwood floor of his large office, repelled by his writing desk and computer. Every day they wooed, then betrayed him. At the tall, mullioned window near the far corner he stopped, spread his feet wide. Hunched over, both hands on his cane, he brooded over the green rolling hills of his estate, the untamed and capricious Pacific Ocean in the distance.

He used to go to the beach to write a couple times a week. Tapping his laptop keys as the surf pounded in rhythm to his pulse. Now he never left the house except for doctor's appointments.

Darell Brooke had no use for a world that no longer had use for him.

The sides of Darell's mouth moved in and out, puckering and unpuckering his lips. Characters' faces in shadow, snippets of scenes filtered through his mind. Fredda Lee. Now there was a delectable killer. Or Leland Stone with his black hair and eyebrows, an intimidating figure much as Darell had appeared in his younger days. *Black Tie Affair*, that was Leland's book.

No. Not right.

Midnight Madness?

Darell shook his head. He used to know. Before the accident, he remembered every story he'd written, every character.

"You knocked your skull pretty badly," the doctor told Darell as he watched the hospital room spiral from his bed. "The dizziness will pass, but you might find it hard to concentrate ..."

As if drifting outside his body, Darell pictured himself standing in front of his office window, a shell of his former indomitable self. The undisputed King of Suspense had reveled in playing the part. Now there was no part to play. That once stern, arrogant countenance—blank-faced. His black hair now an unruly shock of white. The wild gray brows jutting over his deep set, dark eyes no longer intimidating, merely straw-like. The muscular arms—even into his early seventies—sagging. Straight back now bent.

"Pshhh." His lips curled.

Slowly, with defiance Darell raised his chin.

He focused through the glass once more. At least the gnarled trees on his property still looked formidable, their branches scratching windows in the wind. And his mansion looked just as severe from afar, with its black shutters and multiple wings and gables. From the outside looking in, people would never guess ...

Darell turned, glared across the room at the phone near his computer. On impulse he clomped over to it, picked up the receiver. His thick forefinger hovered over the keys.

What was the number? The one he'd dialed countless times, year after year.

He lowered himself to the edge of his chair, flipped through his Rolodex. *There.*

Malcolm Featherling, agent to the country's top writers, answered his private line on the third ring. Clipped tone, terse greeting. Malcolm was always pushed for time.

"Hello, Malcolm. Just checking in to give you an update." Darell pushed the old confidence into his voice. After all, his agent worked for *him*, not the other way around.

"Well, Darell, nice to hear from you. It *has* been three days."

Darell blinked. He'd called three days ago? Surely it was at least a month. Maybe two.

He cleared his throat. Sounded phlegmy, like an old man's. He hated that. "I wrote some today. Almost a page. And another yesterday. You know what they say—write a page a day, and you've got a novel in a year."

He used to write *three* a year. All brilliant.

"That's good, Darell, good ..."

"Maybe I can get that contract back. Just think, Malcolm, fifteen percent of ten million is a lot of dough. I'll make you rich. Again."

"You do that, man, you do that. Keep up the good work."

Darell could hear the disbelief in Malcolm's response. The agent was patronizing him. HarperCollins had waited eight months after the accident, strung along on Malcolm's promise that the King of Suspense would be able to write his one hundredth bestseller—the assumed milestone that had landed him on the cover of *Time Magazine*. But a worldwide publishing conglomerate couldn't wait forever, even for Darell Brooke. Not with half the contract—five million dollars—already paid up front, and doctors advising he may never write again. The deal was cancelled. Darell had been forced to give the money back. Malcolm had to cough up his fifteen percent.

I'll show you, Malcolm. Maybe I'll even get a new agent.

"All right. Well, got to get back to my writing. See you, Malcolm."

Darell clicked off the line.

He sat there staring at the phone in his hand.

Just three days ago he'd called?

With a loud sigh, Darell hung up the receiver. He shifted his legs, focused on the half-empty page on his screen. An emptiness he used to love to fill. Now it mocked him. His killer was still on his feet, frozen. The psychiatrist watched from his chair.

What were they supposed to do next? Where had he been headed with this story?

What *was* the story?

He had to do this. Somehow.

Oh, to regain half the concentration he'd once had. A fourth. A tenth. The thought of spending day after day in this mansion-turned-prison, in this office, unproductive and used up filled him with an emptiness as deep as staring into the face of black eternity. Like Satan and his demons cast from dazzling heaven to the dungeons of hell. Despairing of their loss and hatching vain empires of exacting their revenge on God.

Darell lowered his head. Such melodrama was usually beneath him. But not today. At this moment, steeped in depression, it seemed a worthy comparison.

He straightened and dredged up his self will. Placed his fingers on the keyboard, straining to turn the gears of his mind. One more page, just one. He'd give anything to finish this book. To gain back his reputation, his *life*. Anything.

The gears refused to move.